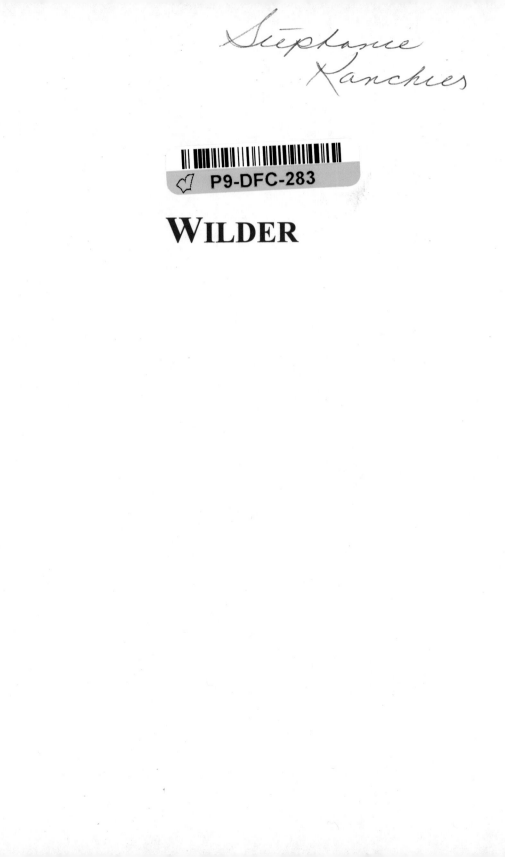

Stephanie
Kanchies

WILDER

WILDER

Loletta Clouse

TENNESSEE VALLEY
Publishing ®

Knoxville, Tennessee
2002

Words have great power and meaning,
but I am unable to find the proper ones
to express my gratitude to:
my husband, who always believed,
my son, who helped me look outside myself,
and my mother, who gave me the stories.

First published in Nashville, Tennessee by Rutledge Hill Press, 513 Third Avenue South, Nashville, Tennessee 37210

Reprinted 2002 by Tennessee Valley Publishing, PO Box 52527, Knoxville, Tennessee 37950-2527

Order additional books from:
    Chicory Books
    PO Box 31131
    Knoxville TN 37930

Library of Congress Cataloging-in-Publication Data

Clouse, Loletta,   1948-
    Wilder / Loletta Clouse.
        p. cm.
    ISBN 1-55853-083-5
    I.   Title.
PS3553.L648W55   1990   90-8885
813'.54—dc20   CIP

Printed in the United States of America
1 2 3 4 5 6 7 8 — 96 95 94 93 92 91 90

WILDER

1

Lacey loved heights. She could stand out on the edge of Buck Rock with her eyes closed, face craning upward, thin arms outstretched and feel her body rise with the first gentle breeze. In her mind, she could picture herself swooping and diving out over the hollow in graceful imitation of the red-tailed hawks that nested above her on the cliff face.

The lush green of the new spring buds spread beneath her like moss on a creek bank. Besides the abundant pine, she could pick out half a dozen other kinds of trees. Her pa had taught her well from his days in the sawmill. The black walnut, a favorite for making gun stocks; the white and yellow poplar sixty feet to the first limb and the chestnuts wide enough "so's a preacher could hold a revival on the stump" her pa liked to say. The buckeye, gum and sourwood filled in the spaces.

The thawing of the last snow always sent Lacey scrambling up the slick to catch the first bloom of the redbud, its stark purity of it contrasted with the bleakness of the mining camp after a winter of mud and coal soot.

Two hawks soared out over the hollow screeching and chasing each other in gleeful celebration of their own natural abilities. Their shrill cries sent chills through her as they whistled past her like bullets. The thought crossed Lacey's mind that it might be a sin to envy the gifts God gave another creature, but it wasn't envy so much as admiration for the grace and beauty of wild things and the way they instinctively knew their purpose.

The pain shot through Lacey's ribs before she felt the rough fingers encircle her waist. Gasping, barely stifling a shriek, she tumbled backwards onto a warm sweaty body. The frail frame beneath her belonged to her ten-year-old brother Ben. Embarrassed at being caught daydreaming, she jumped up huffing and smoothing her shapeless dress down over a fledgling body that strained reluctantly for womanhood. At sixteen, Lacey was "too old to be running the hills like a tow-headed boy" her ma was fond of saying. She knew she was expected to be thinking about marriage. The truth was she did think about it and she had concluded that marrying, at least the way she dreamed of it, was for the pretty ones, the ones whose bodies cooperated giving them full rounded hips and bosoms that strained at last year's dresses. She felt like pointing out to her ma that nobody had been to call except John Trotter. He was so solemn-like. It pained her the way he looked at her so mournful when he thought she wasn't looking on those slow walks back from church. Still he was known to be a clever sort and a good worker. He was eighteen and had a job in the mines working alongside her older brother Will. She knew that was a sight more than some girls ended up with and it shamed her that she could want more.

"Lacey, are you all right?"

She looked down at her brother still sprawled on the rocky ground. "Ben, you 'bout scared the life out of me. I come close to falling right off this rock, and Pa would've had a misery finding all the pieces. What was you thinking, sneaking up on me like that?"

"I thought you was gonna fall, the way you was swaying back and forth all dreamy like. I just meant to pull you backwards a bit."

Touched as always by Ben's "tender ways," as Lacey thought of her brother's gentle nature, she reached out a hand to help him up. He stood before her, one bare foot over the other with sweat making dirty rivers down his face. He was small and thin. At times his quiet, timidness made him appear frail. Freckles fought for space on his nose and pale cheeks. He and Lacey had the same thick, dark brown hair, alive with unruly waves, and the same lavender blue eyes the color of chicory in bloom.

Lacey immediately regretted her outburst but suppressed a desire to hug Ben. He was getting too old for that, although she had held him many times since he was born. She had taken over his raising when he was a baby and she was hardly much more. Since he had been born, her ma had been sickly "with her heart" the doctor said. Knowing that Ben felt somehow responsible, she was always hovering, shielding him from any further blows.

"I appreciate what you done. Guess I 'bout went to sleep standing out there. You done the right thing, and I'm proud of it."

Puffed up by the warmth of his sister's praise, Ben was immediately childlike and expansive again. "I found a spankin' new hawk's nest right up yonder on top of that jutting-out rock. Hits got two eggs in it. Wanna climb up and see um?"

Lacey squinted toward the cliff face and estimated the climb to the nest to be about forty-five minutes. She knew the gift he was offering her and was careful not to make light of it. "I sure would like to see those eggs. It must of took some looking to search out that nest."

"It was a right smart of a climb," Ben replied earnestly. "I seen the nest soon as I got half way up," he went on, skewing his face to one side in concentration, "and I come up on it real quiet so's not to scare the momma off. She weren't there, though. Just them two eggs. You don't reckon that momma done run off and left 'em do you?"

It was like Ben to worry that the momma had deserted her chicks. It was a fear he often experienced himself. He had dreams about coming home from school to find the house empty and his family gone without a trace. Lacey could not imagine what had caused such a fear. Sometimes late at night, when she held him after a bad dream, she promised him time and time again that she would always be there. He would cling to her, his pale lips stretched thin, his body taut until he finally drifted off to sleep. "She's most likely gone off to fetch something to eat," Lacey said. "I reckon that's what we need to be doing, too. Ma's expecting me to stop by the creek and pick some fresh cresses for supper. We probably have a few minutes to sit, though."

Satisfied with Lacey's appreciation of his find, Ben flopped quickly to the ground. Propping himself on one elbow, he began to stack tiny sticks on one another to form a miniature log house. Lacey joined him, tucking her dress under her knees. Ben was completely absorbed in constructing his tiny village. Lacey watched as he squinted in concentration and worked his tongue feverishly on the side of his mouth. She wished that she could save the moment to give to him whenever things went bad.

Lacey contented herself by looking out over the hollows, really a gorge cut by the East Fork of the Obey River on the Cumberland Plateau of Tennessee. The mining camp below, known as Wilder, was owned by the Fentress Coal and Coke Company of Nashville. The little town of some two thousand people made up her whole world. Her family had moved there in 1916, only months before she was born.

The clapboard company houses clamored for space on the valley floor. Most of them stood side by side along the main road through town, while others climbed the steep hillsides, perching like mountain goats on the slopes. On a warm day, barefoot children poured out of the screenless doors to play games of tag on the dirt-packed yards.

The company commissary formed the center of the business district. Owned by the coal company, it was the only place in town to trade. Although the stock was limited, it was more than most of the sawmill workers and hardscrabble farmers who formed the bulk of the mines, had ever known. When a new bolt of material arrived, it was not unusual for half the women in town to show up at church with dresses made from the same print. No one thought anything of it.

All the miners were paid at the scrip office next door. The bookkeeper always deducted for rent, lights, coal, and doctor bills before paying each man. What little was left, or most often a little bit more, was quickly spent at the commissary. Lacey remembered the time Will bought candy for all his friends on Pa's account. He had played big shot for nearly a week before Pa caught wind of it. They had eaten beans all the next week, and Will had eaten his standing up.

The US Post Office was west of the commissary, flanked by the hotel and the company cottage, which was used by families of company officials — "big bugs" as the locals liked to call them, but not to their faces. Their children, away at private schools in Nashville most of the year, would summer in Wilder. They could often be seen riding their horses up the main road to the next camp. Three different camps were strung together along the hollow, each alike and not more than two miles apart, but each with its own distinct personality. Lacey's family had tried to live at Davidson once. It was only a mile and a half from Wilder, but somehow the "feel" had been different, and they had soon moved back. Between Wilder and Davidson was a small community called Highland. It was the junction where trains were switched to tracks that led to other camps in the area. The giant Highland trestle crossed a deep ravine to connect the two camps. Learning to cross the huge trestle without looking down to the long drop below was a skill children learned early.

Across the street from the commissary stood the doctor's office, with a dwelling next door for his family. Everyone was charged a doctor bill whether they used him or not. Lacey was familiar with the sound of the doctor's one-seater car and could recognize it from a distance. She had come to rely on herbs and mountain doctoring more than a real doctor because her pa was not one to call if it was just the younguns. Lacey thought of the time Will had dropped a brick on her head from the chimney. It had cut a gash several inches long in the top of her head and blood had gushed down her face. Pa had told her to put lard on it; the doctor was called only for her ma.

The dirt road that ran behind the commissary was also the location for the school. Lacey had not attended since she turned twelve because her pa was not much for schooling. "Girls don't need it a-tall and a boy just needs to sign his name," Pa had said when she had asked him about going on. Even so, she had tried to go after he left for work in the morning, rushing home in the afternoons to clean house and start supper. It had been too hard getting the chores done, and her ma hadn't liked her being gone.

Next to the school stood the white frame church that had been built back in 1922 when Wilder was still a boom town. As a child, Lacey could remember every seat being filled and the room alive with singing, preaching, and the sound of crying babies. Now, they didn't always have a real preacher. Most often, they had someone in the camp who had received the call to preach the service or someone traveling through. Lacey liked going to church. She enjoyed the hymn singing and preaching, but it also gave her a chance to see and talk to people.

Lacey gradually became aware of Ben staring at her. He always had such an earnest look as though the meaning of something important had just escaped him. "What are you puzzling over now, Ben?" she asked gently as she brushed aside his shaggy curls.

"Did you ever believe that story Pa told us about Buck Rock?"

"You mean the story about where it got its name?" Lacey knew exactly what Ben meant. She had heard the story dozens of times. She and Ben had discussed it practically every time they made the rigorous climb to Buck Rock. It had become part of the ritual of the day, the part that came just before they declared the day over and made their way back down the steep slope.

"Do you think Buck Thomas really jumped off this rock and killed hisself?"

"You know Pa and Buck Thomas was good friends. They come over on the Tennessee Central Railroad from Rockwood in 1915. They found work in the mines and brought the families over the next year. Pa says they worked together in the sawmills before that. Pa was the one that found the body."

Lacey wondered what strange worlds these familiar words conjured up in Ben's mind, for he sat big-eyed and shallow-breathed every time they talked about it. She didn't know if he was pondering how a man could take his own life or if he was speculating on the possibility of life outside the deep gorge with its sharply rising hills on every side that formed their world.

"Why do you think he jumped, Lacey?"

"Pa said after Buck lost his arm in the mines, he couldn't work no more. They say he jumped off because of what it does to a man to have his way of living took away from him. When Pa carried the body home, he said Buck's wife and younguns was takin' on something awful."

"I bet he was busted up purty bad from a fall like that. It don't seem right somehow."

"We better be getting back," Lacey said too quickly. Ben hesitated, the concern still on his face. She wasn't sure what didn't seem right, a man killing himself or the way the mines treated people, but she didn't have an answer to either question. It seemed with all the trouble lately things were getting harder to understand. They had come to count on the company for so much and on things always being the same. "Don't fret, Ben," she said without conviction as they started down the hillside.

2

As Lacey poured boiling water from the kettle into the dishpan filled with supper dishes, the steam added to the heat in the tight little kitchen and the late afternoon sun stirred up lazy patterns of dust. Her folks sat finishing their coffee at the kitchen table, an occasional hand movement breaking up the patterns of dust and sending them dancing off to form new designs.

She wished her folks would hurry. She wanted to finish up and get ready for evening church services. They always ate a light supper on Sunday, and tonight they had had cornbread and salad made from the fresh cresses and poke she and Ben had just picked. Seasoned with meat grease and vinegar, it made a nice change from their winter fare of side meat they got in the fall when someone butchered a hog and the green beans she dried in the summer to make leather britches. Land was scarce around company houses, and the vegetables she was able to put by from their small garden usually ran out by January.

Talk drifted from the kitchen table, the high, breathy voice of her ma chattering on, was punctuated by her pa's deep baritone. Her ma talked as though life was an overpowering experience and just discussing everyday events taxed her strength.

"Maude Sutters come here yesterday with a brand new catalog from the Chicago Mail Order Service. She must of spent a half-hour flipping through, pointing out things her

Buford planned to buy her out of that catalog. 'A Minnesota Model A sewing machine with a genuine dark oak cabinet and seven drawers' and 'a handsome rose design parlor lamp,'" her ma said quoting the catalog from memory.

The image of her ma and Maude Sutters sitting on the front porch laughing, gossiping, and munching on tea cakes all afternoon was fresh in Lacey's mind. She had watched them as she ironed the week's wash. They had ruffled and clucked over that catalog like two hens over their new chicks. Maude was one of those women whose whole purpose in life was to stir up discontent in others. Or maybe, it was just that she was so full of it herself that it spilled over wherever she went. She was known all over camp for her peculiar habit of moving from house to house. Whenever a family vacated a company house, Maude would just up and move her things into it. Buford could be seen wandering from house to house after a hard day at work trying to find out where Maude had moved that day. Then it was his job to tote the heavy stuff over before work the next morning.

"I told Maude," her ma went on, "that I couldn't ask my Frank to go indebting hisself that way and me in poor health. Why, I could be called to my reward any time and then how could my poor Frank raise them younguns and pay off them big debts?"

The air expelled by her mother's sighs moved the flour sack curtains on the kitchen window. Her ma had been dying for as long as Lacey had memory. She was always waking them in the middle of the night with her "attacks." Pa would sit up with her putting wet rags on her forehead and talking calm to her. Usually, by early morning she would be composing last messages to loved ones, often calling the whole family in to hear her dying words. Sometimes if the attacks were too prolonged, Frank would call for the doctor. The examination was always brief and the prescribed medication the same brown liquid. Lacey suspected it was nothing more than paregoric. At dawn when Lacey went to the kitchen to fix Pa and Will's breakfast, her ma would be asleep. It worried her the way these scenes affected Ben. She sometimes found him standing by his ma's bed in the morning, eyes sunken and circled with deep shadows of grief and suffering.

"Was there something special you was wanting out of that catalog Annie?" Lacey's pa asked as she cleared their coffee cups from the table. She marveled at his patience. He was a strong man, often working twelve hours a day in the mines and then sitting up nights with her ma. And yet, he loved this selfish, childish woman with a devotion that often made Lacey feel lonely and excluded. She also knew he kept his ailments to himself. Only she knew about the frequent nose bleeds and the way he sometimes coughed up blood. One night she had found him sitting at the kitchen table, the front of his shirt soaked with blood and a soft look of amazement on his face. She had skillfully packed his nose with rags and then washed out his shirt. "Keep it to yourself, gal," he had said, and she had. The sickness was an unspoken bond between them.

As her ma went on about some mantel clock she would "dearly love" to have, Lacey wrung out the ragged dish towels and hung them on a string behind the cookstove. She knew without having to hear her pa's answer that even with work down at the mines, the clock would be sitting on the mantel over the coal grate before the month was out. Her pa was a proud man. That was one reason she tried never to ask him for anything unless it was necessary. Rarely did she ask for herself.

She slid the heavy lard and flour tins under the work table and covered it with a flowered oilcloth. After covering the leftovers with a clean tea towel, she carried the dishpan out the back door and poured the soapy water over the back steps. It did little to keep out the insidious coal dust that ground its way into the grain of the wood and the skin of everyone who lived in the camps, especially the miners. The lye soap they scrubbed down with at the end of the day was too strong to be used around the eyes, and sometimes as Lacey watched Will and her pa sit around the supper table at night she thought of raccoons eating fish by the creek bank.

"They say Coy Lynn Wilson is back in town," Pa announced simply as she hung the dishpan on a nail by the back door. "Rode in about three weeks back on the morning train."

"Well land sakes!" Annie squealed. "Why ain't you said something before this? Lord have mercy, I bet his ma is fit to be tied. How long has it been, Frank, since that no 'count took off?"

"'Bout four years, I reckon. Him and Will is 'bout near the same age. Coy couldn't a been more'n fifteen when he left here, and Will's going on nineteen this summer."

"And now he just shows back up here. What's he got to say for hisself? I reckon he knows his ma took sick after he left and near died from grief, they say. That child has purely been a burden to his ma. I hope he has come to his senses and has come home to beg his poor ma's forgiveness."

Frank glanced around the room as though searching for an escape route. Never quite comfortable with emotional displays, he had no doubt delayed bringing the news for as long as possible, Lacey thought.

"Pack me a pipe, would ya, gal?" he asked, a pained expression on his face.

Lacey took her pa's pipe from the mantel and expertly packed it with Prince Albert tobacco. She was proud of this simple skill and the way it pleased her pa. As she worked, she thought of Coy Wilson. What she remembered most about him was the way he taunted folks to strike out at him like a dog around a coiled snake. It was as if he was determined to show them his worst side. She had heard plenty of people speak of him. His father had been killed by a rock slide in the mines when Coy was fourteen. He had had to go to work to help support his ma, but he had caused a lot of trouble, picking fights with the other men and laying out of work for days. Finally, one day he had had a fight with the foreman. After that, he just packed up and left. Went out West, everybody said, and worked on a ranch.

"Not staying at his own ma's house!" Annie yelled as Lacey handed the pipe to her pa. "Who can figure that youngun? He always was a wild one. Why when him and Will was just younguns he used to tell stories about joining the Furrin Legion and going off to some desert to fight. Always putting notions in the boy's head. Said he weren't never going to be no coal miner like his pa, and him just a little thing even then."

When Lacey left the room, her ma was still sucking in and blowing out her breath through pinched lips as if she had been the one wronged. As she pulled her only good dress over her head, Lacey wondered what could make someone so unhappy as to run off and leave home and kin. She had never been out of Wilder except to ride the "shopper" to Monterey. It took half the night for the small passenger train to wind the twelve miles through the mountains and the family always arrived itchy-eyed but eager to see the sights and pick up their meager supplies.

They would be greeted there by sleepy-faced, cheerful kin. Sometimes it would be Uncle Pete Phillips, her ma's brother, and Lizzie, his wife. Uncle Pete would always slap Frank on the back and laugh like he was pleased to see him. Annie and Lizzie would immediately be caught up in an endless stream of chatter, oblivious to the children continuing a game of dog and cat they had started on the last visit.

Lacey was tying her long hair back with a blue grosgrain ribbon when Ben ran in breathless to say that Ruby, her best friend, Will, and John Trotter were waiting outside for her to walk to church. Ruby and Will had been walking to church together for several months now, and it looked like they might be getting serious. Lacey hoped so, for Ruby would make Will a fine wife. She was a natural mother with a place already worn on her hip from toting younger brothers and sisters. She was stout and rosy-cheeked with a tousle of red hair and the kind of smile mothers usually reserved for newborn babies.

The knitted loops of Lacey's wrap caught on the peg when she tried to pull it off the hook by the front door. As she wrestled to free it, she thought of how jealous she had been of Pauline Adams the first time she had seen her wearing a sweater. Pauline had strutted down the aisle at church like the queen of Sheba. It had made Lacey feel ugly and plain in her homemade shawl. She was sure Pauline knew it and loved the stir she was making. The memory made Lacey furious all over again and she yanked viciously at her shawl, tearing it free from the hook. Two of the loops stood up like rabbit ears. Twisting them together, she poked them down into the other loops. She would have to fix them proper later. When she looked up, she saw John Trotter talking to the others by the gate. He nodded almost imperceptibly. For shy, humorless John, it was an expansive greeting, and Lacey smiled from the familiarity of it. They had known each other all of their lives, and circumstances and age seemed to be conspiring to push them together. John was, after all, the perfect match. He was handsome enough, with cinnamon brown hair perfectly greased to control natural waves that framed an angular face and eyes the color of hackberry leaves in the spring. He was thin and sinewy, with an economy of words and movement honed by generations of mountain life. "Hardworking and as practical as dirt," her pa had described him.

"Lacey, you just going to stand there with that daf' look on your face?" Will yelled from the road.

Blushing warm around her collar, Lacey quickly pulled the wrap over her thin shoulders and joined the others. She hated to be caught daydreaming, and now she had allowed it to happen twice in one day. Will would not be as easy on her as Ben had been.

Life in a coal camp was tough, and dreams were supposed to have names like *house* and *husband, cookstoves* and *sewing machines*. The truth was she did want those things. In her mind she often pictured standing on the front porch to meet her husband coming home from work, a plump baby in her arms and the smell of supper on the stove. It was the same dream that all the young girls in Wilder had, and they talked about it endlessly when they gathered in groups. It should have been enough. That was the hard part for her. Surrounded by friends and family, Lacey sometimes felt loneliness so deep and jarring that it was like the sound of a rock dropped in a bottomless well. She could never reach its source, and she never talked about it to anyone. There were some things that would change folks' way of looking at you forever if they knew. It was like a crack in a china cup. It might seem a small thing, but they always would wonder about this weak place in her. They could never look at her again without seeing it.

"Yeah, ole Lacey stood there on the porch all blare-eyed looking as crazy as old Aunt Mazy. You remember Aunt Mazy don't you, John? She used to stand out on her porch and call the little sweet younguns up for a nice piece of horehound candy. Soon as she'd get 'em real close, she'd haul off and warp 'em a good one with her cane. She never did get me but one time 'fore I learned to grab that candy outta her hand and hightail it outta there. Yeah, Lacey shore put me in a mind of ole Mazy tonight. Wouldn't you say so, John?"

John shifted his shoulders uncomfortably.

"I don't reckon I do see it," John spoke gently, trying to straddle the fence between love and friendship.

"Sure you do, John," Will went on undaunted. "You remember old Mazy had that crazy bug-eyed stare like she was listening to the angels."

John started to say something about that being enough on the subject when Will turned and headed toward four men huddled in conversation near the post office.

"Will, where you takin' off to?" Ruby protested.

"You just go on to church now and save me a place. I got something I gotta do."

Lacey was half shocked by Will's rudeness, but she was too relieved to be rid of his teasing to say anything. Ruby threw her hands to her hips and puckered her lips tightly, but she stopped short of saying anything. Will was not one to tolerate criticism. Instead, she turned and stomped on ahead, obviously embarrassed by Will's behavior. Lacey looked back long enough to see the other men hunched in the twilight: Joe Morgan, Wilford Potter, Barney Graham and Harvey Long. They all worked in the mines with Will every day. *Why would he leave Ruby to talk to them now?* she wondered.

John said something to her as they neared the school yard. Just as she stepped into a puddle and thick mud oozed inside her shoe, she realized he had been trying to warn her. A booming laugh reached her ears from under a tree in the school yard. A man wearing a wide brim western hat, a loose cotton shirt, and Levi's over some kind of fancy boots was leaning against a persimmon tree. She was sure it was Coy Lynn Wilson. With him was a young woman the town folks called "that no good piece of trash, Lola Mae Simpson." They always said "that no good piece of trash" like it was part of her name. Lola Mae was loud and vulgar, and she seemed quite pleased with herself most of the time. Lacey remembered the many times she had seen the bigger boys crawling under the schoolhouse during recess. One day her curiosity got the best of her, and she had followed the sounds of their voices until she saw a crowd of boys stooped over, laughing and cheering someone on. After a few minutes, the crowd parted and a boy stood up naked from the waist down, his pants around his ankles. Lola Mae lay on the ground, her dress up around her waist. When she saw the horrified look on Lacey's face, she laughed out loud. Lacey could still hear the sound as she turned and ran, bumping her head on the rafters in her haste, shocked and embarrassed by what she had seen. Lola Mae had guessed as much, and it seemed to give her great pleasure. Lola Mae's knowing laugh had never changed in all those years and now, mixed with Coy's bold and boisterous laughter, it brought back all those confused feelings as though she had done something wrong.

John led her, hopping like an oversized frog, to a stump nearby where she sat down helplessly while he cleaned her shoe with a sycamore leaf. She could see Coy drinking something from a fruit jar and whispering into Lola Mae's ear. *It's a sight to ruffle the feathers of every old hen in camp*, Lacey thought.

As Coy staggered towards them, his arm around Lola Mae's neck, the crowd began to gather around the school steps to watch. It was an act both wretched and cavalier, so much so that the women were appalled and the men somewhat in awe. As he neared Lacey, Coy stumbled slightly and dropped his battered Stetson hat. Their eyes met briefly, and he smiled. It was a smile that said he knew exactly what he was doing, and the effect it was having. *My God!* Lacey thought and rubbed the goose bumps from her arms as she watched him stagger up the road.

Lacey banked the fire in the cookstove and set the table for the next morning. It was late and the household was asleep, except for her and Pa. She hadn't been able to get Coy off her mind all night. He had, of course, been the topic of conversation behind every hymn book at church. Ruby had even tried to pick it up on the walk home, but all Lacey could think about were those sober black eyes with their strange mixture of humor and pain. Finally, she told Pa about what had happened and her suspicions. "Pa, I don't believe he was drunk a-tall. He looked like he knowed what he was doing all along. I can't figure it."

Her pa just nodded, frowning into his pipe. Lacey hesitated but couldn't let it go. "Pa, what makes a man like Coy Lynn Wilson come back when he ain't been asked and then set about making folks so angry?"

Frank stoked his pipe thoughtfully, as always, before speaking. "It does seem Coy's always been on the wrong side of people's good nature."

"It was more than that tonight, Pa. He was daring folks to think the worst of him."

"None of us knows what's meant for us when we are brought forth on this earth. Lord knows, if some of us did, we might be for turning back. One thing we ain't got no control over is when and how we was born. It's best to accept it early on, gal."

"What do you mean, Pa?"

"Coy's been fighting life since the day he was born. Wouldn't accept nothing life handed him without a fight. Your ma was right about him. He had a contrary nature even when he was a youngun."

"Are you saying he was just born mean?"

"I'm just saying that life always did rub him like a cocklebur. Kept a sore place on him all the time."

"Something must've caused it."

"I ain't saying he ain't had some burdensome loads with his pa dying and him still a youngun. Well, I never told nobody this but I was in the mines that day when Coy and Lawton Monroe, the foreman, had that fight. They got into it over something, and Lawton called Coy a bastard. Told him his real pa was Seth Ramsey. Seems his ma got herself in the family way before she married Reed Wilson. Coy didn't believe it, but I reckon he suspicioned somethin'. When he went home and told his ma about the fight, she must of broke down and confessed it. That's when he took off."

"So that's why he won't stay with his ma and stays up the holler with the Ramseys. How come you never told the truth of it, Pa? Folks might of looked differently on Coy's leaving."

"The folks that need to know already know the truth. No need to be telling everybody here and yon. Besides, don't you go wasting your pity on the likes of Coy Lynn Wilson. They's plenty of choices to be made in this life on how we're going to face what we've been handed. Ain't nobody makes it through this world without a dose of suffering."

Her pa sat in silence for some time. He ran his hand across the oilcloth on the table as if he were searching for a message in its pattern. Lacey wondered if he was looking back over his life at times when he had wanted to turn back, when the suffering had almost been too much. *Maybe he was looking for a sign,* she thought, *to say there was a reason for it all.* Finally, he looked up. "You just as well learn early," he had concluded, "to swaller hard and keep your head down." He paused again, shaking his head, "No, I'd say if he had it to do over, Coy wouldn't do no better. You see, four years ain't done him no good. Now, you best get in bed. Daylight will be here soon enough." Pa gave her his straight-lipped smile that failed to hide his fatigue.

"Good night, Pa," Lacey whispered with a gentle kiss on his forehead. It was strange how some men could only tolerate weakness in their own kin, if weakness was what it was. She couldn't help thinking it must be a terrible loneliness that drives a man back where he's not wanted.

3

Coy leaned over the back porch rail and vomited the mash whiskey he had drunk with the Ramsey boys. It was their habit to drink until they passed out each night. The way Coy figured it; they were their own best customers. He had to admit it had a favorable affect on their personalities, making them right sociable up till the moment they lost consciousness.

He had walked Lola Mae home early in the evening. She had tugged at his shirt and kissed her warm breath about his face, finally turning on him in anger when he failed to respond. He had left her and wandered on up the hollow, the smell of cheap perfume and her piercing whine badgering every miserable step.

It had all seemed pretty funny when he had thought it up; taking the biggest jezebel in the county to church. Even now he could laugh about the way the old biddies had nearly popped their starched collars. Of course it had given him more satisfaction in the planning. *That was generally the way with things. In the end, nothing changed. Even when it was going good, it was always just a matter of time*. He wondered if he would ever be free. There were days when his life seemed a pure nuisance.

And then he had seen that young girl looking at him. It wasn't hate or anger he had seen in her eyes. He had come to expect that. This had been a different look. It had been a look of puzzlement; one that was just shy of pity. His actions had turned bitter in his throat. He sure as hell hadn't come back to be pitied, especially not by some scrubbed-faced, underfed daughter of a miner.

The back of his flannel shirt caught the splinters as he slid down the corner post of the porch and squatted against the only stable beam. The half moon shed light on two hogs rooting noisily by the steps. It was the custom of the house to throw the few scraps of food leftover out the back door. Since there was no woman to cook, the scraps never amounted to more than a few potato peelings and a hard crust of week-old cornbread. The hogs caught his scent and squealed with excitement for he had been feeding them in the last few weeks and they had quickly come to expect it. He threw a stone and they went greedily in search of it.

It had been three weeks since that day the freight train had brought him back to Wilder. He had come instinctively, not knowing what to expect. As he had started his determined trek up the hollow that first evening, he hadn't really been afraid so much as anxious to have it done. It was a dangerous trip, he supposed, for he had always heard Seth Ramsey and his two boys, Bo and Hoyt, didn't favor company. They had lived off of making moonshine since they came to the hollow twenty-five years ago. If anyone knew where they had come from, it was lost to history. Coy had never heard anyone speak of it. They just appeared one day and set themselves up in an abandoned shack. Hoyt was barely three and Bo was just a baby. Some folks thought Seth was young to have such a family, but something in his way kept folks from prying. He mostly minded his own business and that caused the town to think the worst.

The sun was low in the sky by the time Coy lifted his fancy stitched, soft leather cowboy boot onto the first step of the Ramsey's front porch. One side of the step was propped precariously on a rock. A window pane was broken in the front window and a rag was stuffed in the hole. From the inside, the rag was pulled slowly from the hole and a gun barrel took its place. The front door opened slowly and a tall, dark complexioned man emerged from the shadows. His rugged, angular face and silver hair was like a mirror to Coy's future. Their eyes met without flinching and then a smile broke on Seth's face. Coy found himself in the once muscular arms of his real father.

Seth greeted him like the prodigal son, but by the look of torment in the old man's eyes it was hard to tell just who the wanderer was. The red-rimmed eyes of the old man shone with love for the son he had never claimed. It was the last reaction Coy had expected and they stayed up half the night amid the filth and squalor of the dimly lit shack as Seth explained. "Course, I was just a bit of excitement for Ellen, yore Ma, before she settled down. I don't mean that to be ugly, son. Her Pa was pushing her to marry Reed and she probably would have done it willing. But she was young and headstrong. It was him she loved, of course. I knowed the day she come wandering up here what she was up to. She wouldn't never speak to me after they married," Seth laughed humorlessly. "I wouldn't of told," he went on suddenly serious. "I loved her too much. I still do."

"Why did you let her do that to you, if you knew she didn't love you?" Coy asked. He felt his old hatred for his mother smoldering in the pit of his stomach and his instinct for survival flare up.

"The Bible says a man has free will," Seth stated shaking his head. He sounded like he was still puzzling over the matter. "That don't hardly seem possible sometimes, does it?" He asked with a look of wonderment on his face.

Coy didn't know how to answer. He felt swallowed up by the pain he could still see in the old man's eyes. "Did you ask her to marry you?"

"No, son," Seth said surprised. He spread his hands out before him as though their rough veiny exterior explained everything. "You got to understand. I ain't no good. Fact is I'm about fifth generation worthless. Ain't no woman goin' to say yes to that. Besides, I knowed if you was ever going to amount to anything, it wouldn't be my doing. Ellen made a fine man of you, son. I knowed she would."

Coy raised one thick black brow and started to protest, but Seth stopped him short with a wave of his hand.

"You most likely been wondering after hearing all of this, if there was a chance you was gonna turn out like yore pa," Seth stated flatly, but with the start of a grin flicking at the corners of his mouth.

Coy was surprised by the old man's bluntness and embarrassed that he had read his thoughts so clearly. "I reckon I was thinking it might explain some things." Coy replied honestly, a crooked smile splitting his face like a bad rip. He looked around the untidy, overcrowded room. A bed was nailed to the wall in one corner. The grimy, tattered quilt barely covered a greasy corn shuck mattress. Along one wall was a huge metal trunk piled high with old, yellowed newspapers used to stuff the cracks in the walls. A small rickety table and two straight back cane bottom chairs were directly in front of the fireplace. The walls were pasted with pages from old mail order catalogs. The coal oil lamp on the mantel was dim with soot.

When Coy looked back at Seth, he was chuckling silently. Coy burst out laughing. Together they laughed until tears rolled down their cheeks and they were gasping for breath. Then they slapped each other on the back and passed a quart Mason jar of moonshine between them.

"Don't take nothing to be ordinary," Seth concluded seriously. "Fact is as I look back on it, it took a hell of a lot to make a life this sorry. I don't reckon it could of took much more to make a good life. I just didn't have it in me."

Coy had to agree. It sure seemed like it took all a man had sometime, and still didn't nothing turn out right.

"Life just comes at you like a wild bear," Seth mused. "Don't seem there's no way you can win. But if you don't try atall that old bear just mauls you a little and leaves you there all tore up to die real slow like. That's what it done to me boy. 'Cause I just didn't try. If you're wanting more than this," he said waving his hands back over his head to point out the dreary surroundings, "you best stand up and let that ole bear get a clean swipe at you."

"Seems like that's what I've been doing all my life. No offense, but I ain't sure that's none to smart neither."

Seth chuckled, a deep rumble that moved through his body like a storm. They sat in silence and watched as the coals of the fire died away.

Finally, as morning threatened to reveal it all as a dream. Coy spread his bedroll on the filthy floor. *God help me*, he thought, *I've come home*. And he fell into a fitful sleep.

He awoke with dark all around, the hard planks of the floor cutting into his ribs. For a moment he thought he was in a box car and he shivered at the memory of those weeks hopping freight trains. The cold and hunger had almost done him in before he made it to Chicago.

It had taken him two days to find a job in a slaughter house slitting the throats of prime beef. He had lasted two weeks standing knee deep in blood before he found himself on another freight heading west. By the time he got to Wyoming, he had done his share of stealing, begging, and charming lonely farm wives.

He had mistakenly jumped off the line some twenty miles short of Cheyenne and nearly froze to death before morning. And he would have if he had not found a haystack near a run down lean-to. He had crawled in with a couple of friendly hogs and shared their hospitality till sunrise. He figured there had to be somebody around to feed the critters and he was hungry enough to share whatever they got, but he was craving human company almost as much as food. When he looked outside, all he could see was one lone farmhouse breaking up the miles.

He was met at the door by a wizened old man with tobacco staining the corners of his mouth and clues to last week's meals on his shirt. "Get on in here, you dang fool," the old man greeted him. Within seconds, the old man had dished out a plate of hot biscuits and sawmill gravy and was filling up a speckled blue cup with steaming coffee.

The old man's name was Dovey and he was not alone. It seems he was used to visitors, his place being near the rail lines and the only life for fifty miles around. With him was a rancher by the name of Jake Abbott who owned a small spread up near Horse Creek. He had been down to Cheyenne to pick up a couple of saddle horses when a spring storm had threatened. He planned to stay the day helping Dovey with some work about the place and head out at daybreak the next day.

The next morning, without much discussion, Coy had ridden out with Jake. Looking back on it, he still couldn't figure what had possessed Jake to take on a scrawny kid whose only experience with cows was being kicked over the fence by his Aunt Mabel's milk cow when he was ten.

They had ridden for three days stopping only to sleep at night in crude brush shelters and eat beans from a can. Coy had tried desperately to look like he had sat astride a horse before, but Jake seemed not to notice. He was too busy talking about the ranch.

He had panned gold in Montana for five years; saving enough to buy a small spread that he had stocked with fifty head of Herefords. "In half a dozen years, I've built it up to over 200 head," Jake stated with obvious pride that told of the sacrifices he had made and the difficulty of the task.

Coy learned that most ranching was done by small family spreads. Jake shared his dream with his wife, Bonnie, and their five year old son, Mark. The huge ranches run by rich cattle barons, Jake told him, were more the stuff of the Western serials Coy loved to read. Coy never told Jake that those Western novels were what brought him west. Not just cattle barons, but stories of bold, adventurous men who didn't let anything stand in their way. Well, he had met one even if it wasn't quite what he had expected.

As they neared the ranch, Jake became more animated describing in detail the wonder of owning your own place. The beauty of watching your own white-faced Hereford grazing in rich summer pasture was a pleasure no man should have to miss in this lifetime, Jake explained.

Then on the third day, they topped a small rise and in the valley below was Jake Abbott's ranch. The spread consisted of a small weather beaten clapboard house, a rundown one room bunkhouse that housed four cowhands, a barn with a corral, and three outbuildings.

Coy thought it was the dreariest sight he had seen since the coal soot-stained company houses of Wilder, but he would never forget the look on Jake's face. It was a look that came up from the roots of a man's soul and it made Coy hunger for it.

The work had been the hardest Coy had ever done and the weather the meanest. The herd had to be watched constantly for blowflies, or foot rot, or just dang stupidity. The whole herd would starve in winter with grass lying only inches below them in the snow. In the summer, a cowhand would have to salt ahead to lead the cows to new pasture.

Coy had learned all the skills of ranching, and Jake had never treated him less than a son. It had given him a pride in himself and his abilities to survive. At first he thought that the dream of owning his own ranch could be his, for three years he tried. Just once before he died he wanted to have that look in his eye that Jake had had. He wanted to feel what Jake felt about owning something all his own, but he soon felt the old restlessness return. The emptiness inside him made him turn on even the good things in his life, but he knew if he could just find the right thing, all that would change.

Coy had been more surprised than Jake the day he had told him he was leaving. Jake had seemed to know all along it was something he would do eventually. "A man's got to make it right with himself before he can go on," Jake had stated simply while shaking Coy's hand extra long. Coy wasn't sure what he meant by that. It hadn't seemed right or wrong at the time; just something he had to do.

He had left without really knowing where he was headed. Eventually, he had ended up in a logging camp in Oregon west of the Cascade Mountains at a place outside Klamath Falls. Logging was an ugly, dangerous job that reminded him of coal mining except it had the advantage of being performed outside. It matched the mines for cruelty by pinning men under runaway log slides and killing them in falls that left their insides impaled on stumps. He enjoyed the challenge of felling the giant Douglas firs and he enjoyed the rugged camp life he shared with the other loggers. The dangers that made them so dependent on each other bound them together if only for the season. An older man they called Trump had taken him under wing and taught him how to make a wedge-shaped piece out of the tree trunk called an undercut and how two men could work like one to handle a two-man cross-cut saw the men called a misery whip. Trump had been real good to him. Coy thought about how he had left, in the middle of the night after three months time without a backward glance. He headed south.

For a while his home had been either a freight car or one hobo camp after another along the way. He met a lot of men who claimed to have had good lives back in places like Boston and New York before they lost everything when something called the stock market crashed. He met a lot of other men who never had anything and now had even less. They all looked the same to him.

One day he picked up a newspaper a hobo had been sleeping on in one of the freight cars. The paper was all about a place called Hollywood where they made moving pictures that talked at studios like Warner Brothers, Metro-Goldwyn-Mayer, and Columbia. He had seen a few silent movies in Wilder. A few days later he got off the train in Hollywood.

Coy got a job with Columbia building sets. Then a director spotted him and thought he would look good in a uniform. He played one of the few live soldiers killed on a Civil War battlefield that day. The others were painted on a backdrop behind him. When the director found out he could do more than fall down, he got other small parts, such as sitting on a horse and falling off or standing on a building and being shot off. It didn't pay much, but some folks said he had a real chance to become an actor. Not long after that he found himself on a train headed back to Wilder.

Now that he was back in Wilder, he wasn't sure what he had expected. He had met Seth Ramsey and he had heard the story that had made him a bastard. For all the pain it had caused him, it had been nothing more than two people acting like fools. It was nothing he hadn't done many times. At least Seth had loved his mother, and maybe his mother had hidden the truth out of love. Maybe she had loved him that much at one time. It hadn't helped him to leave Wilder and it hadn't helped him to come back.

As he sat in the moonlight, the sounds of the Ramsey boys snoring inside the house, he realized that his life would never be simple. He had the answers he had been looking for and he felt no better for it. It was just what he had feared the most. The answers were not going to be enough. They had not brought him the relief he had expected. He still woke in the middle of the night with a gnawing at the back of his head, a mass of thoughts working alive. It had always been that way, his thoughts pushing him to do something but never giving him a direction. "Well, Lord, you ain't never been there in the past," Coy said looking up at wispy clouds passing over the moon. "But if you've got anything to say you could start anytime." From under the porch a pig snorted and squealed as he rooted his way to a more comfortable position. Coy laughed to himself in the dark. "Thank you, Lord," Coy said bitterly. "I reckon that was a right smart more than I was expecting." Still shaking his head, he spread his bedroll on the back porch and watched another night turn to dawn.

4

John left Lacey at her front gate and went in search of Will. He hated to leave her so early. They usually sat on the front porch and talked for a while. He loved that time together for they were often left alone. Of course, he knew Frank was nearby in the house, for he never liked to leave his only daughter un-chaperoned, even with someone he trusted like John. Frank and Lacey were a lot alike: calm and self-contained, yet sociable and generous. But a vein of pure steel ran through the core of them. He had known Lacey to sit up for a week without sleep when Ben had pneumonia, and the look in her eyes told John she could pull him back from the grave if it came to that. Her eyes told him lots of things, and their flash could set a fire in him. He just wished someday they would say she loved him, but for now he knew they didn't. He would have to bide his time.

John knew what Will was up to, and he thought it best to find him. There was trouble again in the mines, and the union was trying to rally the men. There had been no union in Wilder from 1924 to 1930. The United Mine Workers had signed up a lot of miners back in 1918, and they had won the right to shorter hours and better pay. After the war, the companies had slowly started to cheat on their agreements until most of the miners' gains were eroded. The men were so eager to work and the changes in working conditions so gradual they had ignored them. When the Depression hit the coal fields in the early twenties, the coal companies felt strong enough to do away with the union altogether. The mines had just shut down for a few months, which broke the back of the union. Every man who got a job in the mines had to sign a yellow-dog contract swearing they would never join a union or go out on strike. Then, in reaction to two wage cuts and worsening conditions, the men had finally organized in '31. They were barely able to stave off a third cut, but they had made no gains.

During the period from 1923 to 1929, when the rest of the United States was enjoying prosperity, the bituminous coal industry had suffered hard times. It was hard for John to understand how the coal companies could be in such trouble. His pa had always talked about the boom years when the mines were always looking for more workers. To meet the demand, little mines had opened up and down every hollow wherever a train track ran. Now all the miners could hear was how more coal was being mined than was needed. Companies were fighting for business, and competition was fast making enemies where once there had been friends.

The Harlan, Kentucky coal operators had started a cut-throat competition with other coal companies that was threatening to destroy the coal industry. They had cut prices and stolen contracts from other companies, and they were the first companies to go non-union and to cut wages. The Fentress Coal and Coke Company, a small company far from the big markets, was forced to go along with the price cuts to keep up with the dropping coal prices. With dropping coal prices, came wage cuts, and the fledgling union, less than one year old and the only recognized union south of the Ohio River, could be in big trouble when the contract ran out in July.

John knew they had to be careful to handle things right. The company had the power over them, and even the law didn't favor unions. The miners were just a small group of people in a county of farmers.

Wilder, Tennessee wasn't like Harlan, Kentucky, where everybody was a miner. There were only three mining companies in the Wilder area, one at Twinton owned by the Brier Hill Collieries of New York, one at Davidson owned by the Patterson brothers, and the largest one at Wilder owned by the Nashville-based Fentress Coal and Coke Company. Few people understood miners, and they didn't understand unions. It would not pay to move too quickly. Will was a hot-headed sort who might just do something foolish. Right now, something foolish could be something as innocent as talking to the wrong person.

He found Will at Harvey Long's place. They had already signed Will to the union and had talked to him about signing up other miners. John could see the excitement in his face.

The men sat around the coal grate. They had talked out their anger earlier, but it revived with the entrance of a new audience. John knew all the hardships of mining firsthand. His pa had been killed in a mining explosion only two years earlier, and before that his pa had been a miner for twenty years. He had grown up on stories of working all day in knee-deep water or in narrow crevices with just enough room for the rats to run on one's legs but not enough room to be able to kick them off. He had heard hundreds of stories of mine explosions and rock slides, and he had waited his share of time at the depot for the bodies to be brought down to be sent by train to the hospital in Nashville if there was any hope of saving them. On many such occasions he had checked for his father's face until one day it was there and there was no need for the trip to Nashville. Nobody had to explain the situation to John, but he listened patiently out of respect for the men.

"By God," Wilford Potter sighed, spitting into the coal grate. He paused to watch the gooey brown liquid sizzle on the remaining hot ashes. "A man first goes into a mine; he's got to make his own place. Got to dig him out a dern hole from nothin', set them timbers and lay his own track. It's yern then, and whatever coal you get outta there, that's yore living."

"And I've worked a many a day twelve hours without stopping. Never teched my dinner bucket ar got a drink of water except when I filled my lamp," Joe Morgan joined in.

"Yeah, nobody never said a man don't have to work hard to make a living in the mines," Wilford replied, shifting his tobacco from one jaw to the other. "But now, it don't even pay a living wage if a man works all dern day. You go into the scrip office and say you gotta have two dollars to buy food, and by the time that paymaster gets through de-ducting for rent, lights, and doctor, you done worked two weeks for nothin'."

"You best be glad you ain't got no wife and six younguns to feed," Harvey Long mumbled, jerking his head toward the other room where his children slept crossways on two small beds, arms and legs intertwined. The men nodded in understanding. "That's something you young boys best be thinking about if yore planning on marrying soon."

Will grinned nervously, but the worn look on Harvey's face caused him to drop the grin and slouch in his chair.

"Why, last week, I didn't have enough scrip to buy powder and fuses," Harvey went on slightly embarrassed. "Them younguns got to eat, and they can't live off yeller squash three times a day," he said, referring to the way some miners begged food from the farmers in the county and distributed it among the other miners. With the miners working only three and four days a week, the union was already running an aid truck. Each week they would scour the countryside for food and bring it back to distribute among the miners. Sometimes they were able to get flour and meal. Most often, it was a truckload of cabbage, squash, or potatoes.

"Well, we can't take no pay cut! We're starving now!" Joe Morgan snapped angrily.

Will picked up on the anger immediately and jumped up excitedly. "By God, we could walk out of there right now and shut that place down. They got to have us to run the place same as we got to have the mines."

"If it comes to that. Right now, we want to see if they won't arbitrate when the contract runs out. Don't nobody want a strike. That hurts us as much as it does the company. Besides, it might take 'em a while, but d'rectly they'd round up enough scabs to run the place," Barney Graham spoke up for the first time since John had arrived. "There's an endless supply of hungry men in this world, so I wouldn't be so hasty to think much of yourself."

He had said it without rancor, but Will's eyes snapped and he paced the floor before coming to rest against the door facing. Barney ignored him and went on talking. As head of the newly formed union committee, Barney knew more about union organizing than anyone else there. The men had respected him enough to elect him checkweighman. He weighed the coal loaded by each man, and he was known to be honest, standing up for the men in any dispute.

John watched Will as he twitched and thumped his body against the door, crossing and uncrossing his arms. John could not understand why Barney would involve someone like Will at this crucial time. However, he knew one thing: he must have his reasons. Like the other miners, John had come to trust

Barney completely. No one knew where Barney Graham had come from, and he didn't talk about his past. He had first moved to Twinton and had married a young widow who worked at the hotel. He took in her two small daughters, and now they had a son of their own. He was a proud man who always wore a suit coat, even if it was worn and patched. He also always wore a gun.

"I wasn't going to bring this up just yet," Barney was saying, "but I reckon now's as good a time as any to tell you. As most of you know a policy committee has been set up of five men from each camp representing Wilder, Davidson, and Twinton. They're good men, all of them. We have the backing of Turnblazer. He's the president of District 19, and he's promised to send us help when we need it. The policy committee has been meeting regularlike at the Davidson schoolhouse and sometimes down here in Wilder. Any one of you wants to can attend. Or if there's something a-worrying the miners, just send a runner and we can meet inside of half an hour, day or night. When the time comes, the policy committee will speak for the miners. John here's been picked to be a member. He's young, but he's good."

The men were up and shaking John's hand before Barney could finish. They offered to help, each in his own way. Will hung back until last, but finally stuck his hand out to John with a crooked, closed mouth smile that meant he truly was glad. Not even Will could dispute that John was the man for the job.

"There may be a time I'm not where you can reach me," Barney went on earnestly. "Anything you need to tell me, you can tell John same as me. You all know that we are part of District 19, same as them mines in southeastern Kentucky. They're having a big rally up there over wage cuts. They're trying to get everybody in the district signed up. I expect after this meeting things will get mighty worked up. I know all you hear is how things is going on up in Kentucky, but we ain't going to let them pull nothing on us. We pay out union dues like the rest of them." They all laughed, and Barney stood up, giving the signal to break up the meeting. "We best scatter. They'll be many a night like this before it's over."

Barney thanked Harvey for his hospitality before they walked out into the cool spring night. The men took off in various directions, preferring the dirt-packed paths to the main road.

John listened to Barney's instructions as they walked, taking in his cautious tone and careful phrasing. "Mostly you got to remember we don't want violence here. We've always tried to settle our differences by talking it out. The best we can do is show 'em we're willing to work with 'em so they don't have to bring in outsiders who maybe don't know mining. Show 'em somehow that they stand to save money in the long run. We don't want to go out on strike unless we are forced into it."

"You don't sound too hopeful."

"Hope's mostly what a miner lives on, son. I've seen trouble come and go in the mines. Wilder's just small potatoes when it comes to mining. A lot a people moved out of here in '24. Besides, there's trouble all over in the mining business. I'm just saying this could be a tough one. We've got to stand strong. I don't intend to see these good men done wrong." Barney looked up at the moon, scanning the night sky as though searching for the words that could explain how a miner could spin hop out of coal dust and blasting powder. "No, son, a man's always got hope. You know that, or you wouldn't be a miner."

John nodded in agreement and then brought up what had been bothering him all night. "I may be out of line here, Barney, but if you're so worried about this unionizing, how come you brought Will Conners into it?"

"Lordy mercy, John! I'm not right sure how it happened myself. Sometimes a man makes a mistake so vexing he can only hope to live a long life so he can get in plenty of regret."

John laughed softly in the dark.

"I reckon I reasoned he might pull some weight with his pa. Now, I'm not so sure it was so smart of me."

He slapped John on the back and chuckled. As they parted, John could still see Barney shaking his head as though he already was working in a little regret.

5

Lacey cut through the dirt-packed backyard sending a few disgruntled chickens squawking. Her feet fell upon the well-worn path through the narrow rocky corn patch she worked each summer. The ground had been turned once for the spring planting, and she had already worked a little ground for leaf lettuce and green onions. The tiny plot of land they had for gardening was rough, and the soil had to be turned just right to get the most out of it. Some miners didn't care about having a garden spot, but Lacey had made sure her pa had traded company houses around until they got a nice piece of land. Her garden was the only plenty she had ever known, and she stopped a moment to relish the joy it brought her, and to think about how she planned to lay off the rows this year.

She cut crosswise of the Will McConnell place and headed up a small slope to the tree line. With one quick glance over her shoulder, she started into the thick patch of scrub pine. It was not that she was trespassing or that anyone would mind her being there, she just needed a privacy that included not being seen. Lately, it seemed, her thoughts crowded her head and she never had a moment to sort them out. She had thought often of Coy since that night two weeks ago when he stumbled and their eyes met. She had gone over and over it. Had she imagined the loneliness in his eyes? It had been almost dark, and his face had been shadowed in the twilight. She was sure of one thing: he had not been drunk that night.

Her pace slowed a bit as her leg muscles began to protest. She was tired. It had been a difficult night. Her mother had awakened the family before dawn with one of her "spells," and after three hours of cold compresses and solicitude, had finally slept. She had dozed half the morning while Lacey boiled water and scrubbed overalls and flannel shirts on the back porch.

Lacey had heard her mother's agitated cry from the bed in the front room and chafed at the thought of having to push the boiling water to the back of the stove or of even having to do the wash another day. She was surprised to find her mother sitting up, pasty-faced and clammy. The doctor, of course, had no understanding of the seriousness of her condition and nobody could know what it was like to live with death always so near. It was a well-worn speech. This time, Lacey thought the look of fear in her mother's eyes was somehow different, deeper.

The sad reality of her mother's fear had melted Lacey's anger and she had promised to go immediately and gather enough sassafras to make a fine spring bracer. "It's just the tonic you need," she had convinced her mother, forcing her to lie back against the pillow and rest until her return.

Relief flooded over Lacey as she headed deeper into the woods. Breathing harshly, perspiration beading up between her breasts, she was reluctant to waste even a moment to rest until she was safely concealed by the thick forest.

Despite the inconvenience of putting her chores aside, Lacey realized how much she enjoyed gathering the sassafras bark and tender sweet birch twigs. First she found some young sassafras trees and gathered a few tender twigs. She could easily peel the bark and mash it into a pulp for tea. She didn't like to pull up the whole tree just for a new root the way some folks did, so she found an old tree and dug around the base taking a few scrapings from each root. Then she broke a few twigs from a sweet birch to add a nice wintergreen flavor and some natural sweetening.

As Lacey topped the hill and headed down a steep slope to the railroad tracks, she wondered if she would have time to pick a mess of wild greens. There was an open field a mile up the tracks where a family named Runion had once owned a farm. Now pike plant and yellow dock grew around where the old barn had stood. She knew that dock greens eaten in the spring could thin and purify the blood. It would be worth the extra effort if it would boost her ma's flagging spirits.

In the distance she could see a flat car coming up the tracks with two people riding on it. She recognized one as a neighbor, Collin Riley. She raised her arm to wave back just as her left foot caught on an upturned tree root sending her to the ground with a hard smack. As pain shot up her leg, nausea caused her mouth to water.

When she opened her eyes to stop the reeling in her head, her eyes focused on a pair of leather boots, fancy stitched and well-worn. She followed them upward — using only her eyes for her body refused to move — to a pair of dusty Levis. Her eyes rested on a smooth polished nickel plated belt buckle. She was too embarrassed to look further, for she knew that it had to be Coy.

His booming laugh confirmed her suspicions and sent a surge of energy to her limbs like air to a billow. She scrambled to her feet, only to snag her dress on the root that had tripped her.

The humiliation of being caught in such a disheveled state and then to be laughed at, was more than Lacey could bear. She yanked viciously on her dress, freeing it from the root leaving a jagged tear. Her instinct was to run but when she turned, Coy stepped directly in her path.

Lacey turned to stare full faced at the man who had been in her thoughts for weeks. His black hair shone like a rich seam of coal under a carbide light and his high cheek bones spoke of the Cherokee blood that was part of his heritage. As his coal-black eyes boldly inspected the length of her body, she was painfully aware of how she must look to him. She felt exposed to his piercing stare.

"Why, Miss Lacey Conners, that was quite a fall. You know you didn't have to go to such lengths to get my attention," Coy said grinning broadly as he began to brush the dust from her dress.

The callousness of his remark and the boldness of his gesture sent Lacey into a rage of humiliation. She pushed his hands away and clutched at the fabric of her dress. "You got no call to be making fun of me. And how did ya know it was me?"

"People do talk. You are Frank Conner's gal, ain't you?" Coy asked as he picked a bit of grass from her hair.

Lacey put her hands to her face palm out, shaken by the assumptions she read in his movements. He was the boldest man she had ever known. He didn't seem to follow any rules that could tell a person what he might do next. "They got no reason to be talking about me. Anyway not to the likes of you," she snapped, her voice betrayed by a tremble.

Coy stepped back, his hands drawn to his sides, the grin fading from his face.

"And what is 'the likes of me,' Lacey? People been talking about me, have they? Well, I don't doubt they have. Around here by noontime most the town knows what a person had for breakfast. 'Course, I asked about you Lacey. I wouldn't of knowed you, it's true. You've growed up in four years since those days when you was just a scrawny youngun roaming in the hills. I see being growed up ain't stopped you none, though."

"I reckon I'm free to come and go," she snapped, ashamed that he saw her as an overgrown child.

"That's one thing there ain't no doubt about, Lacey Conners. I can see it in those beautiful blue eyes."

"Ma's ailing. I was gathering some sassafras bark for tea," she said, hating herself for trying to explain her behavior.

"Are you all right up there, Lacey?" she heard a familiar voice call. It was Collin Riley. She had forgotten about the flat car. Coy must have been riding and jumped off when he saw her fall. Why had he bothered, only to treat her like captured prey?

"I'm fine, Mr. Riley," she called. "If you don't mind, I'll catch a ride into town with you." She bent quickly to collect the twigs and bark she had been carrying. Coy didn't try to help her, but stood over her instead. She could feel his eyes on her and when she looked up, he stepped out of her path. Brushing past him, she ran down the slope, the stones torturing her feet through the thin soles of her shoes. She could feel his eyes like hot breath on her neck, but she didn't look back until she was safely on the train. When she dared to look, he was gone. She stared for a long time at the place where he had stood until the flat car rounded a curve in the track. Even after the spot was hidden by the ridgeline, she tried to imagine him standing there, tall and dark against the sky.

"Law child, you look like you done seen a haint. You scared, ain't you?"

Lacey looked at Colin Riley, startled by the sound of his voice. She realized she must look a sight. She smoothed her hair back into place and picked at the tear in her dress. "No, I ain't scared," she lied trying to control the shakes that were working their way from her insides. "That fall just knocked the wind out of me."

"That boy say something he ort not of said? The way he tore outta here when he seen you fall, weren't no time to stop him."

"He just asked me was I hurt."

"I reckon he knows there's folks here that would fix his wagon if'n he tried anything out of hand."

"He didn't try nothing."

"You be careful round him just the same. He's got a wild streak in him goes clear to the bone."

Lacey didn't answer and they rode the rest of the way in silence.

"Work, Will, that's what it's all about." Lacey could hear her pa patiently explaining from the kitchen table. "A man's got to keep working and it don't matter doin' what."

"But, we're down to three and four days now, Pa," Will protested.

Lacey had cleared the supper dishes and was preparing some more bark for sassafras tea. Luckily, she had been able to collect enough roots from the ground where they had scattered to make the potion for her mother. The picture of her fleeing down the hillside flashed in her mind and made her wince.

Quickly wiping her hands, she took the coffee pot from the stove to refill her pa and Will's cup. Her ma had taken her supper in bed again. Her condition, it seemed, had set in for a spell. Lacey looked over at Ben playing by the cookstove. His bare feet were stained to the ankle with sulfur from playing in the creek beds near the mines and his face was tinged with coal dust. He looked sallow-cheeked and thinner than usual. She wondered if he was worried about their mother. He looked up and smiled his sweet smile. She slipped him a tea cake from the stack her ma saved for 'visiting.'

"This company's been good to us boy. We got this house, a garden spot, 'lectric light and I ain't seen you starve yet," Frank stated his voice clear and slow.

"Things is different now, Pa. You'll see how they act when it cuts into their pockets. They's trouble all over in the mines. Them big mines up in Harlan is trying to cut wages again and when they do you know it won't be long fore they're trying it here on us," Will said rising from his chair to stalk the room.

"I done knowed the foreman, Lawton Monroe, for going on fifteen years. You went to school with Lawton's younguns and played softball with his boys on Sunday."

"He's just the foreman. He don't have no say in nothing."

"He looks after the men. He sees to it we get work when he can."

"And what about Boyer, the general manager and Superintendent Shriver. Are they looking after us at 36 cents a ton?"

"They've always done right by us. It's just that they're hurting too, right now, with the price of coal dropping the way it is."

"And they're going to take the difference out of our wages," Will objected.

"Mark my words on this Will. If they find out you're taking up with the union, they'll have you out of there. And there won't be a mine left that'll hire you."

"A man's got to stand up for hisself."

"And when you are a man you can do just that."

Lacey turned from the stove at the sound of anger in her pa's voice. She turned in time to see Will's back as he stormed out the back door, taking the back steps with one leap. Will was the only member of the family who had ever made their pa angry and he had been doing it almost since his birth. She pushed the sassafras tea to the back of the stove and joined her pa at the table. The anger was gone from his face and sadness tinged the corners of his eyes.

"That boy just don't know. He ain't never been without. There's been many a time if I hadn't a growed it, I wouldn't of had nothing to eat. I give you younguns a purty decent life ain't I, Lacey?"

"I don't think Will's claiming otherwise, Pa. He always has been like a dog on too short a rope."

"I reckon, I have been a might tough on him at times, but he always was one to do whatever he took a notion to do. Maybe John can talk some sense into him."

Lacey blushed at the mention of John's name for she had hardly thought of him in days. She had promised to go to the brush arbor with him on Sunday. Several times a year, preachers would travel through for all day preaching and dinner on the grounds. It was an occasion for socializing as much as rekindling the fires of salvation. Sometimes a preacher would stay for two weeks, living with different families in the community.

"I'll have a talk with him on Sunday, Pa. I'm sure John can talk Will back down. He's just excitable."

"You're a fine gal, Lacey. You've never given me a cause to worry," he said staring at his pipe, embarrassed by the emotion in his voice.

"I'll be fine, Pa. Don't you fret," Lacey answered as she gently patted his rough hands. His face looked tired. The coal dust permanently embedded in the creases around his eyes gave him a haunted look. His simple words of praise warmed her, for she had tried always to please him. There had never been a reason to disobey him, for he was a wise and gentle man.

He sets a powerful store by John, she thought, *if he's willing to bring him into family matters.* She was worried about the brush arbor, when she and John would be together for most of the day. If he had plans to ask her to marry him, it might very well be then. It vexed her that she could come to no decision on the matter. Maybe it was just that she thought the answer should be yes and yet it was still no. It might be best to say yes and hope that her heart would catch up later. *Life was always handing you what you hadn't asked for and denying you your heart's craving,* she thought. She said goodnight to her pa softly, and left him still staring at his pipe.

Lacey awoke with the dark all around and felt for something familiar, finding the quilt she had thrown off in the restlessness of her sleep. She had been dreaming and even though she was safe in her own bed, she pulled her quilt about her shoulders for comfort. The dream had been about Coy Lynn Wilson and it embarrassed her even in the darkness of her room. He had come to her as she sat in a large meadow blooming with Queen Anne's lace and dandelions. He untied her hair and made her lie down spreading it out all around her head. Caressing each lock and stroking her face, he began to tell her a story without moving his lips. Each word was an embrace, a pat, a kiss. Her heart pounded and she reached out to him as though she was someone else and felt him warm and strong as he came to her. As she looked over his shoulder, she saw her father and John standing behind him in the field. They looked at her with sad eyes and turned away.

Even now, as she lay awake in her bed, she trembled. She thought that if she looked in the mirror, she might still show the marks of the dream on her face or that if her pa or John saw her they might treat her differently as if they could know her dream. And yet, even as she lay shaken by the dream, she could still see Coy's face above her and hear him whisper, "I can see what you're thinking, Lacey. I can see it in those beautiful blue eyes." No one had ever called her beautiful before. Suddenly, the thought of it made her want to weep and she turned her face into her quilt to stop the tears.

John sat by the fire carving the delicate spindle to Lacey's four poster bed. He already thought of it as Lacey's bed. He wanted her to have a real bed with a real mattress. The design had been in a mail order catalog. He had carefully copied it, adding only a few flowers on the headboard. *Lacey would like that*, he thought. He had loved her all of his life it seemed. Even when she was very young there had been something about her. He had watched her grow up; waiting for the day he would ask her to marry him.

There was more bad news coming from Kentucky. Thousands of men, angry and frightened, had gathered for the big rally in Kentucky. Conditions were quickly worsening in Harlan. Gun thugs were already being brought in to control the miners and several men had lost their jobs for their union work. John hated how news from so far away was changing his world. If another wage cut was a certainty for Harlan, John felt that the Fentress Coal and Coke Company would then follow their lead. If there was to be another cut, John felt sure it would be in July when their contract ran out. The men were able to get a contract only because the year before the management had been unable to agree upon a lock out. He couldn't ask Lacey until things were more settled.

"John," his ma called from the kitchen, "suppers 'bout ready. You best be getting yourself cleaned up."

"I'm coming, Ma. Just doing some final sanding," John answered. He could hear his mother humming in the kitchen as she set the table. She had adjusted well to the death of his father and he knew that he was the reason. A miner's widow usually didn't fare as well unless she had kin to fall back on, and even then it was a sorry life moving from household to household until she could remarry. Cora, his ma, was showing no signs of doing that. She seemed content to live there with John. With dropping wages and shorter hours, it was going to be harder to take a wife. There was no doubt the two could get along. Cora was a wiry, hard working woman with a sunny disposition. She might even welcome female company in the house, John thought. Maybe he was being too cautious. No, for Lacey's sake, he would bide his time.

Even now Coy could still not believe he had said it. He had gotten up early and pulled on a flannel shirt and jeans. It was barely dawn as he made his way through the woods to a clump of pines behind the Conners' place. The trees dripped a steady beat from the last night's rain. The ground fog almost hid the house but he could tell someone was up and had stoked the fire. Smoke billowed from the chimney.

A determined raindrop plopped into his right eye. *Maybe this wasn't such a great idea,* he thought shivering in his flannel shirt. In his haste he had left his denim jacket on the nail by the back door. He had thought about it all night until he could wait no longer. The words had been spinning over and over in his mind like a wheel coming back each time to the beginning. He had said the words so many times to himself; he thought she might know them already. Now as he stood with the spring rain soaking through the soles of his boots, he was beginning to feel like a fool. He had come to apologize to Lacey. He had seen her fall and instinctively he was off the train and by her side before he could think. He hadn't meant to laugh. At the sight of her pale and hurt, he had wanted to reach out to her. It was that look she gave him that made him put his guard up.

He had never apologized to anyone in his life. Apologizing was like admitting you cared what folks thought. It was like admitting you needed something from them.

Although he had spent the last four years learning not to need anybody, it had started long before that. Something in his mother's eyes — a look of hurt and hate — had taught him early on not to want anything that could turn on you.

"So what the hell am I doing here now," he said to the butt of his cigarette as he sat squatting on his haunches. Readjusting the brim of his Stetson, he flicked the butt of his cigarette to the ground. A noise at the back door alerted his senses like the whinny of a nervous horse. Lacey's pa and brother Will were leaving. They were dressed in denim overalls and carried their miner's caps and dinner pails.

Coy hunkered down to avoid being seen by the men. He'd give them time to get out of sight and then he would head back over the ridgeline. *This was no time in his life to be changing his ways*, he thought.

Then he saw her standing in the mist. She had on the same simple cotton dress, and he suddenly pictured her carefully mending the tear. Her hair was combed free, falling to her waist. She was pumping water from the community well a few yards from the house, and he could see her dress stretch taut around her slender hips as she bent to pump the handle. The strong, sure movements of her young body sent a rush of need that made him shudder. *How at home she is, a perfectly cut piece in this jigsaw puzzle*, he mused warily.

And then he was bounding through the freshly plowed garden, ignoring the path and reaching the porch just as she set the heavy bucket down on the top step. He stopped short as she turned to face him. The morning mist had dampened her hair, and the soft tendrils caressed her face and curled playfully under her chin. The chill of the morning had heightened the glow of her cheeks, and her eyes were wide with surprise. He wanted to stop time, for he knew that in the next moment she would run from him. When the shock of his sudden appearance wore off, she would turn, and God help him, he *would* care. And then she backed up one step and the old Coy was back, protecting him, watching out and making sure he never got too close.

Coy swaggered toward the porch, tilting his hat back and propping a muddy boot on the top step. He could see her reaching behind her, her hand trying to find the door handle.

"What are you doing here?" she whispered breathlessly. "It's barely past daybreak. Pa and Will ain't left for work yet."

"Well now, that's peculiar. Unless you got boarders, I do believe I saw somebody leaving here carrying dinner buckets just a few minutes ago that looked a whole lot like 'em."

"Just how long you been out here, anyhow, and what are you doing lurking around a body's back yard?"

Coy took off his hat and leaned over to rest his arms on his leg. He saw her shiver and wondered again at his ability to cause such fear. His well-rehearsed speech left his brain and caught in his throat. "Up at the Ramsey place they ain't never in a hurry to greet the sunrise. I'm in a habit of getting up early."

"That don't explain why you're here."

"No, it don't at that," he agreed matter-of-factly. Then he noticed the scrape on the inside of her right arm, probably where the skin had been rubbed off when she tried to block her fall. He reached out for her arm to get a better look. He had treated animals on the ranch, and they always responded to his touch.

Lacey backed up quickly and reached behind awkwardly with her left hand. Coy heard the latch lift and felt a sense of panic. Backing down the step in one easy movement, he turned his left palm up as though checking for rain, casually scanning the dreary, gray sky.

"I reckon it might fair off by noon. And to answer your question, I was just worried about you. You took a bad spill yesterday. That's a mean looking scrape you got on that arm."

Lacey looked down at her arm as though it belonged to someone else. "Things must be considerable dull at the Ramsey's for you to be asking 'bout my arm at this hour. Besides, you didn't seem so all-fired concerned when you was laughing at me."

He had been hoping that she would be grateful that he had come, that she would understand. He had half pictured them sitting on the steps, Lacey with her knees tucked under her chin talking away the morning, inviting him for supper later. Well, that wasn't the way with people. Not even it seemed, Lacey Conners. "Well, you have to admit you was a funny sight," Coy chuckled, twirling his hat in his hand. "You smacked the ground like you'd been sawed down, twigs and limbs flying off of you just like a tree falling in the woods."

He could see the anger rise up her body, making it rigid. "Stop it. Just stop it right now! I can't believe you come all the way over here in the rain just to ask after me and then you poke fun at me. Why did you come here?" she asked, her voice questioning. "I don't just mean here today. I mean why did you come back to Wilder? Do you mean to belittle everybody in this town, make them mad all over again so you can turn and spit on them? Do you intend to make fun of the whole town and you've just been practicing on me? Answer me, Coy! Why did you ever come back here?"

He could hardly hear her words for the sight of her so slight, so frightened, making her stand like a wild animal caught in a snare. He watched as the sun came over the ridgeline, falling across her face and licking at her hair like a candle flame. In the space of a heartbeat, nineteen years of pain and hurt and loneliness rushed to the pit of his stomach like the kick of a mustang and almost brought him to his knees. Then he realized that she was staring at him with a puzzled look, waiting for him to speak.

"I reckon I come back for you, Lacey," he said. Then he turned on his heel and was gone, but not before he heard her gasp.

Coy couldn't remember the first time he had seen the look in his mother's eyes. Maybe it had always been there. There was one time, he remembered, when he was five. He had been playing with some wooden soldiers his ma had told him she bought from a peddler. They were hand-carved and carefully painted to look like Yankee and Rebel soldiers. They were his pride, and he played for hours, planning each battle. Sometimes his pa would get down on the floor with him and tell him stories about the burning of Atlanta and Sherman's March to the Sea, and his ma would just sit in her chair by the fire staring at him. It was a look that made him want to say he was sorry, but something else in the look always stopped him. Then one day she got up from her chair and grabbed him up from the floor, shaking him until he could hear his teeth clacking and his head snap. Silently, she gathered up all of his soldiers and put them in the stove, leaving the door open so he could watch them burn, the blues and grays rising in colored smoke as the little soldiers died. After that she never looked at him much. She still cooked, cleaned and mended, and everything went on as before. But he had liked it better when she had had the look.

It was sometime after that, he reckoned, when he and his pa had started to fight. It seemed he couldn't do a thing to please him. Somewhere along the line he just stopped trying, staying clear of them both as much as he could. He stayed clear of most everybody, taking to saying whatever struck his fancy and to hell with them. He got to be pretty good at making up stories, and it became second nature to him. This made folks notice him. It was amazing what some folks would believe, and he got to where he could always give them what they wanted. When he could get hold of a newspaper, he would read the serials over and over. Somewhere in a place called Algiers, men joined the Foreign Legion and led "reckless lives of thrilling adventures." He dreamed about far away places where bold men did great deeds of daring and always won.

He dreamed, all right. He guessed that was what had made him so ready to leave Wilder that day. Hell, there didn't seem to be any way to win in Wilder. Of course, a lot had changed in his life. He had gone west and had lived an adventure. Up close, it had been pretty tough. In Jake's eyes and in his own, he had been a fine ranch hand. Jake had never asked about his past, and what little he had told him had been accepted without question. He could look into Jake's eyes and not see hurt; and he had been a different Coy.

Maybe he had come back to see if the new Coy could survive the trip or if he really existed. And now, he'd gone and fallen in love with a Wilder girl. Not just any Wilder girl, but one so much a part of the place she could have been cut from the mountainside. She was the only daughter of one of the most respected miners in Wilder. And like some dang fool, he'd just gone and told her he'd come back for her, and her looking at him like he was some kind of lunatic. "Coy, son, you sure know how to bring yourself grief," he said out loud to the trees. Laughing grimly to himself, he headed up the steep slope to the Ramsey place.

6

Lacey filled two plates with mounds of food and carried them to a large oak where John was already spreading a quilt. The preaching had been going on for over three hours, and the crowd was drained. They eagerly filled their plates with food the women had brought in covered dishes and spread on long tables covered with white tablecloths. People made their way to the shade of the trees to stretch out, eat their dinners, and rest.

The women were already forcing second helpings on Brother Roberts, the traveling preacher. He had drawn quite a crowd with his talk of hellfire and brimstone and was no doubt entitled to second helpings for the souls he had worked so hard to save, Lacey thought. His face, so recently puffed and mottled with the heat, had gone slack. With his thin, white hair smoothed back into place and the sleeves of his white shirt rolled up, he looked like anyone's favorite uncle, smiling and nodding as the womenfolk flocked about preening and pandering.

In spite of all his descriptive talk of the fate that would befall those who did not heed the Word, many of the men had wandered in and out of the brush arbor during the long sermon to gather in small groups to whittle and talk of other things. However, the women had sat in rapt attention, their faces turned upward at the preacher's heavenly words, glancing down only to shoot meaningful looks at the men and children.

Lacey looked at John who was attacking his food with relish. He glanced up his mouth full, and grinned sheepishly. It was a look so sweet and familiar it tugged at her heart and sent a spasm of guilt to her stomach. She had spent most of the last three hours trying to keep her mind on the sermon. Secretly, she searched the crowd for Coy. She realized it was a most unlikely place for him to be, but she could not keep her thoughts off him. It had been four days since she had faced him on the back porch and had heard him say he had come back for her. By now she was sure that she had imagined it or that he had been making a fool of her again. It confused her more with each rethinking. She had never been so angry with anyone in her life. Most likely he wouldn't even remember what he had said. He was the type, she reasoned, that said whatever struck his fancy without thought to what folks might think, least of all her. Still, he'd had a look about him standing there in the mist, his brow creased, his eyes shadowed, like he had suddenly come to some realization.

Law' me, Lacey, she thought, *you surely are the craziest thing! Coy Lynn Wilson couldn't be nothing but trouble. He just seems bent on destroying everything in his path.* It made her think of a storm that had set down on the Runion place once. The force of the high winds had swirled and twisted the tall grass into tight masses and bowed the heads of the trees. And even then she had wondered why. It was such a senseless striking out. Coy was like that: powerful and beautiful and dangerous. Like a raging storm, he would move on until he burned himself out. Speaking up to him had been like throwing herself in the path of that storm. She had been surprised when her words had stopped him short. His fierce dark eyes had widened and for a moment his body had stiffened in surprise.

"You haven't touched your food, Lacey," John admonished.

"Too many goings on, I reckon," Lacey mumbled. Slowly she came to the realization that she was still at the brush arbor with John. She had the feeling that hours or even days had passed and John had been sitting patiently waiting for her return. "I see you done all right for yourself," she said noticing his empty plate. "Would you like me to get you some more to eat?"

"No thanks. Guess I done eat a cow's bait, at that. Being outside must give me an appetite. That sure was good huckleberry pie. I noticed you brung it."

"You don't have to say so just 'cause I brung it."

"I wouldn't. You know that."

Lacey smiled her thanks and they sat in silence. John didn't seem to have much need to talk and she couldn't think of any news to tell him. He hadn't brought up the matter of them getting married and she was relieved. She needed to bring up the subject of Will, but she wasn't sure how. John had never discussed any of the problems in the mines with her and she didn't know how much she should know. Her pa had always talked to her like she was a man. It might have been little more than his way of worrying out loud, but he was always telling her about the daily goings on in the mines and about the true working of things. He talked about the men who made the decisions that affected their lives and the way they worked. Because he understood power, he knew how little of it the miners had and it had made him a cautious man.

"John, Pa says there may be trouble again in the mines," she ventured cautiously.

"I reckon your pa's got reason enough to believe it."

"What reason you got to believe it, John?"

"Oh, they's been talk of another wage cut. Won't be no trouble if we accept what they give us." John kept his voice low and glanced over his shoulder before continuing. "They been cheating on their agreements for some time now. We the same as don't have no contract. If we accept this next cut, they as same as broke the union in this country."

Lacey was struck by the hardness in his voice. "You sound like you're not planning on accepting it."

"Look around that table over there, Lacey. How many women you think pulled out the last of their canned stuff to set that spread? How many families you think'll have to scrape by tomorrow on fatback and greens? And it ain't just that. We've had three men killed in the mines in the last two years. They don't care nothing about our safety. The mine inspectors just look the other way while the miners cut corners trying to make a living wage. They don't have time to set timbers and shore up walls. And all the time the mine owners yelling they're losing money."

Lacey had never heard John talk so, and she wondered if he was thinking of his father. "You believe in the union, don't you, John?"

He looked at her with veiled eyes that revealed only the seriousness of his intentions, and then looked around cautiously to see if her voice had carried. "A lot of good men believe in the union, Lacey. I'm just one of them. This here is the only miner's union south of the Ohio River. I just happen to believe that's worth fighting for. I know your pa thinks it's a chancy thing, and I want you to know I wasn't the one that brought Will into it. He done that on his own. I know one thing. There comes a time when a man stands to lose it all, no matter which way he sides. I'm a miner, and I'll always be one."

"Pa's not against the union. He's just seen a lot of hard times that made him cautious."

"Hard times is what the union is all about. The union give us the only say-so we've ever had in the mines on how things was to be. Joining up is something a man's got to do of his own free will, or it don't mean nothing, especially when the going gets rough."

"I don't think I've heard you talk so serious, John." In fact, she had never heard him speak so many words on any subject.

"I always wanted to live out my life in Wilder. I thought you felt the same way."

"It's my home, John. You got no call to think you care more about it than I do."

John looked at her shamefaced. "No, I ain't got no call. I know how you feel about this town. The truth is, ain't none of this belong to us. No matter how hard the folks here work, they ain't never going to own the house they live in or the land it's on. The coal company owns it. Lock, stock, and barrel. They do things to suit theirselves. If they took a notion to fire a man and throw him out of his house, it wouldn't matter if he'd worked ever day like a dog in the mines and lived in that house for ten year. They could do it 'cause they got the power to say what goes. The union seems like the only chance we got to hang on to what we got, to build any kind of life here." John scratched at the soft ground with a twig, making circles in the dirt. Without looking up, he whispered, "I'm doing this for you too, Lacey."

She looked at his veiny hand, the coal-stained fingernails nervously pushing at the ground. It was the first hint of his plans for their future. "John, you're into this deep, ain't you?"

John gave her a sidelong glance.

"What'll the company do to you if they find out?"

Shrouding his eyes with a hand, John stroked his forehead and spoke softly. "Everything they can, Lacey. Everything they can."

Lacey sat in silence, amazed at this side of John she had never known.

"It's high time we took a walk and stretched our legs before that preacher starts in again," he announced abruptly.

Suddenly, John was on his feet, holding out his hand to her. The subject was obviously closed, but Lacey wondered just how involved John was in the union. She had heard tales about what happened when the union tried to come into other coal camps up in Kentucky and West Virginia. Her pa had had a cousin killed up in Matewan during a strike. He'd been shot dead in the streets. It was hard to think of such things happening in Wilder. It was hard to think of John being in danger. As he reached for her hand and they started down the path that led to the river, for the first time in her life she felt she didn't know him at all.

"Good weather for a preaching," Lacey said to break the silence as they walked the path along the creek. The brush arbor was being held a mile up the creek from the mines, where the water was still clear of sulfur. Other young couples strolled the path or sat on the rocks along the bank.

"Does seem exceptional warm for April, don't it?"

She could feel him glance at her occasionally as they strolled. Several times she thought he wanted to say something, but it was only to inquire after her ma or to ask how her garden was coming.

As the time drew near for them to return to the preaching, Lacey didn't know whether to laugh or cry about her feelings. One minute she was terrified John would bring up the subject of marriage, and the next minute she was half mad at him that he seemed reluctant to ask. She was so lost in her thoughts that she didn't notice Coy until they were almost upon him. And then he was there, standing not a hundred feet away on the path. The smile froze on her lips, and she was horrified to think that he might assume she was smiling at him.

"Coy, how are you?" John greeted him warmly in his unassuming way. "It's been quite a while. It's good to have you back in Wilder. Where have you been keeping yourself?"

"Oh, I tried my hand at ranching out Wyoming way."

"Seems I did hear something about that. You remember Lacey Conners, don't you?" John said, turning to face her.

"Hello, Lacey. It's good to see you again. You're looking right pretty today," Coy greeted her pleasantly. He looked her squarely in the eye as he spoke, and there was nothing in his manner or look to suggest anything out of the ordinary. Standing tall and dark next to the wiry John, she was struck by how handsome he was. The thought made her blush and she barely managed to stammer a polite thank you before Coy turned his attention back to John. They talked on for a few minutes as Lacey struggled to gain control of herself. Wandering off the path, she pretended to be looking at a cluster of birdsfoot violets in bloom. Snatches of their conversation drifted in and out of her hearing, but her head was spinning too much to make sense of it. The relaxed cadence of their speech and their seeming ease with each other struck her as peculiar. And then, Coy was leaving, saying goodbye politely to John. He was walking towards her.

"Good-bye, Lacey. It was good seeing you again," he said loudly. "I hope I didn't keep you from your walk."

"No, not at all. We was just walking," she said stupidly. "It was good to see you, Coy," she stammered, wishing she were dead.

When he bent ever so slightly towards her, she almost drew back from his closeness but he took hold of her arm, rooting her in place. " Meet me here tomorrow. Please," he whispered.

She felt her eyes widen in surprise, felt herself shaking her head, all the while his eyes pleaded with her. No words of reply came to her rescue, and before she could summon her wits, Coy brushed past her and was gone. She could hear John calling to her, but she was powerless to move. Finally, she turned and wandered blankly back to where he stood waiting for her.

"Are you all right?" he asked.

Aware that he was staring at her, she willed herself to calm the trembling that threatened to shake her whole body, but all she could manage was a nod in response to his question. He took her by the arm and led her gently back to the brush arbor. Neither of them spoke, and John did not ask again. She knew he wouldn't.

The morning had gone on forever. The denim overalls Lacey scrubbed on the washboard were like living things resisting her touch, and they fought her as she tried to hang them on the line. By noon, she sat down on the back porch steps only half way through the morning's chores. She had not slept at all, and that was slowing her down. It had been a starless night, and the darkness had closed in on her. The silence of her room had roared in her ears until she felt like she was trapped in a cave without a light, finally, she had slipped out onto the back porch to suck in great gulps of the cool night air. By dawn the words Coy had whispered by the river, "Meet me here tomorrow. Please," were still ringing in her ears.

When she could think at all, she thought that it was just as well that the work was hard today. It was a test of will, but at least she was familiar with the chores. Not that she had any intention of meeting Coy by the river. It was an act too shameless to contemplate. Why would he ask this of her? She could still feel his warm breath on her neck and the pleading sound of his voice. The whisper came to her as an ache in her stomach and an occasional shiver down her spine. No words of reasoning filled her head. It was just an inner knowledge that this one indefensible act defied the rules of her existence, and he had no right to ask it of her. Once, she remembered, Ben had taken Pa's Tree Brand pocket knife. Pa had washed up and left it by the wash pan, and the temptation had been too great. Ben had brought it back before Pa had missed it, but the blade had been put up wet and by the time Pa found it the damage had been done. The rule had been broken and the damage done, never to be undone. It was like that now. Even if no one found out, the damage would be done by the act itself.

Her head ached, and she decided to walk to the garden and check the newly planted potatoes. She liked to plant potatoes in April, although many folks planted theirs in February or March. Her pa had plowed the rows deep and had prepared them with manure. She had cut up the potatoes she had saved from last year, making sure that each piece had at least two eyes before she planted it deeply in the loose soil. The rows looked beautiful, and Lacey pictured the plants growing green and strong over the ridges. She turned her face to the warm spring sun and closed her eyes to soak up its strength. It was a good and familiar feeling being in her garden with the warm sun on her face. This was the feeling she would have with John, warm and comfortable. She wondered how she could ever want anything else, how she could ever have thought of anything else. She had brought this on herself that day on Buck Rock when she had longed for something she couldn't name.

And then she was running with no direction in mind, her heart pounding and her mind racing. She thought she might scream if she didn't keep running. Where had all these crazy feelings come from, and why did they have to come into her life now? She had always been a person who could do the "right thing," whatever her pa wanted or her ma, or Ben, or even Will. And now, John. John was such a good and decent man. Now Coy, a man who broke all the rules, who made her furious with his every word, who defied the life he had been born into, was turning her inside out. It was time to get hold of herself.

She didn't know when she first thought to go to Buck Rock. She was halfway there before she realized her feet had any direction at all. It would be a good place to be. The air would be clear and clean, and she could be alone to think things out. Maybe she could beg God to forgive her foolishness and give her another chance. If she could just make it there before God decided to punish her wickedness that was exactly what she would do. She felt better for knowing her way and quickly lost herself in the familiar path, her mind caught up in just how she would present her case.

She was upon Coy before she realized she had missed the turn up to the slick to Buck Rock. He wasn't expecting her. He was fishing and had caught half a dozen fair-sized blue gills and was stringing them on a line. After re-baiting his hook and securing the pole in a hole in the ground, Coy resumed his whittling. He was working on a piece of seasoned white pine, turning it into a red-tailed hawk, the wings spread wide in a beautiful gliding motion. She could tell by the precise and patient motion of his hands that he was an expert carver.

And then it came to her where she was. A low moan, like an animal in pain, brought him to full attention. She realized that the sound had come from her. How had she come to be here? Why had she come? She stood before him, frightened and shaken by her self-betrayal. He jumped up as soon as he saw her but made no move toward her.

"I didn't mean to come," she said with a trembling voice.

"Well, it don't appear that way since you are sure enough here," Coy said grinning and putting away his knife.

"You don't think...," Lacey stammered furious at the suggestion in his words. When she wheeled to go, he grabbed her by the arm, nearly causing her to stumble.

"I'm sorry," he stammered. "I mean, did I hurt you?" He spoke slowly, letting go of her arm and making sure she was steadied.

She stood, braced to run. In truth, her limbs were too weak to move. "Don't come near me," she hissed.

"I won't touch you, I promise. I didn't mean nothing by that. I'm just pleased; however you come to be here. I had no right to expect it."

He looked down at her hands, and she gripped them tightly together to stop their shaking. She thought she might never be able to speak again. The words jammed her throat so tight it ached. "No, you didn't. Why?" she rasped her voice a ragged whisper.

Instead of answering her, he reached out and gently took her in his arms. She found herself yielding to his touch, and he held her until the trembling stopped. Finally, he took her face in his hands and looked at her. He looked down at her with such fierceness that she didn't know what he expected from her. She balked and tried to pull herself free.

"No, please, don't leave. I won't hurt you, I promise. You are just so beautiful and I am so happy you are here."

His voice had that same lonely, pleading sound that had followed her for days. Suddenly, nothing seemed as important as the moment there with him and the need to believe that he found her beautiful. Then, without knowing why, she smiled a crazy, crooked smile that made him laugh.

He grabbed her, pulling her tightly to him and twirling her around and around until they both laughed, unable to express why it made them so happy. "Do you believe me Lacey? Do you believe that I would never hurt you and that you are the most beautiful woman in the world?"

"I don't believe any of this."

He laughed out loud. "Lacey, you are priceless."

"You're making fun of me again."

"No, I'm not. You take me wrong."

"How am I supposed to take you? You don't act like noboby I ever knowed. Like asking me to meet you here instead of coming by the house proper."

"Folks have a hard time accepting me, or ain't you heard?"

She blushed at his words because they were true. "You ain't no criminal."

"Worse than that. I don't give a damn what folks think. You wouldn't believe how that puts a burr in their saddle."

This time she had to laugh, and she was surprised by the way it made Coy's face light up.

They sat down by the river under an oak and wondered at the strangeness of their coming together. It was something neither one of them had wanted or expected, and they sat in silence for a moment in wonderment. Finally, they began to talk, talking the afternoon away while trying to piece the puzzle together. He talked to her of things that he had never shared with anyone, of his growing up and his search for a place to fit. She listened as he tried to explain what it was like to feel like the cause of someone else's suffering. How it felt as a child to feel that responsible for someone's unhappiness and not know how to fix it. It made her think of Ben and she found herself wanting to protect Coy from the pain as she had always done for her brother. But his rage and anger frightened her.

Lacey talked to Coy about her love of her family and the town and of her need to bind life together into something whole and good. Quietly, softly, she talked around her secret longings. She did not talk of her sacrifice in coming to him that day. For the first time in her life, she thought only of the moment. At times she wanted to reach out and touch him, but she was afraid it might change something, that she might awaken from the dream. Even then she thought he might turn on her and make her out to be a fool for thinking he could care anything about her. That he could find her anything but scraggly and dull. But he didn't turn on her. He listened, softly, quietly, with a look in the depths of his dark, brooding eyes that she hoped was understanding.

When the tension grew too great between them, Coy swooped her up and threatened to throw her, fully clothed, into the chilly mountain stream. Then he waded in, carrying her until his boots and jeans were soaked and they were laughing so hard he almost dropped her in the water. By the time they reached the bank, he was telling her about the time he almost drowned trying to pull a Hereford calf from a frozen stream and how it had followed him around for weeks thinking he was its mother. She laughed until tears streamed down her face, and she could barely gasp her reply. "Well, you can just take me back and toss me in if you are expecting the same kind of nonsense from me."

And he grabbed her and pretended to toss her in, but he caught her just in time and silenced her scream with a gentle kiss. She felt the passion he fought to control and marveled that he could feel these things for her.

The early afternoon shadows played in the trees and danced on the ground. "I know you have to go," he whispered into her hair.

"I'll be missed. They'll ask questions."

"Will I see you tomorrow?"

"No, but soon," she said and her voice was sure and clear. In her heart she wondered how.

"How will I know where to meet you?"

"I'll get word to you somehow."

They parted slowly, reluctantly, their fingertips lingering. Before she walked away, he gave her the red-tailed hawk, telling her how each time he carved something; it was like setting it free from the wood. When he handed it to her, she realized that it was only partially finished.

7

John stood at the driftmouth of the mines in the cool mist of the morning. It was 5:00 a.m. and the men had been gathering for some time to start the workday. Most of the men had to walk for over a mile to Mine No. 3 since the earlier two mines closer to camp had played out over the years. That, at least, was a blessing to the town since it reduced the coal dust and the smell from the burning slag heap down a little.

They came dressed in their denim jackets and overalls over long cotton underwear and yarn socks. Their dinner buckets held fresh drinking water on the bottom layer and bologna sandwiches or beans and cornbread on the second layer. On their heads they wore the soft canvas and leather miner's cap with its open flame carbide light. Some of the men contented themselves by whittling on discarded mining timbers, not making anything in particular except shavings, but keeping their hands busy. Joe Morgan put down his dinner bucket and squatted on his haunches next to Wilford Potter, who was contentedly stuffing half a plug of Red Devil chewing tobacco into his left cheek. John knew Wilford would soon be offering him a cut off the plug and the teasing would begin. Most of the miners either chewed or smoked some form of tobacco. John did neither.

"Reckon you'll be wanting about half of this here plug, won't you, John?" said Wilford holding the plug out to John, his knife readied at the halfway mark.

"Mighty kind of you, Wilford, but I can't says I will," John answered good naturedly. He was not one for "cutting up," but he had learned to put up with the practical joking of most of the miners.

"John, you ain't afraid you're going to ruin that purty smile of yern and slow them womenfolk down that's been chasing you?" Joe Morgan joined in.

"It ain't seemed to slow ole Wilford down. He's got six younguns and another on the way," Fergie Jensen said laughing uproariously at his own joke. He was the bawdiest of the bunch and liked to regale the men with his talk of topping off some young thing from one of the surrounding towns. No one else liked to work with him because of his constant practical jokes and bragging, but Wilford had taken him on as a helper and they had grown to like each other. "Yes, sir. In fact, there must be something in that stuff makes a feller's pecker stand at attention. Don't you reckon? Now, I wouldn't be a needin' nuthing like that."

"Oh, Lord," the men groaned as Fergie elaborated on his latest conquest. John was relieved to have the attention drawn to someone else. He knew the bragging and teasing were necessary to relieve the tension of facing the mine everyday, but he was just as glad to have his part of it done.

The men talked on, growing louder and bawdier as more men gathered and the time grew near to enter the mine. Finally, the men stamped out the last of their cigarettes, picked up their dinner pails and tools, and quietly made their way to the coal cars. Those who could rode the empty coal cars along the main heading to the place where their working room turned off to the left or right. If a man was lucky enough to work a vein that was high enough, he could walk without stooping all the way to his "opening," the space he had dug out for himself and claimed as his spot. A man was only paid for what he could haul out in a day. Since the strike in '24, there had been no pay for man trips, the time it took to get to and from the work.

The air inside the mine was cool and damp. The men were solemn and quiet, eager to be at their work. In the old days, "company men" would have stayed over to blast the day before, and the coal would be ready to load when the men arrived. Now it was necessary for the men to do their own blasting, and it sometimes took half a day before they were ready to start loading.

Nowadays, with work scarce, a blast at 7 p.m. would signal whether there would be work the next day. Three whistle blasts meant there would be work; one blast meant the men could sleep on. John knew that many of the men could not sleep after hearing the one blast, for it meant a smaller paycheck at the end of the week.

The mine dripped and creaked and groaned its greeting. John worked as Barney Graham's helper. Each miner worked with a helper. The older, more experienced miner usually worked the "face" while the younger loaded the coal into the cars. As soon as John and Barney reached the face, they began immediately to set the safety timbers as close to the coal as possible. The timbers were five or six inches thick and helped to keep the loose rock in the roof from sagging. Many a man had been killed by rock slides and collapsing roofs in the mines and John had no intention of being one of them. The surrounding hills and ridges were filled with widows who had been forced to move out of camp housing into shacks and to live off tiny garden plots and small settlements they had received from the company.

That was why he liked working with Barney. It took extra time to set the timbers and drive the wedges between the jack-props and the roof, but Barney was willing to take it. He knew that because they had to do their own blasting, some of the men weren't taking the extra time to do it right.

The timbers set, John strapped on his thick rubber knee pads and began to cut the coal. A strip of coal had to be cut out about eight or nine inches above the floor and about fifteen feet wide. John and Barney worked to dig as far back as their pick handles would reach, leaving the coal suspended from the ceiling and by its two sides. John then strapped on his breastplate and attached a long auger about two inches in diameter. Pressing the auger as hard as possible against the massive block of coal, he bore a hole deep into its middle. Again and again he drilled until a line of holes covered the block. While John drilled, Barney prepared the charges. Black powder was fixed with fuses and shoved far back into the holes. Dead men, papers tightly rolled with dirt, were then tamped into the hole. Satisfied with their work, Barney called the shot-firer who checked the work and gave the o.k. to light the fuse. John held his carbide light to the fuses, and the men made a hasty retreat to a safe spot. The blast shook the tunnel and dust filled the air. They would have to wait a while for the dust to clear before they could begin to lay the rails that would bring the cars close enough to the fallen coal to begin the loading. It had taken Barney and John half a day to reach this point.

John leaned his back against the cool tunnel and slid to the ground. "We might as well be getting a bite of dinner, Barney. Looks like it's going to take a while for that to clear."

"Dang shame, when a man has to do his own blasting," Barney said more in wonderment than complaint. "It don't pay for a man to be remembering times past. I remember back in the days when all a man had to do was shovel it into the car, a good loader could haul out twenty-five to thirty tons a day. Now a man's lucky to do ten or fifteen tons, and that's working twice as hard as them days."

"Well, maybe they won't be much slate in this pile," John said trying to console the man he admired so much.

"One way to find out. That's eat up and get to it."

"You know a lot of the men don't take the time to eat their dinner now. They say they can't afford to lose the time."

"I know, son. I know," Barney said, a sigh hissing out through his lips.

"Wilford told me he hadn't even been setting jack props 'cepting when it looked like the roof was already bowed might near double."

"Hope you ain't suggesting we try a trick like that. A man ain't likely to die from missing his dinner, but he dang sure might if the roof caves in on him."

"I'm right glad you see it that way."

"Then let's have no more talk of such, you hear. And I promise not to mention the way things used to be. Is it a deal?" Barney said extending his hand for an exaggerated handshake.

"Deal," John agreed.

As their hands met, a low rumbling groan came from deeper within the mines. Their eyes met. "Rock slide," they said simultaneously and headed toward the sound.

It was in the west end tunnel where Wilford Potter and his helper Fergie Jensen were working. Fergie came running toward them from the opening. His face was ashen under the coal dust. "I told him. I told him it was going to give way one of these days. We was jus' taking too many chances. After we blasted I could hear her just a-cracking up overhead."

"Shut up, Fergie!" Barney snapped. "Tell us what happened. Is it Wilford?"

"Buried, under two feet of slate," Fergie gasped and pointed toward the workplace.

"John, get the picks and shovels. Fergie, come with me. He may still be alive."

"Ain't a prayer a man could live through that," Fergie said, shaking his head.

"Well, we sure as hell owe it to him to find out," Barney yelled, grabbing Fergie by the collar and forcing him back toward the opening.

John met Frank and Will Conners and half a dozen other men who had heard the too familiar rumbling noise. They all were carrying picks and shovels. Frank handed John a pick. "Here, John, I brung your tools along. Who is it?"

"It's Wilford Potter, Frank. Roof fell in on him."

"Hurt bad?"

"Don't know, yet. Fergie said it looked bad. Did somebody get word to Lawton?"

"First thing. The whistles done been sounded by now."

The men were silent as they walked on toward the opening, each one aware that his family would be gathering outside the mine, hoping and praying, worry etched on their faces. John tried not to think about the day they had brought his father out. His pa had been setting charges; the shot-firer had checked everything and given the word to light the fuse. The fuse had hissed and spit its way to the charge, but the blast had not come. After waiting long enough to feel the fire must be dead, his pa had gone to pull the charge. The blast had gone off in his face, blowing him several feet and burying him in tons of coal. John had seen it all and relived it many times with each new accident. Somehow, it was the look on his ma's face that had been the hardest thing to bear. The thought of Wilford's wife waiting at the entrance made him desperate to get to the man. "Frank, I'm going on ahead. You get the men started this way."

The entrance to the opening that Wilford and Fergie worked was a low vein, and John had to stoop to get to the face. By the time he saw a light in the tunnel, he was almost crawling. He could make out the shadowy face of Barney Graham bent over a pile of slate, but he was making no effort to remove the rock. John thought he might be praying, but when he got closer he could see Wilford trapped beneath the rock, buried up to his chest. He was trying to talk to Barney who was bent low to catch the faint sounds. Fergie was on his knees beside them, twisting his cap helplessly. Finally, Barney looked up and nodded to John. "He's dead. Fergie, you best get the word out to the rest of the men."

Fergie sat on his haunches, motionless. Tears streamed down his blackened face, and his body shook with great painful shudders.

John crawled closer to him and took him gently by the arm. "Fergie, we need you to go on out now and tell the men what's happened. They need to get word out to his wife. We'll take care of things here. You understand me, now, Fergie," John said, shaking Fergie's limp arm until he looked up. John wasn't sure Fergie understood, but he turned and scrambled toward the tunnel without saying a word. John turned back to Barney, "Fergie's taking it pretty hard. I reckon Wilford was about the only person that ever was halfway decent to the boy."

"It's hard on all of us, son. We've all lost friends and family to the mines at one time or another. It don't get any easier with the numbers."

"There's something else bothering you this time, Barney. What is it?"

"I was just thinking, a man gets killed, and the way things is now, the men won't even get paid for removing this rock slide. A man's life ought to be worth something."

John looked down at Wilford's bruised and battered face. Blood leaked slowly from his mouth and ears, and his eyes bulged in sightless disbelief. "What did Wilford say to you before he died?"

"He begged me not to let his family starve," Barney answered wearily as he grabbed his pick and started to break up the slate.

Rain pelted the pine box as the men trudged the muddy road from the wagon to the cemetery. The Wilder cemetery stood at the top of Glover's Hill on a piece of land that was too rough to live on and no good for mining. It had been left to the dead to give it a purpose. A crowd gathered around the grave for the brief ceremony. Wilford Potter's six children stood like stair-steps next to their mother, already big with the seventh child. Their little faces were sallow and drained from three days of grief and uncertainty. The men set the casket down and stood uncomfortably by the gravesite.

The grave, which had been dug the previous day, was beginning to fill up with water, and the men fidgeted at the sight. John was eager to have it done, for he was bone tired from the ordeal. The Widow Potter had been helpless in her grief, and it had been left to John and Barney to have a casket made and arrange for the service. The funeral was paid for by the burial association. Having a proper burial was a great concern to the men, so the company deducted money from each paycheck for the inevitability of a man's death. The women, of course, had gone in immediately to dress the body and bring food. Many of them had been taking turns sitting up with the family, cleaning the house and caring for the children.

Barney had not mentioned again the promise he made to the dying Wilford, but John knew that it was weighing heavy upon him. The whole accident had left Barney solemn and grim. John knew he was worried about the conditions in the mines. What had happened to Wilford was happening much too often, even in a dangerous business like mining. It was a sign the men were getting desperate. Matters could only get worse if the men did not win a new contract in July, and it would be a heavy burden on them all, even a strong one like Barney. John was anxious to have the funeral done so they could meet and make plans.

The preacher was to the part about greater rewards and streets paved with gold when John looked up and met Lacey's eyes. She smiled a weak smile and looked quickly away. He suddenly realized that it had been a week since they had seen each other. With the accident and all the union goings on, he hadn't had time to think of anything else. He would make it up to her on Sunday if she wasn't too upset with him. He looked forward to sitting peacefully on the porch with her after church.

The preacher had said his last amens, and the mourners were leading the family away. Fergie's face had not been among the crowd. He had not been seen since he fled the mines on the day of the accident. The other bachelor miners he shared a house with on the edge of town said he had not been back to get his things, and since he had no family that anyone knew about, most folks thought he had just left town the same way he had drifted in one day.

John and some of the other men stayed behind to lower the coffin into the watery grave. The rain-soaked clay dirt hit the coffin with a thud as mournful as any hymn they had sung at the funeral. The words of an old church hymn rang in his ears as he shoveled, "Rock of ages, cleft for me, let me hide myself in thee." *There'll be no hiding from what was coming for the miners*, John thought. He wondered solemnly if they would all have to wait for heaven to bring them a better life. "While I draw this fleeting breath, When my eyes shall close in death." The words went on in his head matching the rhythm of the shovels.

John was sitting with Barney at his kitchen table when two men from the other locals arrived to discuss the union's demands for the new contract in July. John and Barney stood up to greet them. "You men all know me," Barney began, wasting no time on cordiality. "I've been a hard worker for the union, and I've been a miner all my life. This here's John Trotter and he's to be trusted same as me. John, this here's Tom Pate, president of the Davidson union, and Oscar Woody from Twinton."

The men shook hands and seated themselves around the table, and waited for Barney to pour a round of coffee for all of them. A woman entered the room quietly and sat in a rocking chair in a corner by the cookstove. "This is my wife, Daisy. She knows everything I know," Barney said without apology. The men nodded their agreement. If they were uncomfortable with the idea of a woman in the room, the tone in Barney's voice had told them to keep it to themselves.

"We know that you men from Davidson have been having it as rough as the men in Wilder," Barney continued without a pause. "We managed to fight off a third wage cut last year, but the men have had a tough time feeding their families on that. Sometimes we don't clear more than thirty-six cents a ton and that ain't a living wage for no man. The company says they are operating at a loss to pay us that much and they's been talk already of a third cut in July. Now, we know that you've been trying to round up union members over in Davidson, same as us. We've got to decide tonight what we plan to ask for in the new contract and when we think we might be strong enough to meet with the superintendents to discuss it."

"Barney, as you know," Tom Pate spoke quietly, "we got men working five days a week, that can't buy food on payday. They's lots of men going into the mine now without breakfast or dinner so their families can eat. Here it is, just barely May, the gardens ain't in yet. We sent some men around to some of the farmers in the county to see if we couldn't beg some of last year's can goods, but you know as well as I do that can't last for long. Our men don't want a strike, but we are ready for anything it takes. We've got near 80 percent signed up to the union."

"We ain't got nearly that many signed up yet," Barney said, impressed by Tom's efforts, "but I figure we will have by June. We had us a bad accident last week. The men lost a good friend to a rockfall. Taking too many chances. I reckon they seen it could happen to any of them. We've all been stretching our chances. That's why I am proposing that we bring it before the superintendents that the wage remain the same as it is now and not be cut."

"My men want to ask that they won't have to work in knee-deep water no more," Tom added.

"That seems fair enough," Barney agreed. "I just have one more thing to add. I want my men to be paid for removing rockfalls."

"I can't quarrel with that one. How 'bout you men?" Tom asked, turning to John and Oscar who nodded their agreement. "Well, that was easy enough."

"Now, if the company was just that easy to see it our way," Barney said and they all chuckled mirthlessly. "Let's talk about how we plan to approach these folks and just what we plan on saying."

They talked on about how important it was to have a good spokesman who could say just the right thing so as not to set the company off. "The general manager of the Wilder mines, W. D. Boyer, and his superintendent, L. L. Shriver, are company men all the way," Barney said. Tom agreed they could expect some of the same at Davidson.

The Twinton contract was set to expire on June 30, one week before the Wilder and the Davidson contracts. Barney turned to Oscar Woody who had been in quiet agreement with the other men all evening. "Oscar, it looks like it will be up to you to approach the operators first. How do things stand with the superintendent up your way?"

"We've always had a right smart of cooperation out of Haynes Garrett. He's been superintendent for near ten years. I tell you though, work's down to about three days a week. They've been squealing hard times for three or four years now."

"We'll hold off down here 'til we see how they handle you up at Twinton. If you men get your contract, there's a good chance of us being successful down here."

"As soon as we know somethin' we'll get word to you."

"All right, Tom. As soon as we hear from Twinton, we'll go in and present our cases. I reckon we'll just have to take it from there when we see how they react."

Finally, around midnight, the men rose to leave. John shook hands all around, and as Barney walked the men to the door, he sat down at the kitchen table to await his return. It had been a very successful meeting, he thought. He was surprised to see Mrs. Graham still sitting quietly in the corner knitting steadily. She had not said a word throughout the long meeting, and he had forgotten she was there. He envied Barney. A woman could see a man through a lot of hard times. He pictured Lacey by the fire, working quietly with her hands, smiling up at him, now and then. It was a thought that stirred an ache in him, and he was glad when Barney came back into the room to stand by his wife's chair.

"Son," Barney stammered, taking hold of his wife's hand and smiling down at her upturned face. "We've talked it over, and we have decided to take in three of Wilford's younguns for a while. Sarah agreed to let us have the two least ones and the oldest girl until she gets settled up north."

Barney's voiced trailed off, and John spoke up. "I think that's real fine of you, Barney. Wilford would be right grateful, I know. What's Sarah and the other younguns planning on doing?"

"She's got a brother up in Detroit that's offered to take 'em in for a while, but he can't handle the whole bunch of 'em right now."

"You're a good man, Barney."

"Well, them younguns'll be a right smart of help to us too, I reckon," Barney said shrugging off the praise. "That oldest gal's getting to be about ten. She can help out with the babies and with chores around the house, and they'll be a company to my younguns. Besides it won't be for that long."

John wondered what help the two babies would be. The little girl couldn't be more than three and the boy was barely walking. It was a lot to take on with times being the way they were, but when John looked at Mrs. Graham's face he realized that she had had a lot to do with the decision.

A knock on the door brought John suddenly to his feet nearly overturning his chair. He grabbed the chair by the top rung and steadied it to the floor then looked at Barney.

"You stay back out of sight, John. Ain't no need for nobody to know you're here lessen they have to." Barney nodded to his wife, and she immediately began to clear the coffee cups out of the way. Barney unbuttoned his shirt and ruffled his hair on the way to the door so he would look to all the world like he had just crawled out of bed. He opened the door slowly like a man half asleep. Will Conners burst through the door breathless from running.

"Pa sent me to tell you. They done found Fergie Jensen. Coy Lynn Wilson come carrying him in about an hour ago. Him and Seth Ramsey found him up near the Highland trestle laying right smack of the railroad tracks. Train cut his legs clean off. The Doc was at our place with Ma, that's how come 'em to take him there. But it didn't do no good. He was bleeding like a stuck hog. You should of seen Coy. He didn't have a spot on him that wasn't red. He'd done took his shirt off and tied Fergie's stumps up in it. Lacey offered to wash out his shirt, but he wouldn't hear of it. Don't reckon you'd ever get all that blood out no way."

"I reckon, we've heard enough, boy," Barney said to stop Will's excited rambling. "Did he say anything before he died?"

"That's why I'm here. He wanted me to give this to you," Will answered, handing Barney a pearl-handled knife. "Didn't say why. He said you would know. I gotta be getting back, now. Coy was gonna head on back up the tracks and try to find Fergie's legs. Fergie was carrying on about not being buried with his legs."

"All right, son. Tell your Pa I'll be down to help with the body come daylight. And thanks, Will. I appreciate you bringing the news."

Barney gently closed the door, and then stood for a moment looking down at the pearl-handled knife in his hand. When he looked up he was wiping at his eyes.

"That knife mean something to you, Barney?" Mrs. Graham asked, concern in her voice.

"Wilford traded it to me for a side of bacon the week before he died. Had too much damn pride to take it as a gift. I give the knife to Fergie and told him to give it back to Wilford sometime. I told him to tell him he won it fair and square in a poker game. Fergie always was a good poker player. I reckon he never got the chance."

8

The steam from the galvanized tub behind the cookstove in the kitchen rose up around Lacey. She had been soaking for some time, and she had had to go to the cookstove twice for more hot water. It was a luxury of time and pleasure she usually didn't allow herself. She had thought that a hot bath might settle her fidgets and ease her aching neck muscles. Still, her back remained rigid and her muscles taut. Her mind would not give in to her body's pleas.

The red-tailed hawk that Coy had given her rested against her chest as she slid deeper into the water. It bobbed gently against her right breast sending memories of his touch quivering down her. Picking it up, she held it gently in her hands. It seemed to be straining to free itself from the wood still clinging to its wings.

"Lacey Conners, wasn't this what you dreamed about that day on Buck Rock?" Lacey said out loud to herself. "Granny Conners always did say to be careful what you pray for because you might just get your prayers answered."

Lacey thought of Granny Conners and all the years she had lived with them after Grandpa Conners had died. She was mostly blind but she still could cook and work around the house. She liked for Lacey to take her out in the yard in the afternoons to sit under the shade of a big hackberry tree. Lacey had been only six, but she had loved sitting and listening to Grandma Conners' stories of when she was growing up. Her life had seemed so difficult to Lacey. Her family had lived way back in the hills of Kentucky without a pump for water and no electric lights. They had come out once a year in a wagon pulled by mules to get supplies.

"Lord, honey," she would say. "I could hardly wait to get out of there. I thought it was the lonesomest place on this earth. I prayed every day for a way out of that life. When I turned thirteen, I run off to Hazard and worked in one of them hotels a-cooking and a-cleaning up after a bunch of filthy drunks and gamblers. I ended up falling in love with one of them no-counts. I married him and him sorrier than Duke Snyder's lop-eared hound. It weren't long before I seen what I'd done. Course he got hisself shot before long and I was back down on my knees a-praying for a way out of there. This time I was real careful how I spoke it, laying it out real plain that I wanted a good and decent man and I would be willing to do without some of that excitement I'd been craving. I'd had my fill of that real quick. Well, the Lord sent me your grandpa, and he was as fine a man ever been made. That's how I learned that the good Lord answers prayers. It's just up to us to be real sure we know what we're asking."

"Did you love Grandpa?" Lacey remembered asking. Grandma Conners had twisted her face up and squinted her milky eyes like that was something she had plumb forgotten to ask for. Not long after that, Grandma Conners had wandered out into the yard and stumbled into a yellow jackets' nest. It had killed her right out. Lacey knew her ma never favored having Grandma Conners there, but Lacey missed her and wished she was there to sit under the hackberry tree and talk about answered prayers.

She knew now that she had fallen in love with Coy that night in the school yard, that she was drawn to him like a miller to a lantern. She had prayed for someone to love, someone to make her heart beat fast and her breath catch in her throat, and the Lord had sent her Coy. He was as wild and dangerous and unpredictable as a flash fire in the mines. She had heard her pa talk of the way the coal dust hung in the air day after day, just waiting 'til one day without warning the flame from some carbide light would set it roaring through the tunnels blowing out everything in its path. She laughed to herself to think of the words she might have used had she known how her prayer was going to be answered: *Please, Lord. Don't make it somebody who will make Ma take to her bed forever and Pa throw me out of the house and the whole town look at me like I've plumb lost my senses.* She shook her head wondering how a person was to think of all that. It was enough to make a person think twice before asking for anything. *I reckon that's pretty much the point of it,* she thought.

As it was, she had spent the last few days trying to convince herself that she would never see Coy again. If she met him again, she might lose her family and everything she had known. And with all of that, all she could think about was seeing Coy again. She had thought herself crazy at times, but never like this. There was just no explaining it. Every moment of that day by the river was alive in her mind. The way Coy's eyes flashed with excitement, the way laughter boomed up from deep inside him and the way he looked at her as though she was something wondrous to behold. For the first time she felt special. She felt beautiful. It was a magic feeling that made her blush with excitement, a feeling so new to her that she wondered how much it showed on the outside. That night when Coy had shown up at her house carrying Fergie Jensen in his blood soaked arms, she had wanted to run to him. She had almost thrown her arms around him when she thought he was hurt, too. If her pa had not been so caught up in helping the doctor, he could easily have noticed. It was not her way to be sneaking around and she would not be able to do it long. And yet, it tore at her insides to think of hurting him. Did she really have the right? Times were getting harder for all of them. Pa and Will had worked only two days that last week.

Time was running out for thinking about it. Everybody in town who had managed to save a nickel would be going to the Saturday night picture show. She had promised Ben he could go with her and, of course, John would be stopping by to walk with them, along with Ruby and Will and half the young people in town. She was nervous about seeing John again. It had to show on her that things had changed. She had never made him any promises, or at least she wanted to tell herself that, but life made promises for you that were somehow just as binding. Folks grew to want things in their hearts and that made it like a promise.

Lacey slipped out of the tub and she started to dry off. Coy would be at the picture show, she was sure, and he would be waiting for a message from her. The decision was hers. That

was the way they had left it. As she combed her long, wavy hair
and tied it back with blue ribbons, she thought about how easy
it would be not to go. It would be such a simple way out and
yet, even as she fixed her hair and smoothed her dress, she
thought about wanting to look pretty for Coy.

Ben had wanted to sit on the front row, but the theater was
already too crowded and they had to sit several rows back.
Lacey was glad when Ben had sat down beside her and John
had to take a seat next to him. They had said very little to each
other on the walk to town and Lacey had been relieved when a
number of other young people had joined them.

The room was already filled with smoke. Men stood around
the walls swapping stories and trading knives, and the women
worked to get the children settled down before the show
started. The mood was one of excited anticipation. With so
much trouble in the mines lately and money hard to come by,
the crowd was determined to get the most enjoyment possible
from their nickels. There had been a time when the theater had
been used regularly by traveling players and even local events
put on by the community, and the company had brought in
entertainment from Nashville and even Atlanta. Now there was
only an occasional picture show.

Lacey looked cautiously around the room, but she couldn't
catch sight of Coy. Someone was blinking the lights, and the
crowd scurried to find their seats. The posters outside had said
it was a Tom Mix western full of "wild and woolly adventure"
and "rip roaring excitement."

Ben squirmed with anticipation and tugged at Lacey's
sleeve. "Who ya looking for Lacey?"

"I ain't looking for nobody, Ben," Lacey answered,
embarrassed.

"Well, you sure are straining your neck for nothin' then."

John was grinning at her from over Ben's head, and she
realized she must have been pretty obvious in her search. "I
guess I was curious about who all was here. I expect about
everybody in town is here tonight. Don't you think so John?"
Before John could answer the movie started, and Lacey was
relieved to have the attention turned to something else.
Everybody around her was immediately caught up in the show.

Lacey lost herself to the action of the flickering lights until she felt someone poking her in the side. It was Ruby. "What's the matter with you?" she whispered.

"Come on. I gotta go."

When Lacey stared at her blankly, Ruby repeated it with a pleading in her voice. "I gotta go to the outhouse. Come on and go with me," she said, taking Lacey by the hand.

They crawled out over Ben and John and made their way out the front door. As soon as Lacey closed the door, she turned to Ruby. "I swear you are worse than a youngun. You mean to tell me you couldn't make it through the picture show without having to take a trip?"

Lacey who had only been teasing Ruby, was surprised to see tears well up in her eyes. It was a three-quarter moon, and Lacey could see Ruby's plump, tear-stained face reflected in the light. She had often seen Ruby cry at weddings and funerals or at the sight of a hurt deer, but never for herself.

"Oh, Lacey, I wasn't gonna tell you. Will's promised to tell your Pa we was getting married, but he ain't done it yet. And now, I'm getting to be a right smart along."

"Ruby, what are you talking about?"

"I'm going to have a baby," she blubbered into her hands. After several minutes, she looked up, still sniffling pitifully. "Now, don't look at me that way. Will said it would be all right since we was getting married anyhow. It's just that ever since I told him about the baby, he ain't seemed so happy about getting married. You don't hate me do you?"

Lacey knew she was staring. The shock of it was still working its way into her mind. She just could just picture Will working his charm on the sweet, giving Ruby and it made Lacey so angry she wanted to pull Will out of the picture show by his ear and march him up before the preacher that very night. Instead, she blurted her anger out at Ruby. "I swear, Ruby. If Will wanted you to jump off the Highland trestle, you'd be out there before daylight to get an early start. When are you going to learn that just because some folks will ask it of you, don't mean they deserve it."

In the face of Lacey's anger, Ruby dissolved into helpless weeping. "You think I ain't no good, don't you Lacey? I knowed you'd hate me. I shouldn't a told."

"No, Ruby, I don't hate you and I shouldn't of said what I did. It's Will I'm upset with," Lacey said, putting her arm around Ruby's thick waist. She used her hand to wipe the tears from her cheeks. "You've been as good a friend as a person could have, and you are going to be a good wife to Will. You'll be a bride before this month is out. Mark my words. You had best start getting that wedding dress ready."

"Oh, I done had it ready for months. 'Course, the way things are looking, I may have to let it out a bit." Embarrassment made her giggle. "It's a good thing I've got plenty of meat on me already." Then they laughed and hugged, Lacey reaching up to pat the oversized Ruby gently on the back.

Lacey stood outside while Ruby used the outhouse. She hated to feel so selfish, but she couldn't help thinking how much harder this would make things for her. Every time Will did something like this, and there had been so many times, she felt she had to make up for it. She knew the words she had spoken to Ruby about folks asking for more than they deserved came more from her own struggle. She had always been able to pay the price, giving up her own wants if it meant keeping peace in the family. Up until now, that had been enough in return. With work falling off in the mines and Will taking on a family, she knew she didn't need to be thinking about bringing more trouble on the family. In her mind, she had pictured a time when she could sit down with her pa and talk about Coy, maybe bring him by the house to meet the family. She imagined that in time her folks would come to accept him.

A strong arm grabbed her from behind and pulled her behind the building. She turned around, and Coy took her face in his hands and kissed her forehead and eyes and mouth. He was warm and smelled of the night air as they held each other, breathless. Coy rested his warm lips on her neck, and she was reluctant to waste the moment on words. "You came," she managed to whisper.

"I can't tell if you are pleased or just surprised," he said teasing her with his smile.

"Both, I reckon."

He laughed out loud, and she put her hand quickly to his mouth to silence him.

"Well, I can't say you ain't honest."

"I'm sorry."

"No, need to be. You probably give some thought to not coming, yourself."

It unnerved her the way he read her thoughts. She didn't know how to reply, and so she looked at him in silence.

"You're not sorry I came?"

"It don't matter," she said nonsensically. She had meant to say it was no use. It had gone too far, no matter what her fears might be.

"It matters to me. Ever since that first day I saw you, I haven't been able to think of nothing else. Being with you, just seeing you is all I want in the world."

"Coy, we don't hardly know each other."

"Tell me you don't feel the same way. Ain't you thought about me just a little? That day down by the creek, ain't you thought about what a good time we had?"

"I have thought about it, Coy. It's not that I don't want to see you. It just Pa and, well, folks," she said weakly.

The creaking of the outhouse door caused her to jump. "Ruby's coming. I have to go."

Instead of letting her go, he wrapped his arms tightly around her. Finally, he whispered, "Lacey, I love you," and there was a pleading in his voice. A thousand good intentions were lost in the moonlight and she told him where to meet her on Sunday.

The warm sun soothed away the uneasiness as Lacey waited for Coy on Buck Rock. It had not been easy to get away. John had walked her home from church and Pa had stepped out on the porch and asked him to stay for Sunday dinner. She had to smile to hide her nervousness. Frank had learned about John's work with the union and wanted to hear John's side of it. They had talked on long after Lacey had washed the dishes and cleaned up the kitchen, with Frank rocking gently back and forth in the cane rocker on the front porch smoking his pipe and nodding as John talked. Lacey had almost given up hope of getting away when suddenly John said goodbye, mumbling something about having work to do.

Will almost bumped into John on the way to the gate, and they exchanged a few words. John must have spotted Will coming up the road and decided to cut his visit short. Lacey wondered if he knew about Ruby and the baby. Seeing Will looking so miserable as he slowly meandered up the path and sat down on the porch step, Lacey hoped he had come to talk about getting married, but she couldn't wait to see. Using the opportunity to escape, she slipped up the garden path only to pass Ben playing ring toss on a nearby tree. He looked hurt and surprised when she had told him he could not go with her.

Now as she sat waiting, she tried to shake off all the bad feelings. The chirping of baby birds brought a smile to her lips, and she looked around for the nest. It was in a cluster of loblolly pines not far away. She watched as the mother flew back and forth, tirelessly bringing food to the waiting mouths. The babies stretched their fuzzy necks and pecked wildly at whatever their mother carried to the nest. Lacey, just watching, wondered how the mother could ever satisfy such a greedy bunch.

When Coy stepped out from the trees, watching her as though he still couldn't believe she was there, she waved to him shyly. He walked towards her, a smile lighting up his face, then took her hands and lifted her up. "You looked so beautiful sitting there with the sun on your hair. I just wanted to stand there and look at you."

"Oh, Coy."

"You don't believe me, do you? Well, you know it's true. You must of had a dozen young men tell you that by now."

"Now you are teasing me!"

"No, I'm not. I'm just naturally jealous of any man who has looked into those blue eyes and felt what I feel now."

She looked up at his wildly handsome face. His dark eyes shone down at her with a wildness that left her breathless, and she broke away from him, her head spinning with the realization that here was what she had dreamed about in her most secret moments. It was so intoxicating in real life. She had to cross her arms and stand with her back to him to steady herself. "The way you talk, Coy. You're not like anybody else I ever met, and you scare me the way you talk."

"Well, that's not the first time I've heard that, but never from such sweet lips." He started toward her, but she straightened her stance and he stopped. "Look, Lacey, I won't hurt you. I know this happened pretty fast and we neither one expected it. I promise you, I don't mean you no harm. And I won't rush you, if you will just be with me."

"If Pa was to find out about us....."

"He would kill me," he said grinning.

"It's not funny, Coy. We can't get away with meeting like this forever. Somebody's bound to find out. And then...."

"And then, you can decide how much I mean to you. Let's not waste the time we have. It's a beautiful day. Dang, if you ain't wearing a look that could sober a drunk."

A laugh exploded from her, unchecked.

"Now, that's better. Sit down. I have a surprise for you."

She joined him under the same pine tree where she and Ben had often rested. The pine needles were soft and smelled of all that was good in nature. He made her sit Indian-style, spreading her dress over her legs to make a bowl in her lap. Reaching gently into his shirt, he pulled out a handkerchief. Slowly unwrapping it, he eased the contents into her lap. It was a handful of ripe, wild strawberries.

"I picked them on the way up. I thought you might be craving a bite of summer."

"Oh, they look wonderful. That was sweet of you, Coy," she said, genuinely touched. No one had every given her anything before, and now he had given her two wonderful gifts. She looked down at the strawberries, some of the red juice already staining her dress. It was a gesture so innocent and childlike; it made her think of Ben. She picked up the biggest berry and offered it to Coy.

"No, the first one is for you." He took the berry from her hand and held it to her mouth. When she bit into it, the juice ran down her chin and she was embarrassed and started to wipe her face. Coy surprised her by grabbing her hand and kissing the juice from her chin. She gasped involuntarily, and he quickly pulled away from her as though remembering his promise. He lay down and rolled over on his stomach, beginning immediately to tell her a story as though nothing had happened.

It was a story about how he used to hop the freight trains when he was no more than eleven or twelve years old. Sometimes he would jump off, and it would take him all day to walk back. Once he had made it all the way to Nashville. He had left with nothing but a few cold biscuits in his jacket. "It took me near three days to get home. It had crossed my mind with some pleasure that my folks might worry about me. When I come in about suppertime of the third day, they hardly looked up from their plates. Ma had gone straight to bed after supper, and no one ever mentioned my being gone. Pa said, 'Coy, your Ma's needing some firewood chopped.'"

"I wanted to tell them about this big adventure and about the old woman who fed me fried chicken and stuffed my pockets when I left. I wanted to tell them about Union Station alive with people and trains, the biggest building I had ever seen. I pictured myself that whole ride back on the train stretching my arms far apart as their eyes widened in amazement. They never asked where I'd been, where I'd slept, nor whether I'd had a bite to eat the whole time I was gone. After that, I took off whenever I got a chance." Coy looked at her grinning. "So here I am telling you, Lacey."

Lacey could hardly believe some of the stories he told her. She couldn't be sure he wasn't making them up. Everything he did was so chancy and full of risk. "Weren't you scared?"

"Damn near scared to death at times. I weren't nothing but a youngun. Sometimes I didn't even want to go."

"Nobody was making you go."

"Yeah, well, nobody never made me do nothing. They was just times things got so's I'd just as soon be on a train someplace."

"She knows you're home, Coy. When are you going to go see her?"

"If you are talking about Ellen, you had best tell her not to set the table for two just yet. Not that she would be welcoming me home with open arms."

"She grieved for you after you left. Wouldn't leave the house for a long time. Then she had to move up on the ridge." Lacey regretted mentioning the move. Coy might think she was suggesting he hadn't taken care of his Ma.

"Don't you fret my little keeper of the flock. I sent her money when I could."

"There's more to it than that. She needs her own flesh and blood there caring for her."

"Whoa now, don't go trying to patch up the whole world, Lacey. There's too many rips in it for a little thing like you to fix."

"Why did you never want to work in the mines, Coy?" she found herself suddenly asking. It was something that worried her, this hatred he had for this way of life. She hadn't meant to ask him about it, and now she watched his face for signs of anger or disgust with her.

"Folks around here act like the mining company done them a favor giving them a job. They don't seem to realize the company gets it back and a lot more. They tell a man where he's to live, sell him electric lights and coal and even pay him in scrip so he has to buy everything else he gets from the company store. You think they don't make a pretty penny off of that? Oh, they get it back all right!"

Lacey had never really thought of it that way, and she was amazed by Coy's attitude. Her pa had always seemed glad to get the work, grateful to the company for giving it to him, just like Coy said.

"Course, it's a whole lot more than that. That black hole is like dying early. Spending your days buried alive. I won't ever do that again. Never, Lacey."

His voice had never changed as he spoke, and he stared off into the distance as though reliving his months working in the dark, damp tunnels of the mines. Lacey sat holding her breath, afraid to move. She dared not ask him what he planned to do with his life if he didn't mean to be a coal miner. And then his look changed and he was smiling again.

"You are just hell bent on being serious today," he said cupping her chin in his warm hand.

"I worry...."

"That you do, gal. That you truly do." He pulled her down into his arms and they lay looking at the clouds. "See that big old cloud up there looks like a horse's head wearing a hat. You can't see nothing like that down in no coal mine. And that one over there looks like a waterfall flowing into a teacup, don't it?"

"What about that one? It looks like a fat woman sitting on a rock."

"I think I know her. Ain't that Miss Fink used to teach fourth grade at the Wilder schoolhouse?"

"Oh, Coy, you're plumb awful! She still does teach at Wilder."

"Well, then admit it. Looks just like her and you know it."

Suddenly he jumped up and straddled her, tickling her up and down her ribcage, nibbling at her chin and ears until she could hardly catch her breath.

"Stop it, Coy. Stop it!" she gasped. "All right, I'll admit it does look a little like her."

"Shame on you, Lacey Conners," he said rolling off of her and looking at her in mock horror. "I can't believe you think that dear old woman looks like a fat toad on a rock."

She punched him helplessly with her tiny fist as he rocked with laughter. His laughter was wonderful, and she loved being able to make him laugh. Everything about him was so unexpected, so exciting. Being with him was like being swept along by a raging river. There was no time to think about where it might lead. . .

"Where you been, gal?" her pa yelled to her from the back porch as she came through the garden path. "Your ma's been asking for you."

Lacey thought there was an edge to his voice that Lacey had never heard before, or maybe it was just her guilt making her imagine more than was there. It was too late to go over her story again. She had repeated it in her mind many times. She had simply been up to visit Flora Lays' new baby boy and had forgot all about the time, him being so sweet and pretty. Pa hardly knew the Lays and wouldn't be interested in a new baby. Maybe he would only half listen, and it wouldn't be like really lying. She had never lied to him before and she prayed for a way out now. As she passed him, her story caught in her throat and she simply mumbled a few words about the time getting away from her. She threw herself into fixing supper with a fierce rattling of skillets and banging of stove lids. As he stood watching her in the doorway, her insides churned with guilt, and her back burned from his stare.

"You brother Will is to be married come Sunday. I suspect they'll most likely be staying here a while 'til they can set up a place of their own."

"I'm happy for 'em, Pa."

"I expect you know how things are."

"Yes, Pa. Ruby told me last night."

"Your ma is a right smart upset. You know how she feels about folks talking."

Lacey could only think that she would be getting a dose of her own medicine. "I'll look in on her Pa, soon as I get supper on. She'll be all right soon as she gets used to it. She's getting a good daughter-in-law."

"Your ma takes things hard."

"And what about you, Pa?"

"I should've expected it outta Will. He always was one to jump before he looked. When he come skulking in here, I knowed it was something. He had a case of the all-overs so bad he couldn't look me in the eye. It didn't take me long to figure things out. I reckon I lit into him pretty hard. Told him I wouldn't have him trifling with no young gal. If he was man enough to trifle, he was man enough to make it right."

As though suddenly realizing what he had said, her pa cleared his throat and shifted uncomfortably. "Well, you're getting old enough to know about these things," he said, pacing about nervously. Finally, he went outside and made a show of banging his pipe on the porch rail and slowly repacking it with tobacco.

Lacey had blushed crimson and had nearly dropped the pone of cornbread she was putting in the stove to bake when the conversation had taken such a personal turn. When her pa returned a few minutes later, her cheeks still felt warm. She hoped he would think it was from the heat of the stove. "I reckon I'll go look in on Ma, now."

"Wait a minute, Lacey. It ain't my way to meddle but you've been right tectious lately. It ain't like you to be so contrary. You and John ain't had a fray, have you?"

"No, Pa."

"You was a might cool to him today."

"You two was talking mining and I just thought to leave you to it."

"Well, you could do worse than John Trotter. That's all I got to say on the matter."

"I know, Pa. You don't need to study on John Trotter and me. We ain't had no fray." She sought to reassure him as truthfully as she could, but it left her sick at even such a simple deception. It was so unlike her pa to meddle that she was sure he must suspect something. The blood pounded in her ears and she hoped her voice sounded calm, "Now, I better get in to Ma before she gets the mullygrubs for sure." She tried to smile at him and forced herself not to run as she left the room.

Much to Lacey's relief, her ma appeared to be asleep in the high bed in the parlor. Her back was turned, and her body was curled childlike into a tight ball. As Lacey peered into her mother's face she almost expected her to be sucking her thumb. The thought made her almost giggle out loud. Backing away from the bed quickly, she made her way to the safety of her room. She would have only a few minutes alone before she would have to finish supper. It was obvious to her that she would not be able to deceive her folks for long. It was not in her nature, even if it were possible to keep a secret in the tight confines of a coal camp.

What confused her most was the way all of this had come upon her and had changed her life. How was she to explain such a thing to her folks? After all, what did Coy have to offer? Certainly, he had none of the things that she had been taught to want. He didn't even have a job and wouldn't take one in the mines if it was offered to him. He most likely would want to take her off someplace strange like Wyoming. She couldn't even be sure of that, for he hadn't talked to her about the future. It was just something they would face when it came, he had said. Even as she argued with herself, she knew it was useless. Whatever he had to offer, it couldn't be explained in any words she had. So how on earth did she expect to explain it to her folks? She could just picture herself standing in front of her pa trying to tell him she was turning her back on a fine man like John for a man who brings her strawberries and carves her birds out of wood. "Oh, my Lord," she cried as the smell of burning bread suddenly penetrated her thoughts. "I've done let the bread burn!"

Ruby looked beautiful as she walked down the aisle to meet Will. Lacey had gone out in the early morning dew to pick forget-me-nots for a bouquet, and Ruby held them clenched against her slightly protruding stomach like a shield. It was hardly noticeable where they had let the dress out on the sides.

The wedding was being held right after church services and most of the folks had stayed on for the ceremony. John sat next to her nervously twisting his hat and alternately shooting her glances. She wondered if he was thinking it should be them getting married that day.

It was just a simple service with just the bride and groom. It could have been held quietly with a justice of the peace, and Lacey was sure her pa had had something to do with having it in church in front of the whole town.

Will looked uncomfortable in his heavily starched shirt and suit. When he turned to watch Ruby walk down the aisle to become his bride, Lacey was glad to see him grin sheepishly and reach out to take her hand. He might be a child in many ways, but at least he seemed to really love Ruby.

As soon as the bride and groom had said their vows, the families and friends rushed forward to offer their congratulations. Ruby's six brothers and sisters hugged and kissed her with genuine affection. Lacey felt a pang of jealousy and hated herself for it. She couldn't help but think that if she married Coy there would be no happy family and friends rushing to congratulate her. There would be only long faces and worry, or worse. There probably wouldn't even be a church wedding and dinner afterward as Ruby's family had planned for her.

John was taking her by the elbow and pushing forward toward the bride. She was embarrassed that she had been so lost in her thoughts of herself that she had forgotten to come immediately and congratulate the couple. "You are a beautiful bride, Ruby. And I am so happy to have you in the family" Lacey said honestly.

"Oh, Lacey, I'm so happy," Ruby said as she hugged Lacey. Then before letting go she quietly whispered, "How did I look?"

"You couldn't tell a thing," Lacey whispered truthfully, knowing she was asking if the pregnancy showed.

"It was the bouquet that done the trick. I appreciate you thinking of it. You are the best friend I got."

Tears suddenly sprang up in Ruby's eyes. Lacey realized the strain she had been under and felt bad for her jealousy. "And you are my best friend, Ruby," Lacey replied, giving her one last hug. Other people pushed forward to speak to the bride, and Lacey stood watching the crowd. Her ma stood among a crowd of women, talking in her breathless way. She had threatened not to come at all, but Frank had managed to persuade her, and now she seemed actually to be basking in all the attention. John was shaking hands with Will and speaking in his soft, solemn way. Her pa came up behind the two men and put his arms on both their shoulders. He looked at them both with pride and affection. Lacey was glad to see that the rift between father and son was once more mended.

John was walking towards her with a gentle, boyish grin on his face. "Your Pa asked me to the wedding dinner over at the Burnett's. I told him I best check that out with you first."

"Well, of course, you are welcome to come. You know Ruby and Will will be expecting you there." Lacey had expected that John would come. He really hadn't needed an invitation, but it bothered her that her Pa would invite him specially.

"You didn't say whether or not you wanted me there."

"Of course I want you there. You know you are practically family." Lacey certainly meant the words she had spoken. She really did feel true warmth and affection for John and he had always been part of her life just like family. But she regretted the way it sounded, the way she knew John had taken it.

She could tell by his sudden broad smile that she was right. "We best be getting over there. I told Ruby's ma I'd help with the fixins." John held her by the elbow as they started off and Lacey felt helpless to pull away.

The dinner had been fun, Lacey thought as she dried the last of the dishes. Ruby's family had teased her with the natural ease of happy people who have a lot in common, and after the meal, the men had taken to the porch to smoke and have a "nip" of moonshine. Lacey could hear their laughter even over the chatter and giggles of the women in the kitchen as they cleaned up. Ruby's ma was as plump and cheerful as Ruby. Although she was several inches shorter, she had flaming red hair and a gentle smile that she used generously on everyone in the room, especially her oldest daughter. Lacey must have been looking at them both wistfully, for Mrs. Burnett came up to her and put her arm around Lacey's slender waist. "Don't worry Lacey," she consoled. "You and John will be tying the knot before you know it." Lacey was so taken aback by the statement, she could only blush. Mrs. Burnett took her silence as shyness and patted Lacey's hand, dishtowel and all.

Lacey was glad when Will came in to get Ruby. They would be leaving early so they would have some time alone at the house before the rest of the family arrived. No one had actually said it out loud. It was just an unspoken agreement that the rest of the family would linger until dark. Will hunched his shoulders nervously before he finally spoke.

"Ruby, you best get your things and we'll be going."

"Yes, Will" she answered, giggling into her hand.

Liola Parsons, May Sims and several other of the most eligible single girls gathered in the yard to get a chance to catch the bouquet. Ruby practically pushed Lacey off the porch into the yard and then tossed the flowers straight at her. Lacey caught them more by reflex than intent. The other girls clapped their approval and Lacey could see the men punching John. She thought how happy it would make them all if she would marry

John. Then she could be the one standing on the porch, while everyone looked on with fondness and acceptance.

After the bride and groom left, the crowd quickly disbursed, offering thanks to the Burnett's. When one of the men offered a last joke about grandchildren being just around the corner, Lacey could see her ma visibly pale. Frank laughed heartily and slapped Ruby's pa, Hyde Burnett, on the back. In the end, even Annie managed a smile to the departing friends and Lacey felt a sense of relief that the day had gone so well after all. Being with friends and knowing that Will and Ruby could now be happy about the coming baby had left her in a good mood. Their worrying seemed silly now, and it was strange that people's tongue wagging could have such power over a body's doings. Then she thought of Coy and the way he had worked so hard all his life to escape from people's judgment of him.

John startled her out of her reverie by taking her hand. She had forgotten he was there, and she smiled at him out of the sheer happiness she felt for the day and all its events. He looked surprised and pleased to see her so happy.

"Let's walk up to the old Runion farm and see if all the wild strawberries are gone yet."

She started to tell him they weren't but let it go. "All right, I think we got time before dark. I could use the walk after being inside all day."

"You do like being out, don't you Lacey? You don't begrudge Ruby and Will their day, do you?"

"Oh, John, you know I wouldn't do that," Lacey said astonished before she realized John was teasing her. It was so unusual for John that she was unable to tease him back. After an awkward moment, she finally said, "It was a nice wedding and Ruby did look pretty in her dress."

John nodded his reply and they walked on silently for some distance. Lacey watched him glance at her occasionally and then look away. He seemed about to speak each time but said nothing. Finally, they reached the meadow behind the Runion's barn where the strawberries grew. The sun set early in the hollow and it was just beginning to settle on the first ridgeline. They sat down on a grassy knoll above the strawberry patch. John didn't seem interested in them and Lacey didn't think she could eat one if he offered to pick her a bushel. They reminded her too much of Coy and their day together on the mountain.

"Lacey, I've been thinking."

After a long moment of silence, Lacey asked reluctantly, "Thinking about what John?" Somehow she knew what he was going to say and she both hated to hear the words and needed to have them said.

"You know I'm not much for words."

John paused again, and Lacey could feel her head begin to throb with a mixture of fear and impatience to have it out. "John, you've known me a long time."

"That's just it, Lacey. That's what I want to talk about," John spoke up suddenly and rapidly as though he had been given the opening he had been looking for. "We've known each other a long time and well. . . . It was a real nice wedding today."

"Yes, it was beautiful." Lacey wanted to help him find the words that would end these tortured moments for both of them, but she couldn't bring herself to do it.

"Not as beautiful as you'd be."

"Why, thank you, John."

"What I mean is, I've been thinking we should get married . . . or what I meant was if you would have me. Times are hard, I know," he rushed on without giving her time to reply, "but, well, everybody has hard times. You look at your folks or half the folks in this town and it seems like they've all had tough times in their lives and they've made a go of it. They get by, so I figured, well, we'd get by. After we talk to the company next week, we'll know better where we stand on a new contract. I've been sorta putting off asking 'til after this union business was settled, but I got to thinking today that we'd get by somehow."

She knew she was staring at him, but she had no idea what to say. He must have taken her silence to mean hesitation because he stammered on.

"It could mean a strike if we don't get a contract. That could mean we'd all be outta work for weeks, maybe months. But, Ma's a good hand to put food by and I ain't too proud to hunt game or beg if we had to." John suddenly stopped talking and looked at Lacey sheepishly. "You wouldn't have to tell me right away."

"You've thought this out considerable, haven't you, John?"

"I think about us a lot, Lacey," he answered simply.

That simple statement tore at her heart like a knife. He had sat alone at night, no doubt, and planned out their lives together. He had thought about how he would take care of her and provide for her if times got really rough. He was even offering her a way out. She didn't have to give him an answer now. She looked into his open, straightforward face and could see nothing that was not deserving of an honest answer, but she could not tell him what she did not honestly know. Finally, she told him the only thing she could. "John, you are a good man and any woman would be proud to marry you. It's just that... I just don't know, yet."

"Well, that's fine. I didn't mean to rush you," he said with a smile. "You take your time."

To her surprise, he took her answer with genuine pleasure. It was obviously more than he had expected. She hadn't said no. He took hold of her hand and smiled, and it made Lacey want to hold him and cry, for both of them.

9

The Twinton mines had renewed the contract without even putting up a fight. John was still trying to absorb the news after Barney had come over that morning to give him the word. Oscar Woody hadn't even made a real argument for the men. The operators had listened without comment, and then they had just signed, giving the men everything they had asked for.

John sat by the lean-to shed that had been built onto the house years before by some unknown occupant. There had been no work for the men that day and John busied himself by repairing gardening tools. He still couldn't believe it. At first, he had been elated, but Barney had warned him that something just wasn't right. "When a company is in as much trouble as Twinton complained of being," he had cautioned, "it just don't make sense to give in that easy. They've got something up their sleeve, boy. I've been around too long not to believe that." However, John hadn't been around that long and he desperately wanted to believe that it could all be solved that simply.

He had asked Lacey to marry him, and she hadn't said no. Granted, he wasn't real proud of the clumsy way he had asked, but at least it was done. Something about being around a woman, especially a young, pretty one that he happened to be in love with, left him tongue-tied. He could talk union or mining all day on the porch with Lacey's pa. That was no problem. But somehow, just the sight of Lacey with her hair tied back in those blue ribbons and her eyes flashing as she talked made him sound like a school boy reciting Bible verses: a few words and a lot of pauses. No, he hadn't done the best job of asking. If fact, he was right pleased just to have it done. He really hadn't planned it, with so much trouble in the making at work. It had just slipped out. When he had seen Ruby and Will getting on with their lives without so much as a second thought as to how they were going to make it, without even a place of their own, he had wanted it for himself. He had wanted their happiness; their new lives together.

He had been afraid of losing Lacey. That Sunday he had sat on the porch talking to her pa, she had been so jittery she could hardly sit still. She was upset with him for paying her so little attention lately. Well, it was all he deserved. Not that he had meant to. After all, it was for her he was working so hard. When her pa had finally asked him about the union, he had to take the time to explain to him how important it was to the men. He wouldn't have to do it ever again if things went well with the union; if they got their contract without all the problems he had imagined in the weeks past.

John thought of how he loved Lacey. It wasn't just that he couldn't find the right words to tell her how much. There just couldn't be words found anywhere that could explain it. It always made him weak when it hit him just how much.

He looked up, surprised to see Cora watching him.

"Barney's here to see you, son."

"What is it, Ma?"

"I best let Barney tell you, son." She turned quickly and went back into the house.

Barney stepped through the back door and into the yard where John sat on an old nail keg sharpening a hoe blade and he continued working, only stopping long enough to motion Barney toward another keg. "Sit down, Barney. What brings you here? More news of Twinton?"

"I'm afraid so, John," he sighed pinching his creased brow with his right hand as though trying to sooth away the pain of the news he carried.

"Well, what is it Barney? It can't be so bad you can't say it!"

"Damn close. You know I told you something was squirrelly with that Twinton deal?"

"Yeah, you said it went through too clean. . . . Something's happened to the contract. They've backed down on their signing. How's that possible, Barney?"

"No, son. They ain't backed down. Least ways not the way you think. It's worst than that."

"What could be worse than that for God's sake?"

"They closed the mines."

"For how long?"

"Forever. They just shut it down lock, stock, and barrel. The whole dang company is pulling out. They put near two hundred men out of work without so much as an hour's notice. When the men started to leave work today, the foreman told 'em to go by the scrip office and collect their final pay. Told 'em the company was shutting the mine down cause they was losing money every day they operated. Didn't even say how sorry they was or nothing. Oscar was so stunned he said he couldn't think of nothing to say."

"Where was the superintendent when all this was going on?"

"I reckon he was too much a coward to face the men after he signed that contract without a word about the company pulling out."

"What does this mean for us now?"

"It dang sure ain't going to make things any easier. They're sure to figure they got us over a barrel with so many men out of work within a few miles of Wilder."

"These men wouldn't try to come in here if we was to strike. They're union, same as us."

"Hungry's hungry, son. We'll have enough trouble feeding our own if there's a strike. They're good men. They'll hold out as long as they can, but it sure don't leave us much to bargain with. Well, I sure hated to ruin a man's fine summer day like this, and you did looked to be enjoying yourself out here in the sunshine." Barney looked around the back yard as though trying to draw strength from the familiar sight of a garden bursting with summer growth and the smell of clematis trailing up the back porch rail.

"Barney," John spoke, his voice almost in a whisper. He was reluctant to disturb any peace that could be gathered from the moment. "What now?"

Barney turned to look at John in such a slow, languid move; they could have been discussing the virtues of honey over sorghum molasses on a pan of Cora's fresh hot biscuits. "It's our move, now. We'll talk if they're willing. It could mean a strike, if they won't listen to our demands. The going could get mighty rough."

John frowned, studying the blade of the hoe. He ran his fingers along the edge testing its sharpness. Satisfied with his job, he leaned the hoe against the shed and looked at Barney. "I reckon we take it as it comes."

Barney nodded. "That's the way life is, son. Sometimes all a man's got is knowing he toughed it out. I don't know about you, son, but I intend to see this through to the end if it kills me."

"I'll be waiting right here to hear from you the minute the meeting's over," Daisy said, straightening Barney's tie for the third time. "You send word if you can't get back to let me know what happened."

"Now, Daisy, we will all know soon enough what's to happen."

Barney's three children stood anxiously staring up at him as they watched him strap on the inevitable gun. Wilford Potter's three children huddled just inside the kitchen. A tiny face peeked around the door facing. "I'll do my best, Daisy," John said with genuine admiration in his voice for her strength and courage.

"Lord a-mercy Barney, I ain't worried about that. I know you'll do your best. It's them I'm worried about. They're a tough bunch."

"Ain't you told me yourself that I was tough as two-year-old leather britches."

Daisy gave him a look of impatience. "That was different and you know it."

"John'll bring me home safe and sound as soon as the meeting's over. Now you younguns take care of your ma while I'm gone. I want to make you all proud. I'm doing this for your pa too," he said nodding to the faces in the kitchen doorway.

Three well-scrubbed faces appeared from behind the kitchen door. They were as pale and thin as young willow saplings. John wondered how Daisy managed to stretch the meager vittles to feed so many mouths. He knew that Barney was always giving away to others what his own family needed. He had told John once that he could always get more for his family, but he couldn't stand by and watch another man starve. The children were meek and almost soundless. John suspected they missed their brothers and sisters. *It was too much on little ones to lose their pa and their home in one month,* he thought.

"All right, you can come in," Daisy instructed, motioning them forward with her hand and a smile.

Slowly they came toward Barney and stood huddled together shyly as he took turns patting their heads. "That's my sweet little 'uns. Now you take care of Daisy, here and if you're real good, I'll bring you a treat. That goes for all of you," he said looking at his own children.

"Licorice?" the little girl asked.

"Now, that I'm not tellin'," he said cupping her under the chin. "You'll just have to check my pockets when I get home."

He smiled one last smile at Daisy and turned to John. "We better get on with it, son. This is no time to keep the boss men waiting."

As they walked at a fast clip up the main road toward the scrip office where the meeting was to be held, John could feel a hundred eyes on them. He watched Barney throw back his shoulders in confidence They had gone only about a quarter of a mile when Barney's face began to pale and a thin band of sweat broke out on his upper lip. The July sun was just making a dent in the cool morning air, but it was not warm enough yet to make a man sweat. "Are you all right, Barney? You're looking a might peaked."

"Must of been something I et," Barney said with a chuckle.

John knew that with three extra mouths in the house to feed, it was more than likely that he hadn't eaten at all. Just then he caught sight of Seth Ramsey and Coy Lynn Wilson coming up behind them in a wagon pulled by two mules. As the wagon came along side the men, John spoke casually nodding his head in greeting. "Seth. Coy."

"Morning." Seth greeted them dryly. "Surprised to see men out so early."

"I reckon, we could say the same about you two."

"That you could."

John approached the wagon. "I never got a chance to thank you both for what you done for Fergie."

Seth cut him off short with a simple wave of his hand. John turned his back to Barney and leaned closer to Seth. "I'd take it as a favor if you'd carry us on into town."

Coy looked over at Seth and a look passed between them. "Hey, Barney, I've been wanting to talk to John for a spell. Why don't you climb on up here and me and John'll chew the fat in the back of this wagon till we get to town. That is if that don't interfere with your plans."

"Well, I reckon I can handle that," he answered sounding relieved.

John shot him a look of gratitude as they climbed on the back of the wagon.

"What brought you out today, John?" Coy asked, nodding his head toward Barney as though to say it had to be something important or they were both fools.

"We got a meeting with the mine superintendent, L. L. Shriver and W. D. Boyer about the union contract. The contract runs out July 8, and they're trying to pull another wage cut on us. They say they're losing money."

"Well, if I had knowed what kind of trouble makers I was loading into this wagon, I might of thought twice. You know I got my reputation to think of."

"Considering your reputation for not giving a damn about what folks think, this could add to it considerably," Seth said chuckling.

Coy laughed out loud. "Now, ain't that the gods' honest truth."

"John," Barney said. "Don't let me forget them younguns' licorice. I reckon I got enough draw left to buy a penny poke of candy. If'n the company ain't deducted it for some new fund."

"Probably to pay the devil his due," John said

They all laughed. John shrugged and smiled.

They rode on in silence until John said, "You know I used to hunt 'sang up on the ridge past Seth's place years ago. You still find any 'sang up that way?"

"Yeah, I spotted a patch on a hillside just the other day when I was out . . . working. I used to wander up that way myself when I was a kid. I was just sure ole Seth was going to jump out from behind a tree an' slit my throat wide open. Maybe even nail my hide to a tree 'til it tanned like a rabbit skin."

John was surprised at the way Coy and Seth went on at each other. He noticed that Coy was grinning and looking at the man. Seth just drove on, refusing to turn his head and acknowledge him. It was true that most of the children in town had been afraid of Seth when they were growing up and more than one had sneaked up the hollow to test his fate when growing up. The strange relationship that had grown up between the two men was curious to John, and he wondered what had drawn them together. However, he had no time to ponder it, for they had arrived at the scrip office. He tried to calm himself for Barney's sake and the sake of all the men who were counting on them.

"Good to see ya, Coy," John said as they came around the side of the wagon. "Thank you, Seth, for carrying us to town."

Seth nodded.

John watched as Barney climbed slowly from the wagon. When he reached the ground, he paused a moment and looked up at Seth. John saw a wordless thanks pass between them and then he turned. "Let's go, son."

The scrip office was open for business even though there was no work in the mines that day. Leland Miller, thin and pale, stood nervously fidgeting with a stack of papers behind the desk. His oversized head, which looked silly atop his skinny neck, bobbed in the direction of the backroom office. As they entered the room, Boyer jumped up from his desk and greeted them heartily. "Good morning, men. Barney, it's good to see you. John, come on in."

Shriver had been standing in the corner, arms folded, leaning against the wall. He stepped forward silently and shook hands with Barney and John. He appeared solemn in the face of Boyer's cordiality. John wasn't sure which attitude made him the most nervous.

"Sit down men. I know you are here to represent the men and I just want to say a few words on behalf of the company. It has been a tough year for the Fentress Coal Company. Why with the price of coal dropping the way it has we lost money more months than we made any. We've always tried to deal fair with our men. When things was going good, the company saw to it that some of the miners got new houses and the school house got some new desks. We even bought uniforms for the softball team. Even with hard times, the company was willing to hold off cutting wages again for a whole year. Now that year cost the company a lot of money but we done it. We have always tried to provide good working conditions for the men and Shriver here can tell you my instructions to him have always been, 'Look out for our men.' And we are here today to hear you men out on what you're asking us to do."

John looked at Barney to speak. Barney's face was tight with control, and he seemed to be trying to gather his thoughts. Slowly he began to speak, and John was impressed by his words, "The men appreciate everything the company's done to hold off on this last wage cut. We know things is hard all over for the coal business."

"That's right, Barney," Boyer said excitedly. "You know coal has just bottomed out. They's too many companies mining and no place to sell it all."

"Hear me out on this now," Barney said.

Boyer snapped his mouth shut. He put his elbows on the desk and interlaced his fingers. He wound his thumbs around each other slowly.

"Truth is, we've got men working all week without eating breakfast or dinner or taking a break, who can't draw scrip 'cause they ain't made enough. They can't feed their families on what they're a makin' now and we know there's been talk of another cut. We got men takin' chances they shouldn't been takin' and they're a dying because of it. We can't take no wage cut." There was a touch of anger in Barney's voice.

"Now, Barney, you just hold on right there. You know the company was losing money last year when we signed this contract. Out of the goodness of our hearts and money out of our pockets we held off cutting wages for a full year. It cost us, Barney. It cost us."

"You been hungry? Either one of you'uns been hungry 'cause we didn't take a wage cut? You ever seen your wife do without supper so the younguns could have something to eat?"

John could tell that Boyer and Shriver didn't like being challenged and they moved closer like animals stalking. Barney motioned them back with a jerk of his head, and he looked at John to speak. John knew he was afraid of losing control of his temper. "You know what Barney says is the truth. The men can't make a living wage on what they're being paid now. We've had to bum food from the farmers already. These are all hard working men. They don't want nothing give to 'em. I speak for Barney and all the men when I say, we don't want a strike. A strike hurts us the same as you. We just want a chance to earn a decent wage. We are proposing that the wage stay the same in the coming year and not be cut. We ain't asking that it be raised. And we are asking that the men be paid for removing rockfalls. That's all we are asking. It's as simple as that."

"Barney, you and John are fair men," Boyer said, leaning back in his chair and tapping his fingers together, "but I'm in a tough spot here. I tell you what, let me mull this over and present it to the men in Nashville and we'll meet on this again tomorrow." He jumped up suddenly and was shaking hands all around. He escorted them both to the front porch before they had time to say another word in argument of their case.

"Well, they made quick shed of us," Barney said as they stood in the morning sun. "I'm afraid I didn't make much of a show of it."

"You made a fine show, Barney. Ain't nothing we can do now but wait to see what they got planned." John looked up, surprised to see Coy bringing the wagon around the side of the commissary.

"Well I wasn't expecting to run into you men again today," Coy said. "I reckon, from the looks of you two, that them men was just real cooperative."

John and Barney nodded.

"Just what you might expect, Coy," Barney said.

"Well, I'm heading your way if you two want to climb in."

As they headed down the road, Barney rode in silence until finally he looked up at John. "Thanks for speaking up in there. This dang temper of mine sometimes gets the best of me."

"That's all right Barney. I hope I spoke it right."

"As good as I ever heard. Dad blame-it! I forgot them youngun's licorice."

"Don't fret on it now, Barney. They'll understand."

"I do hate to disappoint them, John. Things mean a powerful lot to you when you are a youngun."

"I know, Barney. They know you got a lot on you right now."

Coy let them off at the road and they marched sadly to the front porch where Daisy stood waiting. "What happened down there? Did they listen to what you had to say?"

"They let us speak. That ain't no sign they listened. No decisions to be made 'til tomorrow. They want to stew on it a while."

"You think we got a chance?"

"I think they've already made their decision," Barney said angrily slamming his fist against the porch rail. "They're just buying a little more time. John, we best send some runners out to the men. They'll be anxious to hear what took place."

Shadowed faces gathered in the doorway.

"I want you younguns to know, we done what we could. We don't aim to give up on this. I aim to see to it that your pa didn't die for nothing. I can't stand to see good men done wrong."

They all stood mute and wide-eyed. Daisy gathered the children around her like a brood of chicks and rustled them off toward the kitchen.

Coy bounded toward the front porch as she turned to go. "Ma'am, I got something here must of fell out of Barney's pocket. I think he meant it for the little ones."

He handed her a crumpled sack.

"Why it's licorice! Look here, ain't that something," Daisy said dabbing at her eyes with the corner of her apron. "Your Pa done remembered your candy with all he had on his mind." She divided up the licorice to the eager little faces and hurried them off to the kitchen to eat their treats.

John looked over at Coy in wonderment. "You're a good man, Coy."

"Things mean a powerful lot to you when you're a youngun," he said quoting Barney with a crooked smile. Then he turned on his heels and was gone.

The company was not long in presenting its proposal. Barney had met the next day to hear the word. It was simple enough. The miners were to take a 20% pay cut and the mines could stay open. If they refused, the mines would close. They had no other proposal to offer and refused to discuss it further. Knowing he had the full support of the men, Barney turned it down flat. Within an hour the foreman, Lawton Monroe, had posted a notice that any man who wanted to work at a 20% cut could do so. Not a man had shown up to work that morning and the mine had ceased operation.

As John walked home from another meeting with Barney, he thought about how complicated his life had become. He had never wanted it that way. He was just a man who wanted to do his job and live his life. Sometimes he thought that the more there was against Barney, the stronger he got. It was his way to stick it out and that's what he planned to do. Summer was a slow time for the mines. That was something for the company side, not that they needed any more in their favor. He was sure the company would try to reopen the mines on a nonunion basis, although they probably wouldn't do it until fall when the demand for coal went up. The men could be pretty starved down by then. They would just have to find some way to hold out. "Please God," John prayed, "give us the courage. Give me the courage."

10

"**H**and me that fair-sized plank, Ben, and I believe we'll be about finished with this job."

"It looks good, don't it, Coy?" Ben said, standing back to admire the back porch of the Ramsey place.

"That it does," Coy replied with understanding at the boy's pride in a job well done. "I don't see how I could of done it without your help though."

"It was a right smart of a job, weren't it?" Ben said, a sudden smile flashing across his face, which glistened with sweat in the hot August morning. "I was glad to help. You got any other jobs around here. I'll be more'an happy to lend ya a hand."

"That's right neighborly of you, Ben," Coy said seriously. "I wouldn't want you to be neglecting your chores at home."

"No, I wouldn't do that. Lacey needs me to help her," Ben said with a sense of self-importance.

"Well, right now I need you to draw us some cool water from the well. A man gets mighty hot a-working, don't he?"

"He sure does," Ben said, grabbing the bucket from the nail on the porch. He was happy to be doing anything for Coy.

Coy thought back to the first time he had looked out to see Ben standing at the edge of the rocky path that led up to the Ramsey place. He had been holding on to a fence post, swinging nervously from side to side, and when Coy walked out onto the front porch, he had almost bolted. He had come to tell Coy that Lacey could not meet him.

"She has to tend to Ma. She's sick again," he explained. Coy had slowly coaxed the boy to come up to the porch, where he told him that Lacey must have had a heap of trust in him to give him such an important job. The praise had been genuine, but it touched something in Ben. He sat down on the porch next to Coy and they talked for an hour. Coy recognized the loneliness in the boy, and the guilt Ben felt at his ma's sickness ate at Coy's heart. A genuine friendship had developed between them. The truth was, Coy enjoyed Ben's company, and the boy was getting to be a pretty fair carpenter in the bargain.

"Here's ya a cool, fresh drink, Coy," Ben said, struggling to set the heavy bucket on the step. "I let the rope go all the way down to get the coldest water."

"Thank you, Ben. I knew I could count on you to do the job right." Coy took a long drink from the gourd, emptying it twice before he spoke. "Now, that's good water." When he lowered the gourd and looked down at Ben sitting on the bottom step, the boy was looking up, squinting gravely into the sun. "You been up here most of the morning. You reckon your folks is missing you?"

"Lacey might be needing me. We're purt near done this part, ain't we?"

Coy was amazed at how Ben had caught on and was even sometimes ahead of him on figuring out board sizes and the angles to cut. He marveled at Ben's need to ponder things, and that oftentimes as they worked he would turn and ask why they were doing something a certain way. Coy was beginning to recognize the signs of a serious question by the way Ben squinted his eyes and furrowed his brow.

"Coy, can I ask you a question?"

"I ain't never stopped you yet.'Course, I don't guarantee an answer."

"You planning on marrying my sister Lacey?"

"Lord, son, you sure know how to ask 'em!"

"Well, the way you been fixing up this place. And the way you're always meetin' her some place. She won't let me say nothing to nobody about it."

"It ain't likely folks would be right pleased about it. I'm not the most favored man in these parts. I bet you don't go telling 'em where you're a-going when you come up here, do you?"

Ben's neck turned patchy scarlet. "But you would be if folks got to know ya. Why, I like you a whole lot."

"Well, Ben, I appreciate that, but I don't know as how your pa would feel the same way, Lacey being his only daughter. And besides, Lacey has some say in the matter."

"Oh, she loves ya. I can tell that by the way she stares off at nothing all the time. And she smiles to herself a lot."

"You don't say," Coy said, laughing out loud. "Well, we best keep that piece of information to ourselves."

"Do you love her, Coy?"

Coy felt himself squirm under the boy's steady gaze.

"If you love her, then don't you think you best own up to it?"

"Ben, if you ain't the dangest boy I ever met!"

"Well, you 'bout got everything on the place fixed up, and if you wasn't going to marry her, maybe you was thinking about leaving when everything's all done up."

"And that's been worrying you the whole time you been helping me up here?"

Ben nodded his head, wide-eyed.

Coy shook his head in consternation. In a few short months, he had undone four years of shaking himself free of everything and everybody. Every move he now made just seemed to dig him in deeper. He was collecting a heap of folks who had a heap of expectations. He reached down and tousled the boy's curly hair. "A man couldn't ask for a better friend than you, Ben. Now, let's get back to work."

The sun set early in the hollow, and the high ridges robbed the miners of a few extra hours of sunshine they could have used. Coy sat on the front porch and propped his feet on the railing. Taking a sack of tobacco and his papers from his pocket, he skillfully rolled a cigarette. Of course, it didn't matter about the sunshine any more since the miners were no longer working.

It had been a tough summer in Wilder since the mine shut down, and there were no signs of it letting up. The men had all stuck together, and not a miner had gone back to work when the sign announcing the wage cut was posted. Lacey had been having all she could do at home to scrape enough food together to feed a house full of people, and sometimes Coy hunted rabbits or a squirrel or two to help out. Sometimes they gathered wild plants and berries from the woods. According to Lacey, just about everything that grew was good to eat. He had some doubts about that.

Seth came out carrying two cups of steaming black coffee and handed one to Coy.

"No 'shine tonight," Coy remarked, taking a cup and sipping the strong liquid with pleasure.

"Don't seem to crave it as much since the boys left. Maybe I'm just getting old."

"Next thing you know, you'll be telling me you got religion."

"I do plan to get it some time before I die."

Bo and Hoyt had left for West Virginia shortly after the strike had started in June. They had found a sudden urge to try their luck someplace else. They had relatives in West Virginia, Seth had said. Since then, Seth had given up drinking. Coy was glad, for he had never liked it much. Like Seth, he had only done it to be sociable. "You forget, I've tasted your 'shine, and I'd say you are most likely just getting smart."

"Now you may be on the trail of something there," Seth said with a hardy laugh. He sat down on a powder keg and set his coffee on the porch rail. Coy tossed him the tobacco, and he absent-mindedly rolled a cigarette as he stared off into the distance at the smoke from the burning slag heap.

"You're mighty serious all of a sudden."

"This town's a-dying, son. Been dying for a while now. Looks like this time it's going to go for sure."

Coy was still getting used to Seth's unceremonious way of jumping into a subject, and he was shocked sometimes by the powerful truth Seth could pack into a few words. "You don't expect the mines to reopen, do you?"

"Don't much matter. Folks can't live on what they're paying nohow."

"What do you think will happen to all the folks around here?"

"Oh, they'll hang on long past time to quit, 'til they're dang near starved to death. This is a hardscrabble bunch if I ever seen one. They'll fight to hold on to this town. You know, it's enough to make a man regret some things looking back."

"What do you mean?"

"I see how hard these folks is working to keep this place alive; sticking together and helping one another out. I've lived in this place near twenty-five years, and I ain't never been a part of it. That was the way I thought I wanted it when I come here."

"What made you decide to come to Wilder? Nobody ever seemed to know much about you when I was growing up."

"I worked it that way. Kept to myself. Oh, I guess there ain't no harm in telling you the story. I was born of a no count family up in West Virginia. They hadn't never done nothing but raise a ruckus and make moonshine. They was six of us younguns and not a one of them worth shooting, but early on, I was determined to make something of myself. Worked ever job I could find from the time I could walk. Finally, when I was seventeen, I just up and left on a freight train headed west. So, you see you come by it natural," Seth said, pausing to grin at Coy.

"That don't explain how you come to end up in Wilder."

"You're also short on patience like your pa," Seth said, shifting his weight on the keg as though he was looking for a more comfortable way to tell what had happened.

Coy took the remark about his lack of patience with good humor. He knew it was the truth. "I got all night," he said to let Seth know he was prepared to listen.

"Well, I didn't get far before I was hungry. I wandered onto a farm near Lexington, Kentucky, that was the prettiest sight my young eyes had ever seen. Gentle rolling pasture with cows grazing peaceful-like. Belonged to a man named Andrew MacCracken. He was a good man. His folks come over from Ireland. Worked like dogs, according to Andrew. They both died before they was fifty and left everything they'd made to their only son. They was the saving kind, and he used the money to buy a farm. Made a good living raising corn and tobacco and a few cows. He was good to me, and I worked hard to show him I appreciated it. He come to think a right smart of me. He had a only daughter named Gillian. Ain't that the prettiest name! I still love to say it. Anyway, it wasn't long before we was in love. I don't reckon I was the man Andrew had hoped for, it being his only daughter. I sure didn't have nothing to offer but hard work. I promised him, though, that I'd make her happy and she wouldn't never regret marrying me. I meant it, too. We worked out a pretty good life for ourselves there on the farm. We'd been married going on three years when it happened."

Seth paused and leaned back against the porch railing as though lost in the sadness of a memory. Coy watched silently, wondering if he should say something. Finally he spoke. "Seth, you don't have to tell me this."

Seth opened his eyes. He slowly seemed to realize what Coy had said. "No, I need to tell it. I ain't spoke to a soul about this in twenty-five years. It's time it was told. I hadn't heard a word from my folks in all that time. I wrote them maybe once a year to tell 'em I was doing fine. Just so they'd know where I was. They never wrote back, and that was fine by me. Then one day I get this letter in the mail. It come from my sister, Frances. She said the folks had been dead for going on two years. Pneumonia took them both the same winter. Can you beat that? She hadn't even bothered to write 'til she needed something. Seems as if my sister Bertha had got herself caught in bed with a man, and her husband had shot them both to death. Now he was in the West Virginia State Penitentiary, and they was two little baby boys didn't have a home."

"You mean to tell me Bo and Hoyt don't belong to you?" Coy could hardly believe what he was hearing. Seth, lost in his story, seemed unaware of the impact of his words.

"That's right," Seth went on matter of factly. "I had told Gillian about my family early on, and being a good soul she had me send for them boys right off. Lord, she was a good woman. Treated them babies like her own. We was a real happy family, and it wasn't long before we was expecting a baby of our own. Coy, I'm telling you I was one proud man. I felt like there wasn't nothing I couldn't do with Gillian there helping me. Trouble was, she died giving birth to our son, and the boy died two hours later."

"I'm real sorry, Seth."

"You see now why you always meant so much to me? You're my only real son, and I'm right proud of it no matter how it come about."

'Seth, I don't know what to say. I always thought Bo and Hoyt was yours."

"I know that's what folks thought, and I just left it at that. You see, after Gillian died, I could of stayed on the farm. Andrew always treated me like a son, but I wasn't fit for nothing. I just wanted to get away from everything that reminded me of her. Figured I had been fooling myself about ever making anything of myself. I was just worthless without her. Reckon I thought God had played quite a joke on me. So I picked the most God-forsaken place I could find: Wilder, Tennessee."

"What made you decide to start making moonshine?"

"Only thing I learned from my pappy that ever done me any good."

"Did you ever tell Bo and Hoyt what happened?"

"Not 'til just afore they left. I got a letter from their real pa. He was about to get out of prison, and he wrote and asked if I would tell them the truth. You see, I wrote a little to him all along so's he'd know how they was getting along."

"Seth, you are a remarkable man." Coy tried to imagine what it took to write to the man who had killed his sister.

"I wished I could agree with you there, but I made some powerful mistakes in my time. And even when I knowed I had done made 'em I stuck with them. Pride and foolishness a-plenty, I reckon. And cowardness."

"You don't sound like no coward to me."

"The worst kind, son. The kind that's afraid of living and afraid of dying. You end up living in a hell somewhere in between."

"What would you change if you had it to do over?"

"Well, I couldn't change Gillian a-dying, and I don't regret giving the boys a home."

Seth pondered silently in the darkness. Unable to take in fully all that Seth had told him, Coy watched the fireflies light up the night. He felt Seth's urgent need to tell him the painful story of his coming to Wilder, and yet he felt there was more to come. A message was still wrapped up somewhere in the story. "Maybe you regret coming to this God-forsaken place," Coy said, urging him on.

"This may surprise you, son, but I don't regret it. If I hadn't of come here, I would never of met Ellen and I would never have had you. I couldn't regret a thing like that. I do regret the way I lived my life, though. That's a hard thing for a man to say. To look back on your life and know you've been a fool. Seeing you makes me wonder what would of happened if I had spoke up to Ellen. If I had asked her to marry me when she was carrying you. I give up too easy. I always did. That's been my big fault in life. I just give up without a fight."

"Well, hell. You're not dead yet. You are acting like you're a-getting ready."

"What do you mean?"

"I know you take stuff up to her place ever week or so. You leave it on the porch in the middle of the night."

"Ain't no harm in my looking out for her. Besides, it's just a little flour and meal. Sometimes a tin of lard. Nothing special."

"That ain't the point. Do you ever wait around to see if she'll come out and speak to you?"

"Lord, no. If I let Ellen catch one glimpse of me, she'd never take that stuff. She'd leave it there to rot."

"How do you know? You never give it a try. It ain't too late to change that mistake you made."

"You sure know how to turn a man's words back on him. I'm a-telling you this story so you won't make the same mistake."

"I figured you was trying to tell me something."

"Well, I hate to see you waste your life the way I done. I thought I could hole up here and never have nothing to do with nobody if I didn't so choose it. I paid a heavy price for that freedom, son. I see you trying to walk the same road. You don't want to lose that Lacey gal. She's a fine young woman, and you'll not have her without a price. If you want her, you best own up to it."

"That's the second time I've heard that today."

"Well then, you take heed."

"Yes, Pa," Coy answered like a dutiful son.

"Mark my words, son. You're trifling with that gal's life. She needs you to step in there and take hold of things. Face up to her pa like a man. For once in your life, think ahead to what your doings mean. You got more to think about than yourself now, and that's new to you. That's all I got to say on the matter. Now, I best be getting up the ridgeline and get this stuff to your ma before daylight."

"Can't teach an old dog a new trick, huh, Seth?"

"I may be too old to learn, but I ain't too old to pass along some advice. Life ain't a fence you can straddle until you can decide which side looks best. Like I said, that's all I'm going to say on it. If it makes you mad, I can't help that none. You wait right here," he said leaping from the keg. "I got something I want to show you before I go."

Seth went inside, and Coy could hear him rummaging through the old trunk in the front room. He came back holding something in his right hand. "I used to leave you stuff on the porch, too. It might have been wrong of me, but I done it. One winter, I carved a whole set of Yankee and Rebel soldiers. Hand painted them myself. I left 'em on the porch one night. I always wondered if you ever got them soldiers."

"I got them, Seth. Ma told me she bought them from a peddler." Coy was too stunned to say anything else. All he could think about was what a waste it had been that he had never known this man when he was growing up.

"That was right and proper of her even if she knowed I left 'em. I made an even dozen of each, but I kept one Yank and one Reb. I used to hold them at night and imagine you playing with them. You'd be making up battles and working out plans. Did you ever do that, son?"

"They was my favorite toys, Seth. I used to play for hours just like you imagined. I always wondered why they was such an odd number."

"Now you know. Here's the last two soldiers, I want you to have them. It may seem like a strange present for a grown man."

"Thank you, Seth." He held on to Seth's hand as he passed him the toy soldiers. "It don't seem strange at all."

"I don't reckon you know what become of them others, do you?"

Coy thought of the open cookstove and the gray and blue smoke curling up around the bodies of his fallen soldiers. "No, Seth, I don't reckon I remember."

"Well, it don't make no never mind. You was just a boy. I'll be getting on over the mountain now. Good night, son."

"Good night, Seth."

Coy sat for a few more minutes trying to absorb all that Seth had told him, then poured the remains of his cold coffee over the porch railing onto the hard-packed ground. He could hear it splatter in the darkness below. Flicking his last cigarette out into the night, he went inside. The trunk in which Seth had searched for the soldiers was still open, and Coy patted his shirt pocket where he had safely tucked them away and began to look though the contents of the trunk.

There was a photograph of a beautiful young woman with long, dark hair standing next to a dark, handsome young man that could have been Coy. Their open faces were full of hope and happiness. Seth was wearing a well-tailored dark serge suit that made him look to the entire world like he had "amounted to something." There were other photographs of Gillian, Seth, and the boys, but there were no pictures of Seth's family, only some old newspaper clippings of the shooting of Bertha Sloan and her lover, Dade Williams. The murderer, Thomas Sloan, had turned himself in to the local sheriff and was awaiting trial. A clipping about the life of Bertha Sloan told the worst of Seth's family.

Coy thought back on something Seth had said the first night he had come to the Ramsey place. "I ain't no good, son. In fact, I'm about fifth generation worthless." He must have believed it was his fate to carry on the Ramsey tradition, and when Gillian had died he had gone back to what he truly believed he had been all along: worthless.

Is he trying to tell me it doesn't have to be that way for me? Coy wondered. "I have a chance to make something of myself," he whispered to himself. "What was that he said? 'I just give up too easy. That's my big fault in life.'"

Coy put everything back in its place in the trunk and closed the lid. The coal oil lamps were beginning to flicker. Not being part of the mining camp, Seth had never bothered with electric lights. Coy leaned back in his chair, suddenly aware that the hot August night had finally cooled off. Lacey had made it easy for him not to get too involved while she fought to hold on to him and to her family and the life she loved. He thought of her thin shoulders trying to carry the weight of it all. He had let her do it, knowing what it was costing her. Well, he'd put a stop to that. If she wanted to stick it out to the end, he would help her stay in Wilder until she could see her way clear to leave. He didn't believe the town could be saved, but he would give a part of himself to the dying if it would win him Lacey's respect. And he might just earn a little piece of self-respect in the bargain.

"Come daylight, I got some things I'm going to own up to," he said firmly to the first rays of morning sun coming over the ridge. Getting up, he stretched his long limbs, and then started a fire in the cookstove for coffee. Suddenly, as he noticed that Seth's bed had not been slept in, he looked out the back door to see Seth bounding up the path to the porch. He took the steps in one leap then stopped suddenly, looking sheepish when he spotted Coy.

"Good morning, Coy. You're up early," Seth greeted him cheerfully.

"Looks like neither one of us made it to bed. It seems to of done you a right smart of good losing a little sleep. Don't tell me you finally stayed to watch the sunrise on Ellen Wilson's front porch?"

A huge smile crossed Seth's face. "I done more than that. I done had my breakfast at Ellen's kitchen table!"

"Let me pour you some coffee, and you can tell me all about it."

While Coy poured coffee for the both of them, Seth pulled up a chair and sat down, excitement causing his body to twitch. He pounded the table with his fist. "Dangest thing! I meant to just leave the stuff on her porch and take off. Instead, I skulked around there for more'n an hour like a dog with a sore paw. I was just starting to roll me a cigarette when I seen her standing right out on the porch. Her hair was combed all down over a white cotton gown with her toes just a barely showing out from underneath. Next thing I knowed, I was a stepping right out from them trees brave as you ever seen. If I startled her, she never let on. She just stepped closer, and that's when she said it." Seth grinned and slapped his hands together, staring daftly at Coy like a moonstruck young boy.

"Seth, if you'll pardon my saying so, you sound a bit touched. What did Ellen say that had such an effect on you?"

"Well, like I said, she stepped a bit closer, and I could see her face in the moonlight. And then, just like that she said it. 'Seth,' she said. She recognized me right off."

Coy raised his eyebrows in impatience.

"All right, I'm getting to it," Seth said, taking deep breath. "It's just I have trouble believing it even now. She said, 'Seth, I wondered when you was gonna stay for breakfast.' And I just up and said, 'I reckon it's high time.'"

"So you not only stayed for daylight. You stayed for breakfast."

"I sure did. We had us a long talk, me and Ellen. They's been mistakes on both sides. She asked about you, Coy. She knows she done wrong by you, and she's grieved about it since you left. I see that look on your face, but before you go getting your neck hairs up, she ain't asking you to forgive her."

"I wasn't planning on it nohow, Seth. I'm happy things is working out for you and Ellen. You two can talk all you want. As for me — "

"Son, let me tell you. I am as much to blame for your bringing up as Ellen. It was my cowarding ways that made her so bitter. She weren't nothing but a little girl. I should of done right by her."

"But I thought she loved Reed."

"That's just it," Seth said jumping up to grab the water bucket. "Lord a-mercy, this place is a mess! I'd best get some water to boiling and set about cleaning this place up."

"What are you talking about? Seth, you ain't making sense."

"It was me she loved, son. She done told me. It was me she loved. Now help me get this place cleaned up. I done invited your ma to supper."

Coy could only shake his head as he watched Seth take the back stairs in one leap and click his heels as he headed to the well.

11

Lacy stretched her back and rested her arms on the hoe, looking back over the garden rows she had just worked. It was hard work keeping the weeds hoed out. Ben had collected ladybugs to put out to help keep the beetles and potato bugs from eating everything in sight, and now he was dusting the rows of potato plants with ashes from the cookstove to fertilize the ground. She had managed to get a hold of a few more seed potatoes late in the season, and she hoped they would produce. They needed the additional food to get them through until the mine reopened. When she had first planted them, her ma had told her she was being foolish and that they should have eaten the brown, shriveled potatoes for supper. It made her proud to see them now tall and green and heavy with blossoms. "You gonna need some more ashes there, Ben?"

"I have might near enough to finish out this row."

"Do what you can there and I'll get you another bucketful." Lacey leaned her hoe against the back porch railing and went in to fill another bucket with ashes from the cookstove. The stove was almost empty. To keep the kitchen cool, she had started an open fire at the pit in the backyard to cook supper. It was the same pit where she made lye soap and hominy in the fall. She thought of the pot of fresh green beans and new potatoes cooking there now and closed her eyes in silent gratitude for one more day of food. It would take the last of the corn meal for pone, but she couldn't worry about that now.

Voices drifted in from the front porch. Ruby and her ma spent much of every afternoon sitting on the porch talking. Ruby spent many hours patiently listening to Annie's ailments, her hands on her swollen belly and a sincere look on her face. In return, Annie often rallied to care for Ruby, grown huge in her seventh month of pregnancy. Although they couldn't be counted on to be of much help around the house, Lacey was relieved to have her mother distracted.

Lacey carried the heavy bucket of ashes out back and stood squinting in the bright August sun, allowing her eyes a moment to adjust. Ben, barefoot and covered with dust, worked on steadily, his face and hands browned by the sun. They had spent many hours together in the garden trying to scrounge enough food to feed the household.

The strike had had its effect on all of them. In some ways it had made life harder for Lacey, but it had given her a freedom she had never known. With Annie and Ruby wrapped up in themselves and Pa and Will scouring the countryside for day work, no one seemed to take notice of her comings and goings. And since her trips to the woods often meant wild onions, dandelion leaves, or a mess of poke, they were generally welcomed by the household.

Only she and Ben knew the trips had another purpose. Since it had been necessary to confide her secret to Ben, he had developed such an attachment to Coy that he would have risked death rather than betray him. He begged to be allowed to go along on each trek, and Lacey could hardly deny him. Like her, he was caught up in the energy of Coy. She set the bucket on the back porch and took a drink from the water bucket. "You'd best come up and get a drink before you try to do much more of that, Ben. You got to watch this heat, even if it is getting on toward four o'clock."

Ben loped up toward where Lacey stood holding the drinking dipper in her hand. Wiping his face with the cleanest part of the back of his gritty hand, he grinned broadly as he drank deep, gulping swallows. He poured the second dipper over his head, shaking the water from his hair and soaking Lacey in the process. "Ben!" Lacey shouted, laughing and wiping the water from her face, "It'll take a heap more than a dipper of water to clean that face."

"I know that. I was thinking about heading up to the river to cool off before supper."

"And was you thinking about taking a cake of lye soap with you?"

"Yes'm, that was exactly what I was thinking of doing," he answered sincerely.

"Well, as long as you already had that in your head, I reckon you better go on," she laughed.

"You sure you don't need me to finish up here?"

"It won't take me but a minute to spread this last bucket. Besides, it's might near time for me to get supper on. You go on so you can get back before Pa and Will get home."

"I won't stay long, Lacey, I promise."

"I'll hold you some supper on the back of the stove," Lacey reassured him.

"I'll be back d'reckly," Ben yelled as he raced off to the river.

"You take care." With so many folks to worry over, it was hard to work them all in. Coy could never understand her feeling responsible for other people's lives. Even if he cared about somebody like he had Jake Abbott, he didn't feel responsible for what happened to them. She had tried to imagine what that felt like, but it was too foreign to her. Even as she roamed the woods with Coy, caught up in the excitement of being with him, she always thought of what it would do to her folks if they knew. Part of her still believed that her time with Coy was a dream, that someday it would end and she would go back to her life the way it had been set out: to marry a miner and live in Wilder forever. She could not believe that anything else might be her fate, and so this intoxicating summer with Coy had to be a dream.

Of course, the dream was real enough to be punished for, of that she was sure. She had never been one to believe that it was possible for a person to escape the consequences of one's choices. God had a punishment for every sin and every sinner. It might be swifter in coming to some than to others, but everybody got their due in time. Retribution was out there circling like a red-tailed hawk ready to swoop down and catch its prey at the most unexpected moment. Coy had laughed at her when she had first told him her beliefs. He said he had seen plenty of folks slide right through life evidently just ahead of the Almighty without a sign of them having to pay for their sins this side of the grave. It wasn't God she should be fearing, he had gone on to say, but the downright mean-spirited orneriness of human beings.

It didn't seem much different to Lacey. To her way of thinking, folks was just a form God used to exact the price, like risking her family in exchange for loving Coy.

It had been a week since Lacey had seen Coy. Sometimes, when the days went by and she didn't hear from him, she thought that might be the price. One day he would just be gone.

Will and Pa came over the rise in the road just as Lacey looked up. She couldn't tell if they were carrying anything. Pa and Will had been gone all week looking for day work. It was hard to find any kind of work with so many men looking, but each week Pa would roust Will out of bed at dawn and they would go back out. Sometimes all they got for their work was meals.

She set aside the hoecakes she had fried golden brown in a skillet over the fire and stirred the beans before she went to greet them. *It won't do to burn supper, even if I am glad to see them*, she thought.

Annie and Ruby were chattering excitedly to the weary men when Lacey reached the front porch. "What was the farmhouse like? Did they have lace curtains?" Annie asked.

"We wasn't in none of the house 'cept the kitchen. It didn't have no lace curtains," Will said irritably.

"We spent four days pulling stumps from a patch a ground as hard as any rock I ever dug in the mines," Frank said, dropping into the chair Ruby had been sitting in. "They just had one mule, and I reckon they used us as the rest of the team."

"What they give you for working?" Annie asked without hesitation.

Lacey cringed at the question she hadn't wanted to ask. She saw the tin bucket Will held behind his back ashamedly. Her Pa looked over at her, his eyes glazed with fatigue. "How you doing there, gal?"

"I'm fine, Pa. You're looking a bit done in. I got supper ready. Would you like a cool drink before you eat?"

"They ain't told us yet what they got for pay," Annie whined.

Will slowly brought the tin around and held it out to Ruby who took it, looking at it stupidly. "What is it, Will?"

"It's a five-pound bucket of sorghum molasses. That and meals is what we got for four days of working like dang mules.

Damn near broke us, it did. Why, Pa went down once. I thought it had him."

"Pa, what happened?" Lacey asked, trying not to rush to his side. Slipping up next to his chair and squatting beside him, she quietly laid her hand over his on the chair arm. The calluses were thick and rough, and briar scratches cut deep red patterns in his skin.

"It weren't nothin' but the heat. Don't fret yourself, gal."

"Well, I can't believe decent folks would work a man like that and then not give him more than a bucket of molasses," Annie screeched.

"We never asked the man what he'd pay us. I always expect a man to do right by me just as I'd do right by him. We take what we get, Annie, and be grateful for it."

"I still say you ought to a de-manded they pay you a fair wage."

"Maybe I should oughta send you out ahead of us, Annie. See if you couldn't wrangle us a better deal. Then me and Will will just step in after you get the feller fairly well wore down."

"Now, Frank, I ain't about to let you turn this into a joke. How we gonna live on a bucket of molasses?" Annie crossed her arms and sighed heavily.

Frank looked at her wearily. "Ain't I always took care of you, Annie? Have a little faith. Something will turn up. It always has. Now, let's eat us some supper before it gets cold. I'm hungry enough to eat that bucket of molasses."

They all laughed, and Lacey was relieved to have the tension broken. As they turned to go into the house, she thought she heard Ben's voice. He was shouting her name, and the voice was getting louder. Just then he topped the rise and Lacey could see he was driving a wagon and waving one arm for all he was worth. Riding next to him was Coy. Lacey's heart lurched and caught high in her chest, making her gasp.

"Hey, Lacey, look at me! I'm driving this here wagon. Coy let me drive the wagon all the way from the river. Ain't that somethin'! And lookie here, he's done brought us a whole mess of grub. Just come out here and look at this stuff. There's flour, lard, cornmeal, and dozens of eggs. You gotta see this, Lacey. Pa, come on out here."

Lacey looked at Coy who was grinning with amusement at Ben's excitement and with obvious pride at the bounty he had brought. Will was already running to the wagon when Lacey turned to her pa. His face was set in stone as he stepped off the porch and headed to the wagon. Annie and Ruby were uncharacteristically speechless, seemingly powerless to move. Lacey followed her pa to the wagon but stood back a few feet, unable to bring herself closer.

"Howdy, Mr. Conners," Coy said cheerfully, greeting him with a tip of the hat and a broad smile.

"Howdy, Coy," Frank answered without returning the smile. "Ben, let's be for climbing down from there now and leave the man be."

Ben jumped down undaunted and buzzed around the side of the wagon like a bee after a flower. "Look at this, Lacey, taters, squash, even a side of bacon. We ain't had bacon in a month."

Lacey blushed at Ben's innocent confession. She could see her pa's jaw muscles working. "Ben, why don't you go get Coy Lynn some water. He might be thirsty after his ride."

"Why, I'd appreciate that, Lacey. I've been out since dawn. Been up near Livingston doing some trading for a week now. I reckon I must of stopped at every farmhouse between there and here on the way back. Folks was mighty nice to me though, and it appears I got more than me and Seth can use in a month of Sundays. Frank, if you and the family would be interested in taking some of it off my hands, I'd be much obliged."

Despite Lacey's fear, she couldn't help but beam at Coy with pride at what he was doing and the way he was handling himself. She felt a surge of hope that her pa might come to see Coy as she did. Only she knew what it had taken to bring him there.

"Coy Lynn," her pa said, sucking in his breath. His face was red, and the veins in his temples were beginning to bulge. "I done got along this far in life without taking nothing that was stole, and I reckon I don't need your thieving to see me through."

Lacey could hear Ben drop the water bucket behind her. She felt her pa's words like a punch and bent forward holding her arms around herself, powerless to move. Everyone around her stood motionless, and the only change was the familiar cloud that moved over Coy's face as the unexpected cruelty of Frank's words soaked in. Coy looked at her through the slits in his eyes, and then drove away without a word. When he was just out of sight, Pa turned on his heels and strode off toward the house. Lacey continued to stand rooted on the ground until her pa yelled back at her, "Let's eat."

His words felt like gunshots fired at close range, yet she moved about serving supper, spending what she knew might be her last moments in this house doing familiar things. No one spoke, and the silence was like a roar in her ears. Ben sat hangdog over his plate and refused to eat, only occasionally glancing up at Lacey wide-eyed.

When supper was finally over, Pa pushed back his chair and spoke without looking at anyone. "Now y'all clear on outta here. Lacey and me has got some things to talk over."

Ben hung back until Lacey motioned for him to go on. She busied herself with clearing the table while her pa sat silently and watched. As she stacked the dishes, her eyes went over every familiar object in the room like a caress. She ran her hand over the blue flowered oil cloth on the table by the stove and straightened the tins of salt and baking powders. It was strange, but she couldn't even remember when she had cooked her first meal. She had to have been around five years old because she had stood in a chair to reach the stove, and it had taken both hands to lift the heavy skillet of cornbread into the oven. A lot of family meals had been eaten in that room, and she had had many late night conversations there with her pa. Suddenly it came to her that she was saying goodbye to the things she had known. Tears stung her eyes, but she refused to let them fall. When the table was clear, she stood back and looked at her father. "Why, Pa?" she asked simply.

"You think I don't know what's been going on between the two of you?"

Lacey blushed crimson, and fear clawed its way up her spine and stuck its talon in her throat. The red-tailed hawk had struck its prey. "I didn't mean to hide it from you, Pa. I knowed how you and the town felt about Coy. I just hoped after he was back a while you would change your mind about him."

"What's to change, gal? That boy's the same no good he always was."

"He didn't steal that food, Pa. He wouldn't do that. He was just trying to help."

"I don't need the likes of him to feed this family. I been feeding you since you were brung into this world, and now you're looking to somebody else, I reckon. Can't count on your own Pa, is that it?"

"No Pa, that ain't it at all. You always done right by us."

"It ain't bad enough you been sneaking around seeing this boy behind my back. Now you have to bring him to our front door to shame me in front of my family."

"I didn't... He didn't do it to shame nobody, Pa. He's not like that."

"You seem to think a right smart of him."

"I love him, Pa." The words surprised her. They made other young girls foolishly happy. Somehow they became more grown-up when they were in love. Now, the same simple words were bringing her so much pain, and there was nothing she could do. She loved him, and her words were as true as any she had ever spoken.

"Gal, you don't know what you are saying. Loving that boy will be like holding fire in your hand. Lord have mercy on you, child! You've set yourself a hard row to hoe." Lacey watched as he dropped his face into his hands and sat rubbing his temples. She wanted to go to him, but she could only stand and wait for the long seconds to tick away. Finally, he looked up, his face slack and ashen. "I never expected this from you," he said, his voice a raspy whisper. "You was the one most like me. You was always the one that done me proud."

"Was, Pa?" His words burned deep until every nerve was seared.

"I never tried to stop one of mine from doing what it come to 'em to do. And up 'til now, not one of 'em ever put more on me than I could hold up under. I'll tell you this just once. If I ever hear tell of you seeing that boy again, they'll be no place for you here. Make your choice."

They looked at each other for a moment until she could bear it no longer. The challenge was in his eyes. Grabbing the kettle from the stove, she went outside to put water on the fire for the dishes. As she knelt to put more wood on the fire, the heat swirled around her face making her deliciously sleepy. It was a strange feeling to have. She thought perhaps she should be making plans, but she was too tired. What she really wanted was to lie down on the ground and go to sleep, a long, long nap that would prove that everything was a dream. Something told her that it was not to be. It was the same part of her that knew that this time would come. With every muscle exhausted, she lifted the water kettle from the fire and carried it back to the

kitchen to wash the supper dishes. When she opened the back
door and looked about the kitchen, her pa was gone.

The hours dragged on until the house became totally silent.
Ben had been to her door several times in the evening, but she
had been unable to let him in. She tried as best she could to
reassure him that she was just fine. It was a lie, she supposed.
At the moment, she didn't know if anything would ever be fine
again. The flour sack she held in her hand was still stitched on
one end. She planned to use it to pack her few possessions. A
comb and brush, some talcum, the carving of the red-tailed
hawk, her only good dress, and two blue ribbons were spread
out before her on the bed. Packing would not take long. With
the house quiet and everyone asleep for hours now, she already
could have left.

She could understand her pa's surprise, for there had been
no mark on her, no outward sign, that she would be the one to
bring such heartache. It had come as a surprise even to her. But,
when she thought of how she was to endure the pain, she could
only think of her pa, his quiet strength and determination to
survive. "You are right, Pa. I am the one most like you," she
whispered into the dark. Quickly, she threw her things into the
flour sack and quietly went out through the back door. Before
she left, she bent to kiss Ben and to brush the unruly locks from
his forehead. He had been sleeping on a pallet on the kitchen
floor since Will and Ruby had married. Beads of sweat had
collected on his face and left a salty taste. It made her think of
her tears earlier in the evening. Without looking back, she
made her way down the steps and headed up the railroad tracks
toward the Ramsey place.

Even in the dark, Lacey could walk sure-footed on the
tracks from years of practice. Most folks used the railroad
tracks as the closest way to the next camps. Lightning from a
gathering thunderstorm began to light up the sky, and a breeze
worked its way through the ever-yielding trees on the ridgeline.
It was when she cut up the hollow to the winding path that led
to the Ramsey house that she was less sure. Not only was she
less sure of her footing, stumbling over an occasional
unfamiliar root or dip in the path, her courage faltered with
each step. *What if he doesn't want me?* she thought. It must
have cost him a lot in pride to come to the house like that. Her
pa should have understood that, if nothing else. This strike

wasn't even Coy's business and it probably seemed foolish to be helping folks to hang onto something he so despised. And now he might be too mad to want to see her again.

Lightning cracked the sky wide open, and the rain pelted down with heavy thudding drops. Lacey hugged the flour sack closer. *My family could bear the shame of me better if I were dead,* she thought. The thought chilled her even in the crackling heat.

She couldn't see a single light through the rain. Between each flash of lightning, the sky became black as coal, and the moon was covered by a thick layer of swollen clouds. She wasn't sure how far she had come on the trail or if she might be getting near the house. She was confused and afraid, and the warm tears mixed with the rain on her face. She felt the urge to bolt and run back toward home. The path ahead of her was now cascading toward her like little rivers. Suddenly, her foot slipped on a muddy rock and sent her sprawling face first into the torrent. When she tried to pull herself up, she realized that her foot was lodged between a rock and the exposed feeder root of an oak, and the mud from her hair washed down her face with each drop of rain. Her panic rose as the gritty dirt filled her mouth and eyes, and with one violent twist of her body, she wrenched her leg free. Crawling along the tree root, she found the base of a giant oak and sat there gasping for breath.

Never had she felt so alone, sitting hurt and afraid in the dark with no sure way to turn. Ahead of her was a man she hardly knew who had made no promises to her. What was she thinking? That he would greet her cheerfully, glad to take her in just after her pa had humiliated and accused him of being a thief? He might at that very moment be on a train headed back to Wyoming convinced at last by her own family that Wilder held no promise for him. Behind her was the family she had shamed by her love for Coy. She had brought this burden upon her pa at the worst time of his life when his pride, tattered and sore, was the only shield he had left to hold up to the world as a defense. She prayed to die, but she knew God well enough to know there would be no quick release from her suffering. Hugging the tree, she rubbed her cheek against its rough bark, seeking any solace the contact might offer. For the first time in her life, she had no one, and great racking sobs matched the rhythm of her rocking.

After some time she became aware that the storm had stopped, that a quiet had settled over the hollow, and she came alert to the sound of someone on the trail. It had not occurred to her that she might meet anyone. Coy had told her that Seth was a good man, but she had no desire to meet him in the dark. The sound of her name came through the darkness. Someone was calling her. It made her want to weep with relief. When she had walked off the back porch into the night, she felt like she had disappeared off the earth, swallowed up by the blackness of the night, forgotten forever. The voice drew nearer, and still she could not call out. All at once she was too ashamed at being caught on the trail, filthy from the mud and unsure if she could even walk. Then not twenty feet from her the voice called.

"Lacey, where are you. Laaa—cey, It's me, Ben."

It *was* Ben. He had come out in the storm to get her. How had he known she was gone? "Ben, over here by the tree. Over here, Ben," she called to him, trying to stand up. He came through the dark to her, and they fell together, clinging to each other silently. Then Lacey realized how frightened Ben must have been while wandering through the storm to look for her. "What are you doing out here, Ben? You're soaked through to the bone. There ain't a dry rag on you."

"The thunder and lightning woke me up, and I went to your room," he said weakly, his voice trailing off.

He had been terrified of lightning since he was a baby, and Lacey had often found him asleep by her bed after a storm. His coming out in the storm was almost more than she could bear. She had been so alone. So she hugged him tightly and tried not to cry. "You shouldn't have come after me, but you done a brave thing in doing it. You're a better brother than I have a right to."

"Why'd you do it, Lacey? Why'd you run off and leave me? You didn't even tell me you was going."

It did seem ugly and foolish to her now. Running off in the middle of the night like that and leaving everything she had known was wrong. And she hadn't said good-bye to Ben, either. "I didn't do it to hurt you. I just had to leave. Now, I can't go back, Ben. Pa wouldn't let me in the house."

"He was mad over Coy, wasn't he?"

"His pride was hurt. But I was the real cause of it."

"Coy didn't mean no harm."

"I know."

"Was that where you was going? Was you going to meet Coy?"

Lacey didn't know how to answer. To be running off in the middle of the night to meet a man was not something she thought she would ever have to explain to her brother.

Ben looked at her, puzzled. She realized she must look a sight with mud caked on her face and hair. She tried to smile, but it wouldn't come.

"Come on back to the house with me, Lacey."

"I can't, Ben. Pa'll turn me out for sure."

"No he won't, Lacey. When I snuck out, he was still sawing logs."

She almost laughed at Ben's innocent reference to her pa's snoring, and she felt foolish that she had pictured the whole family sitting up angry and worried about her. They were sleeping soundly in their beds unaware that she was even gone. "I hurt my foot. Can you help me walk?" She put her arm around Ben's neck, and he slipped his arms about her waist.

"Don't you worry about nothin'. I'll get you back home, Lacey."

Slowly, painfully, they started back down the hollow and away from Coy.

12

"They're going to try to reopen the mines," Will yelled as he burst through the back door. "They posted a big sign up at the mines. Anybody that wants to work at thirty cents a ton can come back."

Lacey looked at her pa sitting at the kitchen table. He had never joined the union, and it was only from John's efforts and the respect of the other men that there had never been any trouble over it. The men had not been so easy on the other miners who had not joined the United Mine Workers. Late at night they had visited the homes of these men and had stolen whatever there was to take of value and left behind only a sign of warning to join the union or else. The Conners had never found a warning, but often they had found food on the porch in the mornings. She thought maybe it was because Will was a union member or maybe because of John.

"When they set to open her back up, son?" Frank finally asked.

"Says here, October sixteenth. That's Monday week, Pa."

"I reckon they figure we're pretty near starved down by now. We won't be so choicey about working for thirty cents a ton."

Lacey looked around at Will and Pa. They were all as thin as birch bark. The garden had fed them all summer, but with winter coming on, the hard times were still ahead.

"They ain't going to break us that easy. Barney Graham's got a big meeting called down at the schoolhouse tonight. The men's bound to be set for a ruckus on this for sure. I'm heading on down to the commissary to see what's a-stirring."

"Will, you mind that bunch. They's likely to be worked up over this, and you don't need to be getting mixed up in nothing if there's a chance of getting back on at the mines."

"Pa, ain't none of these men going back at thirty cents after all we been through. We mean to last it out."

A thin whine could be heard from the other room, and Ruby entered the kitchen swaying rhythmically with each step and loudly singing an old church hymn. The baby's screams increased with the pitch of the song, and Ruby looked up helplessly at Lacey. "Oooh," Ruby moaned. "I just don't know what to do with little Rachel, Lacey. Don't seem that nothing can satisfy her."

"Could it be your singing that's got her riled? Ain't she a might young to be hearing about sin and temptation and 'Nearer My God to Thee'? She just got here," Will said, snickering.

Ruby looked at Will like he was as useless as a gnat buzzing around her face, and Lacey stepped between them to take the baby from her arms. "I sung for all my brothers and sisters when I was home, and they loved it. I never heard of one of them complain."

"The Burnett's is all tone deaf. Ain't they, Lacey? Everybody in church done discussed it, and that's the conclusion we come to."

Lacey had to turn away to keep from laughing. She caught a grin starting on Ruby's face as she grabbed a wet dish rag and stung it after Will's disappearing backside as he retreated across the room. It felt good to hear their good natured jostling. It had not been easy, all of them living in the house. Sometimes, even though Lacey was glad, it was hard to see how well Will and Ruby got along. They were perfect for each other. Ruby's patient, giving nature tempered Will's selfishness. He was learning to stop short of taking too much because he genuinely loved Ruby and their tiny daughter. She was happy for them, but the sight of it made her feel lonely, causing an ache that spread out to every muscle and nerve in her body.

"Remember, Will," Frank spoke up from the table. "While you are down there playing big man with them union men, remember about that baby girl of yourn. Does she mean to last it out, too?"

Lacey shot a look at Will as though she could stop the words. Will was looking back at his pa through narrowed eyes. The baby had been born frail after many hours of struggle. Ruby's milk had not been good, and it had been difficult to find a steady supply of cow's milk. None of it had been Will's fault, and she wanted to stop her father's cruel words before they reached him. There was a meanness that had come out in him since the strike, and she knew that it was just the fear and humiliation swelling up inside him. She felt it, too, when there was nothing left in the house to eat and everyone looked to her at suppertime, or when she looked out to see the garden spot empty except for the skeletons of summer bounty.

Will left without answering. Lacey turned away and mixed the last of the honey with some warm water, then dipped the corner of a clean rag into the bowl. Rachel sucked greedily on the treat as Lacey bent to kiss the translucent skin on her tiny hand. She rocked the baby gently and stared out the kitchen window, unable to turn and face her pa just yet. They still talked the way they always had, but things between them were not the same. Her pa had never brought up Coy since that night, and if he knew that she had tried to run away, he never mentioned it. In some ways, not being able to talk to anyone about what had happened made it more difficult. But at least she had been saved the shame of it.

Coy had left the next day without a word. He had ridden out on a freight train in the early morning hours as she had lain sleepless in her bed. Ben had been up to the house to report back that it had been cleaned out of everything except a few powder kegs and a rickety chair.

Word drifted through camp that Seth Ramsey and Ellen Wilson had married and had moved to Kentucky to live. The news had shocked the camp and had given her mother something to cluck over for a week.

No one had been surprised over Coy's leaving, and his name still came up in conversations. Hearing it felt like ripping open a wound just as it was starting to heal. She only said it sometimes when she was alone on Buck Rock, and it always came out like the high, keening sound of an animal caught in a trap. He had never tried to get word to her, and she hurt from not knowing if he ever gave her a thought. She wondered what would have happened if she had made it to the cabin that night. Would Coy have welcomed her with open arms and taken her away some place where they would have built a life for themselves? Would her folks have forgiven them both in time? There was no point thinking about it. Hope had died with the last strains of the train whistle that had carried Coy out of town.

A tremor shook her body as she came to herself: the baby was asleep, Ruby looked at Lacey with a concerned look, and she wondered how long she had been staring out the window. She smiled and handed the baby over to Ruby's waiting arms.

Her pa sat holding his unlit pipe between his teeth, his chin in his hands. There had been no tobacco for his pipe for some time, so there was no need for Lacey to pack it for him. *If things are not the same between us*, she thought, *it's because I'm not the same*. To her pa the matter was settled and forgotten. That was his way.

"Pa, I got your traps oiled if you want to set 'em tomorrow on your way to Jamestown." He still trekked across the mountain to look for work or to hunt for rabbits, even though both were scarce. She knew the idleness was hard on him.

"Them traps is so old they's slower than I am. They're most handy for scaring the game off." When he looked up to see Lacey standing over him holding the traps, his expression softened. "Lay them out for me, would you, gal? I don't reckon it could hurt to tote 'em along."

Ruby appeared in the doorway. Already she looked peculiar to Lacey when she was not holding the baby. "John's at the door asking to see ya."

"Thank you, Ruby. I'll be right there."

"Pa, I'll put the traps here by the back door so you won't forget them in the morning." Lacey laid the traps just inside the back door so they would be safe. In the past, she would have hung them on a nail outside. Now, with so much borrowing going on, she thought it was best to leave them inside. As she came through the front room, she could see John unloading something from a dust-caked Model-T pickup truck. The truck had been bought with union money to bring in aid for the miners. John spent a lot of his time working at the aid station or driving through the county picking up food. Sometimes the truck would park at a spot, and the miners would come with their pokes and divide it up. "I hope he brought something good," she whispered and then looked around her to see if anyone had overheard. He had been so good to them all.

The sunlight picked up the red in John's hair as he walked to the porch carrying a small wooden crate. His green eyes told her how happy he was to see her. She had promised to marry him in the spring, although she did not love him. He would never know. She would see to that. It had taken all her will to sit on the porch with him that Sunday after Coy left and act like her life could really go on with any meaning, but she had done it. No one would ever know about the time she had looked into a pair of coal black eyes and thought she had seen love. She had been foolish, and that was hard for her to admit. It made her stubborn in her determination to put it all behind her and make a life with John. No one would know, least of all John. She would do what life had set out for her, and she would do it proud.

"Morning, John," She greeted him with a smile as he set the crate down.

"I brung you a few things."

"That was good of you, John. You know we can always use it. I hope it didn't put you out."

"I was taking this load down to the aid station, so I had to come by this way anyhow."

"We appreciate it."

"You heard about the mines?"

"Will come in telling about it just about an hour ago. He already went down to the commissary to see what news he could pick up on it. You know he never could stand to wait around when there was some excitement."

John nodded his agreement. "Barney's called a meeting of all the men," he said hesitantly. "It's important we all know where we stand. If the men go back, the union's dead."

"Pa thinks there may be trouble."

"He don't think what we have had these past months is trouble?"

"I'm sorry, John. I know Pa ain't union. And it's good of you to bring this stuff to us, knowing how he feels about it."

"Well, I shouldn't of said what I did. Your Pa's right. They's likely to be some men pretty worked up over this, especially if they try to bring in scabs to work the mines."

"He worries about Will."

"Will's got to grow up sometime. He might as well start by standing up for what he believes in." John reached into his shirt and pulled out a small brown package and stuffed it under the other contents of the crate. "It's some hog meat. You can tell your pa where you got it. I come by it honest. It didn't come from the meat committee."

Lacey knew John was referring to the group of miners who raided farms in the area and killed livestock to bring meat back to the hungry families of Wilder. "John, you done more than enough. Pa should be proud to get this food. I'll tell him you come by."

"I better be getting on. Barney's expecting me at the schoolhouse."

"John, was you worrying that Pa might go back to work?"

"Lacey, I never worried a minute about your pa. He may not be union, but he's a good man. I don't guess he told you."

"Told me what?"

"Boyer offered him five dollars a day to be a mine guard. Promised him he'd keep money in his pockets. Your pa turned him down flat. Told him he would just wait 'til he could come by it honest. He said he didn't see how guarding that mine against his friends could be worth five dollars a day, so he must be paying him for something else."

Lacey stood staring down at the porch, shaking her head in disbelief. Last week her pa had walked five miles and worked all day for a sack of corn meal. He wouldn't join the union, and yet he had turned down the general manager of the Fentress Coal and Coke Company on an offer to make more money a day than he had made in three months because he wouldn't go against the other miners.

When she looked up, John was already headed down the steps. It was a few seconds before she realized he was leaving. "John, you take care."

He grinned his simple straight grin and waved his hat back at her. She watched the truck until it was completely out of sight. It was some time before she could pick up the food and carry it into the house.

The family gathered around the supper table and watched as Lacey set the steaming bowls of food in front of them. The smell of fried meat made their mouths water, and Lacey couldn't help but smile with happiness. The crate that John had left had contained a home-canned jar of peaches, and she set them down by her pa's plate because they were his favorites. He had not asked about the meat after she told him that John had brought it by. She tried not to think of the day Coy had ridden up with a wagonload of food and had been turned away as a thief.

As soon as the food was served, Lacey sat down, and Ben said a quick blessing before diving into his food. Lacey waited until everyone was served before she filled her plate. She looked around the table at her family as they savored fried potatoes, turnip greens, and side meat. *This is as close to the way it used to be as it might ever be again,* she thought.

Will had news of the meeting and was eager to tell it even as he crammed cornbread and side meat into his jaws. "Pa, there must've been two hundred men there. They had to end up holding the meeting in the school yard. Barney Graham stood on the school steps and shouted out to the men, 'Men we knowed this was coming. We knowed if they was going to try to reopen the mines, it would come about now. It's been a long, hungry summer, but we made it. If we are going to make it now, we have to stick together. Now tell me, are you going back in there?' You should of heard them shout. They stuck together to a man. It was something to see."

No one said a word, waiting to see Frank's reaction to the news. Even Annie looked up from her plate, blinking like a slow-witted child. He chewed his food slowly, seemingly unaware of their attention, and finally he rattled his cup and Lacey jumped up to pour his coffee. It was murky in the cup, thinned with too much grain. He seemed not to notice and slurped it deeply with enjoyment as he had in the past. "That was a good supper, gal."

"Thank you, Pa."

"Will," he said without looking at him. "How much you getting from the union?'

"Two dollars and fifty cents a month."

"How much you think one of them gun toting company guards get?"

"I don't know. A right smart, I reckon."

"Five dollars a day."

Will whistled involuntarily and sat back hard in his chair. With his point made, Frank pushed his chair back from the table and leaned back. The distant baying of hounds that had haunted their supper conversation grew louder. "I swear, I can't figure who would be running hounds this time of year, and it not hardly dark yet at that."

Will looked uncomfortably around the room, his eyes darting from window to door. Lacey caught the look and wondered what Will knew about the hounds. "Pa," Will spoke up hesitantly. "The men know who has the power. Ain't a man who has ever worked in the mines don't know who had the power." Something in Will's voice told more than the words he spoke. "When you see a man like Barney Graham who believes in the union, who believes in the miners, you just have to stick with him. Somewhere along the line, you have to take a stand."

Frank looked at his son as though he was trying to remember who he was. Before he could speak, a ruckus erupted on the front porch. The sound of dogs barking and clawing at the front door mixed with the pounding fists and shouting voices.

"Will, do you know anything about this?"

"Yes, Pa. A trestle got blowed up past Twinton today."

"Did you have anything to do with it?"

"No, Pa." Will stopped and stared straight on at his pa. After what seemed like minutes to Lacey as she held her breath, Will spoke again, trying to be heard over the din without shouting. "Pa, I know who done it."

At that moment the door burst open, and a pack of hounds filled the room. They clawed at the table, eating what scraps were left and knocking dishes from the table. Ruby, holding the baby, jumped up from the table and backed into a corner. Rachel screamed, and Will threw himself in front of Ruby just as a dog made a jump for the baby, and the hound clawed the back of his shirt as it slid to the floor. Blood marked the tracks of its paws. Lacey saw her pa grab a chair and break it over the dog's back, and the hound yipped in pain. Ben sat wide-eyed, holding his cheek where one of the hounds had nipped a chunk of flesh in the frenzy. Lacey was holding a dry rag to the wound to soak up the blood when she looked up to see the sheriff and two deputies standing in the doorway. Sheriff Watson called the dogs, and the two deputies began to put leashes on the animals as they came back to them.

"Ernie," Frank spoke, his voice raspy. "What the hell's going on here?"

"I'm sorry about this, Frank. A trestle got blowed up about five miles up the track from here today, and the dogs tracked the scent to here." He could hardly be heard for the sound of the dogs still barking and scratching at the floor. "Get them hounds out of here, boys."

"But Sheriff Watson, we done tracked them union men to here."

Lacey saw a look of murder come across her pa's face. It was swollen almost black with anger, and his veins bulged. The sheriff motioned with his thumb for the men to take the dogs out.

"How long have I knowed you, Ernie?" Her pa spoke through lips that showed clenched teeth.

"I'm real sorry about this, Frank. They're paying me to do a job here."

"You didn't answer my question. How long have I knowed you?"

"Twenty years."

"And in them twenty years, have I ever done a harm thing to you?"

"No, sir."

"I notice you don't limp so bad like you use to. I reckon, that leg of yourn healed up right nice." Ernie looked at the floor in shame. "Maybe, you don't recollect back when you was just a lowly miner like the rest of us, the time I stayed down in the hole with you for twelve hours till they could dig you out from the rockfall. Maybe, you don't recollect begging me not to leave you."

"Frank, I got to do what they tell me. I got family to feed. The dogs come to this house, and I got to ask you if Will here was involved in that dynamiting. That's my job."

"Damn you to hell, Ernie. We had us a little taste of hog meat for supper. That's what your fool dogs broke down our door for. The company ain't made it against the law for a miner to have meat, have they?"

"Frank, don't make this any harder on me."

"No, Ernie. Lord knows, I wouldn't want things to be hard on you. So I'm going to make things real plain for you. My son Will didn't have nothing to do with what happened, but if he did, it wouldn't make no difference. You'd have to come through me to get to him. Is that easy enough on you? Now, you get the hell out of my house!"

Ernie started to speak but thought better of it and turned on his heels and was gone. Lacey watched as her pa surveyed the room. The bare light bulb hanging from the ceiling still swung from its cord, casting shadows in the hollows of each frightened face. Broken dishes lay strewn around the room, and the muddy paw prints of the hounds covered the edges of the table. Annie sat cowering in her chair as Lacey washed Ben's face and set about straightening the place.

"You all right, Will?"

Will looked around, surprised by his pa's concern. "Yes, Pa. And I'm real sorry about this."

"Weren't your doing. I'm to blame."

"What do you mean, Pa?"

"I just knowed you was a fool to join that union. I always thought if a man didn't make it in this world, it was his own damn fault. He didn't need nobody else taking up for him. And I reckon I didn't see no way the union could win. That don't matter now. I see things real clear. You done that for me son, and I want to thank ye."

"Pa." Will seemed overcome by his pa's acknowledgment.

"If you're up to it, get my hat. We got us a little trip to take."

"Where to, Pa?"

"Barney Graham's place."

"Why you going off to Barney Graham's at this hour, Frank, and leave us here alone?" Annie whined. "What if the sheriff was to come back with that pack of hounds?"

"He won't be back," Frank said firmly as Will handed him his hat. "Ready, son?"

"Yes, Pa."

"I'm going to Barney Graham's 'cause that's the best place I know for my son to sign me up to this here union." Will grinned and grabbed his pa by the arm.

"If you go to Barney's place at this hour, the sheriff will know what you're up to, Frank," Annie warned.

"That's exactly what I had in mind. The time comes when a man has to take a stand. Ain't that right, son?"

"That's right, Pa."

Lacey wanted to shout after them to be careful. Instead, she stared after them into the night. Some things were more important than being careful.

13

"**J**ohn, I'm telling you we're making the papers all over Tennessee. They just don't intend to let nobody here know about it. I had to get one of them railroad men to sneak me a copy of the *Knoxville News-Sentinel*."

John sat on Barney Graham's front porch, rubbing his chin between his right forefinger and his thumb. His head was cocked to one side as he frowned intently at a spider making its way up the porch rail.

"Listen to what Boyer has to say about the union," Barney went on. "'We offered them a union contract at a 20 percent cut in wages. They refused.' Damn right, we refused! Sounds like they was doing us some big favor, don't it. 'Now we won't have anything to do with the union,' he read. 'We tried it out a year, and it didn't work. It lost a lot of money last year.'"

"What conditions you reckon he's talking about?"

"I can't figure it. The only condition we had in our contract was that they wouldn't cut wages a third time. It was right mean of us to make them pay us wages just for working," Barney snorted.

"It sure makes it sound like we turned him down flat though, don't it."

"Oh, they got it down here where I told that reporter that we asked to talk it over with the operators, but they wouldn't give us a hearing."

"What does Boyer have to say about that?"

"He says we never asked. Says he wouldn't even consider it now, this being the only union mine left in the whole damn South. Says he just couldn't make money competing with all them nonunion mines. Now, how do you figure they plan to make money paying all them guards five dollars a day when they was only paying us three?"

John laughed a quick, bitter snort through his nose. The spider had made its way up the porch rail and was industriously spinning a web from post to rail. "The men chalk up a few railroad cars and fire off a few shots into the air, and they got half the county deputized."

"It's worse than that. They're bringing in hired gun thugs like they done up in Harlan. Men that don't know you as a neighbor and would just as soon shoot you as not."

"They got a man stationed on every bridge and trestle for five miles around since that trestle blew the other night."

"Yeah, I seen some of them scalawags with their high boots and leather jackets. The company gives 'em whatever they want on credit. They got one by the name of Jack Green that's supposed to be as mean as a striped snake. The men call him Shorty, and I reckon he's their leader. He ain't never worked a day in the mines from what I heard."

"They're set for us to do something come Monday when they try to open the mine up. Word is they got about thirty of our men ready to go back in."

"That ain't too bad out of three hundred."

"They've scraped the hills around here for a few dozen scrawny farmers. It will be a while before they haul a load of coal out of here at that rate. They ain't none too happy about it, neither."

"What do you mean?"

"After the meeting the other day when they heard the men weren't coming back, they sent a company man up here to tell me I had three days to pack up the family and move."

"What did you tell 'em?"

"I didn't tell them nothing. I wasn't even home. When they come up here, Daisy was sitting on the porch peeling apples with that switchblade knife of mine. She heard him out, and then she stuck that switchblade right up in his face and told him straight out, 'We ain't gonna move. We won't do nothing. Now you clear outta here.' And he took off like Snyder's pup. They ain't tried that trick again." Barney said, slapping his knee and throwing back his head in laughter.

John admired the pride in Barney's laughter. He could just picture Daisy facing down a grown man with a knife. It hadn't been that long since she had busted a woman square in the face at the company store for calling her a "punkin roller." John wasn't sure where the term had originated, but it had come to be a derogatory name for a striker. Daisy was fierce in her support of Barney and the union. It made John think of Lacey, and he had a sudden need to see her. She had promised him they would go for a walk later in the evening before dark. He looked forward to it.

He couldn't believe his luck that Sunday in July when she had turned to him as they sat on her front porch in the sweltering afternoon heat and without warning had agreed to marry him. He had never pressed her for an answer since he had first asked the day of Will and Ruby's wedding. He had never had the nerve. There had been an urgency in her answer that made his heart beat fast, but when he had asked her to set the day, she had said only a vague "in the spring." Since that day he couldn't get enough of her. He wanted to be with her, and when he wasn't, he thought about being with her. He pictured her in the kitchen when he came home from work. The heat from the cookstove made her cheeks glow and the steam had dampened the tendrils of her thick hair that escaped their ribbons. When she turned to him, she smiled and said his name, "John."

"John . . . John."

He looked up to see Barney talking to him with a look of consternation on his face.

"What's the matter with you, John? You been staring at that spider for five minutes with the craziest look on your face."

John felt himself grow hot and knew his face had gone crimson. "Sorry, Barney, I guess I was thinking about something."

"From that look, I'd say it wasn't the union," Barney said, grinning. "It's good to know that courting can still have a place in a young man's mind with all that's going on. Things must be considerable easier for you over at the Conners' place now that Frank's joined the union."

"You know he never did hold it against me. 'Course I never expected to see him come into it fists a-swinging like he has."

"Well, a man can change his mind real quick when he sees his family threatened. That kind of thing has just started. Them thugs they brought in is just nosing around trying to find something to shoot at. They're cocked and ready to go. Lord, most of the men around here don't have any idea what these men are like. Up in Harlan they brought in a bunch of these low-downs. They're just hired killers is all they are."

"What's the UMW doing to help the men out up there?"

Barney shook his head grimly. "'Bout what they're doing down here. Told the men to hang in there while they high-tailed it in the other direction. That's all Turnblazer had to say when he come down here. 'Stay in the boat, fellows. We're going to win.' He didn't offer us no money. I asked him point blank what happened to all them dues we been paying in. He said it went to international dues. Can you beat that? They give us four hundred dollars and told us to buy a truck. It's a good thing most of the men don't know what sorry shape the UMW is in right now."

"What do you think our next move will be?"

"We got to keep our men fed so they can hold out. The more people that finds out about Wilder, the better off we are. We are isolated here, and that's the way the company likes it. You know there's months here you couldn't get a truck or a wagon out over these roads. They's people that can help us if we get our side of the story out."

"How we going to do that?"

"I got a letter from a man by the name of Myles Horton. He runs some kind of place he calls the Highlander Folk School."

"How's a school teacher suppose to help us any?"

"It ain't a regular school. They teach grown men like us who are up against a big company how to fight them. He believes in poor folks having the right to a decent life. That's what he says his school stands for."

"Does he think we have a chance?"

"It don't matter what anybody thinks. I done told you, I intend to see it through to the end, son. That's all I know. I'll win, or I'll die trying."

John looked at the spider. It had finished the web and had settled back to wait for its victim. Within seconds a fly was caught in the intricate trap, entangling itself more with its desperate struggle. The spider had only to wait. The outcome was assured. The thought gave John a chill as he said good bye to Barney and left him sitting alone on the front porch.

Lacey sat alone in her room hugging her knees to her chest. Resting her chin on her knees, she tried to block the thoughts of Coy from her mind. The thought of his wide, bright smile and the way he had of looking at her like she was a cool drink on a hot day made her close her eyes and throw her head back to savor the moment. Even as he had pulled her to him and had kissed her lips, his arms warm and strong, she had known she was wrong to think about him. John would be coming to pick her up soon, and she really should be getting ready for him. She wondered when the longing would stop.

Lacey tried to picture John in her dreams, but she couldn't make his face appear. *He's a good man*, she reminded herself. Her folks were proud that she had decided to marry him. Will had slapped John on the back and had gone on like he was welcoming a new member to a secret society, and Ruby had hugged her, squeezing her so tightly she had almost lost her breath. Even her ma had given her a quick peck on the cheek while patting her gently on the hand. Although her pa never said as much, Lacey could tell he was relieved that she had come to her senses. It was for that as much as anything that she had told John that she would marry him.

Now everything was as it should be. She had put everything back in place just the way it had been before Coy had ridden into town. Like the furniture in a room, it had all fit neatly back into its well-worn spots. Once everything was in place, there was no sign that anything had changed. Only she knew. Only she was haunted by the memories. No, that wasn't entirely true. Ben knew. He had taken Coy's leaving almost as hard as she had. They couldn't bring themselves to talk about it, and they would just sit together sometimes and stare off into the distance.

She looked up surprised to see Ben standing in the doorway.

"John's here," he said.

"Oh my goodness, Ben. I ain't even combed my hair. You talk to him on the porch while I fix myself up."

"No need to hurry. Will's got him cornered talking about them gun thugs driving a car through town with their guns stuck out just to show folks they mean business."

"I'd a-thought you would a-found that right interesting."

Ben shrugged his shoulder and stood staring at the floor as he made circles with one bare foot. "Where you going tonight?" he said into his chest.

"Walking. Probably up through town and back. Just to be out since they's not much social doings lately." It was hard to have a pie supper, she thought, with food so hard to come by and sugar next to impossible. "You want to come?" she asked, thinking he might be hurt that she hadn't invited him along.

"John's not much fun to talk to," he said sheepishly.

"Ben, I know what you got on your mind, and you are just going to have to put it behind you. You can't go comparing John to . . . other people," she faltered. She knew Ben was thinking of Coy and the times they had been together.

"Coy made things different, didn't he? He just had a way of talking about stuff that made it seem exciting, even something you seen every day."

"John is a good man."

"But why did you have to go and promise to marry him?"

"Coy's gone, Ben, and he's not coming back."

"You don't know that. You can't give up on him just like that."

"Ben, he give up on us."

She could tell by his expression that she had hurt him. How could she help but think otherwise? If she could be so completely charmed by Coy's magic ways, what was she to expect from a ten-year-old boy? "I'm sorry, Ben. You come and go with us. Go tell John I'm coming."

Ben hesitated in the doorway as though still not satisfied that he should accept Lacey's apology. "I might go a little ways with ya."

Lacey smiled and tousled his thick hair. "Now, that's my Ben. You run on, and I'll be right there."

She stared into the mirror, absently brushing her hair. Ben was right. Coy had changed everything. "Damn you, Coy Lynn Wilson," she said out loud to the mirror. She guessed that wanting something she couldn't have was just the contrariness in her nature. It made her think of when she was younger and had so wanted a wristwatch like the other young girls that she had taken a poison ivy stem and drawn one on her tiny arm. At first the design had popped up perfectly, looking very much like a watch, and she had been so proud. Childlike, she ran to tell a friend what she had done when she noticed the design had begun to spread up her arm and over her face to cover her whole body. She had been in pain for a long time before her body healed itself. *It should have taught you a lesson about wanting things you can't have, Lacey Conners. It's time you was growing up.* Suddenly she felt cheerful. She wanted to enjoy her walk and put her foolishness behind her. With one last swipe at her hair, she put down her hairbrush and went out to meet John.

She found John sitting on a powder keg on the front porch, his legs crossed and his hands clasped across the knees. He squinted in concentration as Will went on with his story about the gun thugs swaggering down Main Street with their guns in plain view. Will was whittling angrily on a stick of oak and waving his knife around as he talked. John looked up, relieved to see her, and she smiled. His face beamed back at her, and when he rose to meet her, she reached out a hand to him. He stood staring at her outstretched hand for a moment until she almost took it back. Suddenly, he seemed to realize she meant to hold hands with him, and he awkwardly clasped his rough hand around hers. Ben stopped swinging on the porch rafters long enough to shoot her a look. She ignored him and turned to Will. "Will, you've been bending John's ear long enough. We are going for a walk now and get away from all this strike talk."

"Ah, Lacey. I was just telling John here how being married is the best thing that ever happened to a man." Will gave John an exaggerated wink and grinned big at his embarrassed reaction.

"Will, hanging's too good for you," Lacey declared, stalking off the porch and pulling John behind her. She turned long enough to crook her head at Ben, who jumped down from the rafters and followed after them in hang-dog fashion.

"You look real pretty tonight, Lacey," John ventured shyly.

"Why thank you, John. I should have tied my hair back in a ribbon." She felt self-conscious of her long, wavy hair hanging past her shoulders when all the other girls had long ago started to bob their hair and get permanent waves.

"No, it looks real nice."

They walked on in silence, enjoying the cool night air after an unusually warm autumn day. With the mines not in operation and no one yet burning coal to heat their homes, the air smelled of autumn leaves and cornstalks drying in the gardens. Only the smell of the slag heap that burned continually up by the mines tainted the freshness of the night.

"How's your ma been getting along, John?" Lacey asked to break the silence.

"Oh, she's doing right well. She said to tell you she's got you a quilt top made, and she'll be quilting it for us as soon as she can get a hold of some batting."

Lacey noticed that John had said "for us."

"You tell your ma, I'm just real pleased, and I'll be happy to help her if she needs me."

"She's been working with a bunch of folks out of Nashville that calls themselves the Wilder Emergency Relief Committee. They say they are collecting clothes and food to bring in here. It's due in on the next train. I reckon Ma would be right proud if you could help get it out to folks. Some folks around here don't much like to take from strangers. If you could be at the aid station, I reckon they wouldn't care to take it from you."

"Tell Mrs. Trotter I'll be there."

"She said to tell you to call her Cora."

"I know. It's just strange to me yet."

"You ought to come and spend some time with her. She'd appreciate the company."

"I might just do that, John." They walked in silence. Only a few people were out on their porches to wave as they passed.

"You got mighty quiet all of a sudden. What you thinking about, Lacey?"

"I was just thinking that if it weren't for this strike, we would be having a corn shucking about now. Remember the time Will got the red ear and got to kiss the prettiest girl!"

"He made out like he was going to kiss the Duncan twins."

"And them both uglier than homemade sin."

"Lacey!"

"Now, John Trotter, don't you act so shocked. I've heard you and Will say a lot worse, and besides you know it's the truth."

"You got me there, I reckon," he admitted laughing. He turned to her suddenly with a frown on his face. "I know this ain't the way you would have wanted it. Young girls have dreams. That is, they like things to be special."

At first, Lacey didn't know what he meant. For a few stomach rolling minutes, she thought he might be talking about Coy, that he somehow knew that marrying him had been the way she wanted it. Then she realized that he was talking about the strike and the way it had changed all their lives. He was talking about the way there would be no dances or candy pulls or ice cream parties that filled the courtships of other young girls. "You are a sweet man, John Trotter." She could see him blush crimson even in the fading light. "But you can't make the world perfect for me."

"I would if I could," he said solemnly. "I'd give you a house with lace curtains and a new cookstove and a big garden spot out back."

She felt the weight of his love like an anvil on her chest. To break the tension, she looked back to see if Ben was still following. He had stopped at the Jenkins' house and was in deep conversation near a small oak tree with his friend Ted. When he looked up and caught Lacey's eye, she motioned for him to come on. "Me and Ted's going to stay here and ring toss awhile," he yelled.

"All right. Be home before it gets good and dark, though." She turned back to John with a frown of worry still on her face.

"He'll be fine. Them thugs won't bother a bunch of younguns, if that's what you was thinking."

John had read her mind. "I do mother hen too much, don't I? I can't expect to keep him under my wing for much longer. He's getting to be a good-size boy."

"I always liked the way you took care of Ben."

She never knew he noticed the special care she took of Ben. "I worry about him if he spends too much time with me, and I worry if he don't." She had to laugh at her own silliness, and John laughed with her. It felt good to laugh, and it felt good to be with John. They were nearing the main part of town, and the street lights in front of the hotel had just been turned on. Laughter and loud voices could be heard from the company cottage nearby. The gun thugs had made the hotel a busy place, with more strange faces appearing in town every day. The company cottage had become a gathering place for drinking and cards among the mine guards and gun thugs.

"Listen to them in there, Lacey. They're having the time of their lives. It's enough to make a body sick."

"Maybe we better turn around and walk back to the house. I don't know if it's safe to be out here calling attention to ourselves."

"They got no call to bother us."

Just then shots rang out from behind them. Lacey could feel the wind from the bullet as it sang past her head.

"Get down, Lacey," John shouted as he pulled her down and threw his body across her.

She lay with her face pressed into the dirt, hardly able to breathe, her heart pumping madly as the bullets crisscrossed above her head. Someone was firing from the hotel roof and from behind the buildings across the street. John began to drag her along the ground, inch by inch, as they worked their way behind the barber shop. When they were finally behind the porch, they sat there panting for breath.

"Are you all right? You weren't hit, were you?" John had her by the shoulders, a look of terror on his face.

"I don't think so. Some of those bullets came mighty close."

"If anything had happened to you . . . Damn, I shouldn't have brought you out here."

She had never seen him so upset. "John, really, I'm fine."

"Sorry about the way I throwed you down. I reckon I ruined your dress," he apologized, looking at the tear where the seam of her dress had pulled loose at the waist.

She looked down at her dirty, torn dress and almost laughed. "Don't worry. As long as I'm alive, I can mend a dress."

A crowd of men had gathered on the porch of the hotel and the company cottage. Most of them carried guns, and they were shouting orders and arguing among themselves as to what to do.

"Who do you think was doing all that shooting, John?"

"Probably some of the strikers mad over the mine opening up with scabs. 'Course it just takes one bullet to get the whole gang of 'em going. They're looking for something to shoot at."

"I don't know how men can go against their own that way."

"It comes natural to some of them. Come on, now. I better get you home before Frank Conners hears about this and has my hide."

She stood up and dusted off her dress, trying to pick the leaves from her hair.

"We better walk home a back way. No need to be seen by this bunch," John whispered, taking her by the elbow.

As they started to the back of the building, Lacey turned and took one quick look behind her. Just as she did, someone on the porch of the hotel struck a match to light a cigarette.

Even in the dark, shadowy half-light, she recognized Coy's silhouette. She stopped the scream in her throat, but it worked its way out as a moan.

"Lacey, what's the matter? Are you hurt?"

"I guess I must've sprained my ankle," she lied.

"Here, put your arm around me. Does it hurt much?"

She didn't have words to answer him.

"Lord, Lacey, honey, I just about laughed 'til I cried," Cora said, chuckling as she wiped fresh tears from her eyes. Her strong hands never missed a stitch on the quilt piece she held as she rocked and laughed.

"What did you say to the woman, Cora?"

"I wouldn't have said nothing to her if she and them other biddies hadn't been so proud. They rode the train all the way from Nashville to personally present the town of Wilder with five big crates of donations. When they opened them up, there it was, hundreds of moldy yeller books. Ever woman in the Saint Holier-than-thou church must have cleaned out their attics to get that many books. And them women just stood there puffed up like banty hens."

"They surely thought we had a lot of time to read with everybody being out of work." Lacey tried to match the speed and efficiency of her stitches to Cora's relentless pace. They sat in a corner at the back of the general store where an aid station had been set up for the miners. Cora worked there almost every day, and Lacey had been coming in to help out when she could. Cora's personality was neat and even like the stitches on her quilt pieces. They looked as good on one side as they did on the other. Lacey had come to appreciate her simple honesty. She was much like John, except without the apologetic nature.

"Huh! Them women was just trying to put stars in their crowns by helping out the poor folks. Trouble is they ain't never been poor, so it never come to them we might be needing something as simple as food. I said to the woman, 'What do you think we are, a bunch of cutworms?'"

Lacey laughed so suddenly she snorted loudly through her nose and stuck herself with her needle. She rocked back and forth holding her sides and trying to suck the blood from her thumb.

"Mama, I don't believe you said that," John spoke up. "You know Barney Graham said we need folks to know about what's going on here in Wilder. We don't need to be making them mad when they're just trying to help out."

Cora and Lacey stopped laughing and looked up at John as though he was as peculiar as the three-legged stool he sat on. He squirmed under their scrutiny.

"Son, I got the word out that needs to be got out. If they can't see from looking at this skinny, ragged bunch of diehard miners that it's food we are needing, then I just made it real plain for her. Now she can take the word back to the rest of them fine folks."

"Folks from all over has sent us food and clothes. We ought to be grateful. Times ain't getting any better around here."

"What am I going to do with this boy of mine, Lacey? He's as solemn as a mule. Reckon you can josh some humor into him?"

"Lacey likes me sour, Ma," John quipped dryly before she could speak. He rose from his stool, stretched, and wandered languidly over to talk to the store clerk, turning back only to give a slow grin to the two women.

"Lord, that boy," Cora said with obvious pride, "I am glad he has you, Lacey. This strike is all he has talked about for months. Don't get me wrong. I believe in it 100 percent. It's just a worrisome thing for a mother to have her only son wound up in something so dangerous."

Cora patted Lacey's knee, and Lacey reached out and held her hand for a moment. She tried to smile a reassuring smile. "Well, they's not been as much trouble over the reopening as John expected. Will hid out and watched some of them scabs go to work. A couple of them got fired on, but nobody was hurt."

"What about the two of you nearly getting gunned down in the middle of town not more'n a week ago?"

"That was just foolishness, us being out like that," Lacey said, keeping her eyes on her work. She had tried to forget that night. It had taken all of her will to allow John to lead her home and to accept his solicitations. The family had gathered around to hear the story, and John had repeated it over and over until each one had been satisfied by his telling of it. The men talked out their anger in loud, jumbled voices, devising schemes for revenge until she thought she would scream. Finally seeing how pale she was, John said goodnight, and she had escaped to her room. Once there, she had thrown herself upon the bed and held on as it spun beneath her, the face in the shadows spinning with her. Every attempt to shut it out brought it to another corner of her mind.

She had believed that she would never see Coy again. Later she had found out that he had been back in town two weeks when she had seen him on the porch and that he had spent most of that time drinking and playing cards with the mine guards and the hired thugs. He had made no effort to see her or to get word to her that he was back. It seemed cruel beyond her imagining for him to show back up like this, and she wanted desperately to know why he had come. It was foolish to think he had come back for her. If he had, he would have come right to the house and claimed her to her pa's face like she had dreamed of him doing so many times.

Ben had been up to the house to scout things out. She hadn't wanted him to go and had given in only when he promised to stay out of sight. He was as hurt and confused by Coy as she was. There hadn't been much to see, just a bedroll on the kitchen floor and a coffee cup on the table. He was traveling light.

A noise at the front of the store brought Lacey back from her thoughts, and she looked up to see if Cora had noticed her wandering mind. Cora's fingers worked steadily on the growing quilt pattern she was creating. As Lacey looked around to see who had come into the store, she was startled to see Coy walking toward the counter where John stood. He began to talk casually to John and the store clerk. Her pulse was beating so loudly in her ears she couldn't hear their conversation. She prayed not to be sick at her stomach as the room began to swim around her.

"You all right, honey?" Cora asked. "You look a bit puny-like."

"No, I'm most likely just tired."

"I bet you ain't had nothing to eat today. That's it, ain't it? You're not doing without for that family of yourn, are you?"

"Cora, I'm fine," she answered too sharply.

"Now, that was right ugly of me. I didn't mean to pry. You're a little thing, but then I was always little. It don't mean nothing. It don't mean we're not strong. I always was strong as a mule and suspect you are the same way. 'Course, I have an appetite to go with it."

Lacey let Cora talk, unable to say anything and wanting only to escape. She wondered if Coy had noticed her sitting there. She might be able to sneak out the back and never be seen.

Cora stood up, putting her work down in the chair behind her. "John," she called out. The three men turned to look at her. "I'm just going to run up to the house. I'll be back d'rectly." She looked down at Lacey and whispered, "I've got a little corn pone and some honey up at the house that will fix you right up."

"Cora, I feel fine, really," she said weakly to Cora's disappearing backside, and then turned away from the counter, closing her eyes to steady herself. When she opened them, Coy was standing there smiling at her. He had lost some weight, and it had hewed out hollows in his face beneath his cheekbones. His dark, clouded eyes belied his smile. If he had reached for her at that moment, she would have forgiven him everything.

"Lacey, don't you look nice. I have just been over congratulating John on his good luck. I hear the two of you will be marrying real soon."

"Coy . . . I." She looked up at him. No words would come to her.

"The way I see it, the two of you were just made for each other. John being a miner and all. That probably sets well with you. I hope you will be real happy together."

His words stung her like a whip. She had betrayed him. She had not believed he would be back, he did not believe she had really loved him. Suddenly he took her chin in his hand and looked into her eyes, and spoke softly, "You look as beautiful as ever, Lacey."

_14_

"Your deal, Sawyer."

"Just hold on there, Coy. Don't rush me. I got to have time to roll me a cigarette. You're in an all fired hurry to lose some money."

Coy watched as Sawyer slowly rolled his cigarette and struck a match, sticking it to the end until it flamed. Then he shook the match and tossed it behind him to the filthy floor. The company house where the gun thugs had been living for three weeks was filled with smoke and reeked of sweat and corn liquor. Coy had been playing poker almost every night since he had come back to Wilder, and he had managed to win a considerable sum, more money than he had made in a year at ranching. They didn't seem to give much thought to the money. From what he could tell, not a man there had any family or any loyalty to a place. "You call it. I can play it. We'll see who wins."

"Five card draw. You cut the cards."

"You fellows in?" Coy asked the two other men at the table as he tapped the deck without looking at Sawyer. Sawyer was the one to watch. Coy had known that from the first time he had seen him, and nothing had happened to change his mind. He was as cold and as mean as a Wyoming blizzard, and he could trap you just as quickly if you let him sneak up on you. He was maybe forty, but his face showed the scars of too many knife fights to make guessing easy. Roy was maybe ten years younger. He liked to talk tough, but it was most likely just talk. Perry was the youngest and was well on his way to being a drunk. It hadn't helped that he was also a fool by birth.

"Deal me a good one, Sawyer," Roy Wilkes said, scooting his chair closer to the table.

Coy watched as Perry Horn finished off the last of a quart of moonshine and pulled a chair to the table, straddling it backwards. "Dammit, Sawyer. You better do me right. I ain't won a hand all week."

"You ever think it might be your playing and not my dealing that's your problem?"

"Hell, no! Look at this hand. You done it to me again, dammit!"

"Could just be your poker face," Coy said dryly without looking up.

"Let's hear it, Roy," Sawyer said.

"I'll ride this one."

"Perry?"

"Well, sorry as it is, I reckon this hand's worth a dollar."

"I'm good for that," Coy said.

"Me, too. You Roy?"

"Hell, I guess. You know, I'm getting mighty sick of poker every night. Things is just too damn quiet around here."

"Don't start pissing just because you got a bad hand. Card?"

"Give me three."

"Shit, I knowed it," Perry shouted. "He don't have nothing, so he starts in on these ragged-ass miners so we won't notice he's taking three cards. I'm good."

"Who you trying to fool, Perry? You got a sorrier hand than I do."

"I didn't take no damn three cards, did I?"

"Now, I mean it. If something don't happen around here soon, they ain't going to pay us to sit around here on our asses forever."

"Well, why don't you get out there and stir something up?" Sawyer said, chewing on his cigarette.

"Truth be known, I'm not above firing into a house or two. It sure sets them womenfolk to screaming, and you can see some stupid miner trying to jump into his overalls and get to his shotgun. I got half the town sleeping on the floor now."

"You're a devil all right. Coy?"

"One will do me."

"Dealer takes three. Bets."

"Hell, I'll bet a dollar. I'm telling you, men. I seen some real action in Harlan. Why, if there weren't a man killed might near ever night, we got downright bored."

Perry frowned at his cards. "You're a big talker, Roy. How come you ain't still in Harlan then? Just wait 'til they try to haul that load of coal outta here next week. They's bound to be some trouble then. I'll see that dollar and raise you five."

Sawyer whistled loudly. "That's just what these mine operators likes the newspaper folks to think. They're already making it up to be more than it is. The way they tell it, you'd think we was the only thing that was keeping it from being all out war in this holler. These puny miners don't know where to start to make trouble. 'Course, as long as they are paying us good money, I ain't got no complaints. Yeah, Roy there has a point. If something don't happen next week, we better be working on a plan to get these folks in the fighting mood." Sawyer looked to Coy. "You ain't said much tonight, Coy. That's six bucks to you."

Coy tossed six one dollar bills onto the pile in the center of the table. "That's a fact. What you got in mind to do, Sawyer? You don't think half starving these folks to death is enough to get them riled?"

"Now, don't you go belly-aching over a bunch of miners. Everybody knows they's no love lost between you and these hill diggers. In fact, I 'bout half expected you to hire on as a guard. I figure we need to rough up one or two fellers. Somebody that's real well liked. You know how these folks stick together."

"You thinking of anybody in particular?"

"How about Barney Graham?" Perry asked.

"We don't have to go that far just yet. I reckon it'll come to me. I'll think of just the right one, and then we'll do him up real good so even his mama won't claim him. I'll call you on that hand, Perry. You ain't going to bluff me, you dumb sonofabitch."

"You're the dumb sonofabitch, Sawyer. Look here at three beautiful aces."

"Well, I'll go to hell," Sawyer swore, slapping his cards on the table.

Perry laughed gleefully and reached to rake in his winnings. "You thought I didn't know how to play the game, huh?

Thought ole Perry didn't know how to bluff. Well, that will teach you not to mess with the best."

Coy slowly reached out and stopped his hand. "You know, Perry that is just what I was thinking." Perry was still grinning as Coy spread the full house out in front of him. "Now, Sawyer, why would I want to work as a guard when I can make more money off you men in a night than I could make in a week playing tough guy?"

"Damn you, Coy," Perry whined. "You stole that from me."

"Smoothest I ever seen," Roy whistled his admiration.

"Deal 'em up there, Roy. I want a chance to beat this asshole."

"I got all night, boys. I got no place to go, and I don't have to work tomorrow," Coy said, settling back into his chair.

"Seven card stud," Roy said. "What's a good-looking feller like you doing sitting here playing cards all night with a bunch of old farts like us anyway, Coy?"

"Speak for yourself, Roy," Perry said preening. "You're just trying to get out of a losing streak. I happen to have a way with the ladies myself."

"Perry, you got about as much charm as a pole cat with his tail up," Sawyer grunted.

"You're just jealous 'cause I got them little Wilder things swishing their tails up main street just to get a chance to walk by me. And some good looking stuff it is."

"I bet Coy could tell us how good it is, couldn't you, Coy?"

Coy didn't like the sound in Sawyer's voice. He had run into it too many times. He was a man who liked to goad and pick at a man's sore spot until he could get a rise out of him. Sawyer was feeling him out, first about the mines and now this. "It don't matter, boys. You don't think they'd fool with the likes of you after they've met Coy Lynn Wilson, do you?"

"Whoa, he got you there, Sawyer," Perry yelled, grabbing the rungs on the back of his chair and rocking them in rhythm to his laughter.

"Maybe Coy done spent too much time with nothing but a bunch of cows to keep company with and he done lost interest in the ladies."

Coy saw Perry and Roy fold their cards and look first to Sawyer and then to him. They were waiting for him to rise to the bait.

"Roy, how many people you figure that schoolhouse will hold?"

"Lord, Coy, I don't know. Maybe a hundred."

"That's a shame. I was hoping I could get might near all the women in there that could tell Sawyer here how a real man rises to the occasion. I reckon, you're just going to have to ask 'em one at a time. In the meantime, could we play cards?"

Perry and Roy settled back in their chairs, pretending to hide their grins behind their cards. Sawyer's face showed nothing of what he was thinking as he concentrated on his cards. Coy hoped he would be content to drop the subject. "Your bet, Perry."

"I'll go a dollar on this hand."

Coy had a seven showing with two aces down. Perry was high with a king showing. "I'll see that dollar."

"I'm in. I'll tell you the first one I'd ask." Sawyer said.

"Same, here," Roy answered dealing out another card. "What you talking about, Sawyer? Perry, you still got the bet."

"Coy says I got to ask them women one at a time. I'm saying the first one I would ask would be that Conners girl. Lacey Conners."

"Damn, Sawyer, you're old enough to be her pa. I believe I'll bet another dollar. What you say about that, Coy? You going to stick with that hand? A seven and a four ain't much to put up against a king and a six."

"With what I got in the hole, I think it'll do," Coy said, hoping his voice told nothing. It had been all he could do to hold on to his cards at the mention of Lacey's name. What was a grub worm like Sawyer doing thinking about Lacey? He tried to keep his mind on the game.

"That's the way I like them, Perry. Young and tender."

"Where you going to take her, Sawyer? Sunday school?"

"She ain't that innocent. I watched down at the creek one day. She had her dress hiked up, wading that stream with that long hair combed down around her waist. I bet you money she knowed I was there watching. I tell you, it was a sight to make a man rutty."

Coy had a .45 in his coat pocket on the back of his chair. His first instinct was to reach for it and mix Sawyer's brains with the pink and green wallpaper, and he had to get out of there before he let Sawyer see that he was getting to him. He looked around the table. Roy had already folded. Sawyer had nothing. Perry had two sixes showing. Roy dealt the last card down.

"Shit!" Sawyer swore, lifting his last card.

"Looks like it's just you and me, Coy. And I'm good for five big ones."

Coy raised his last card. It was an ace. "I'll call that bet, Perry."

"You're a damn fool, Coy, and me with two sixes showing. Lookie here, boy, three beautiful sixes. Count them. One, two, three. Now, try to beat that."

"I'm afraid you got me there, Perry. I can't beat that," Coy said throwing his cards into the pile.

"I knowed you'd lose your touch soon enough. Your luck had to run out soon."

"I guess you are right there, Perry. I should have quit with that last hand. Reckon, I better give it up for the night."

"What! You not going to give me a chance for a run on my luck?"

"Hell, you just about wiped me out with that one hand."

Perry grinned broadly as he raked in his winnings. "I'll drink to that. Let's all drink to the best damn poker player alive."

"And who would that be, Perry?" Roy asked.

"Don't you start with me, Roy."

Coy said goodnight and left them still arguing the question. He stepped out into the night glad for the fresh air, his head aching from bad liquor and stale cigarette smoke. He was sick to death of playing cards and listening to a bunch of misfits who made their living off the misery of others.

As he stepped off the porch into the night, grateful to lose himself in the dark, Coy thought about the mess he had gotten himself into. There seemed no escape. Even as the town died, it meant to trap him in its jaws, and it was using the only thing he cared about as bait. He had run off in anger for the second time. Humiliated by Frank Conners' attack and by the look of shame in Lacey's eyes, he had hopped a freight the next morning for Wyoming.

In the two weeks it had taken him to make it back to Jake Abbot's place, he had done a pretty good job of convincing himself that Lacey would never leave her family to be with him, and he was sure he could never live in Wilder and be a miner. Jake and his family had taken him in as they had before without question, and by dawn the next morning, he had been astride a horse, riding out in the clear, crisp air to repair a fence row in the south end of the ranch. At first the majestic snow-capped mountains that encircled him were exhilarating. His eyes told him they were just as he remembered them, but now there was a loneliness in their beauty. He had wanted to show them to Lacey the next time he saw them.

Weeks went by, and then one day he saw a young doe, drinking from a stream, and it made him think of Lacey as she held back her long hair with one hand and cupped the other to get a drink. She had laughed shyly that day when she had found him looking at her. Even in memory it had the power to take his breath away, and it hadn't taken him long to realize that his life on the ranch or any life he might choose from then on, would become ashes in his throat without Lacey. He had always been a dreamer, and until Lacey nothing in his life had ever matched his dreams. That was when he made up his mind to go back and do whatever it took to have her, even if it meant being a miner.

Coy passed the days on the long trip back by picturing her running to meet him, arms outstretched and long brown hair flying behind her. He had never given anything of himself to anyone. It had become a way of life for him, and in the beginning it had suited him fine. He would give a part of himself for Lacey, and as he caught the last train on his return to Wilder, he was convinced that he could give whatever it took.

The engineer, Ezra Poore, recognized him and let him ride the engine the last long miles from Monterey, filling him in on all that had been happening in the mines. They had not reopened, and folks were beginning to get mighty hungry. Barney Graham was urging the men to hold on. Some big shots had been in from Washington, but it hadn't made much difference. Folks were still suffering and no end was in sight. Gun thugs had been brought in, in case of violence, and there had been a trestle blown up and some shooting. They had set the hounds loose to find out who had done it. He told him about the attack on the Conners' house.

"Was anybody hurt?"

"Mostly their pride," Ezra surmised. "That's how ole Frank Conners come to join the union."

Coy thought the sheriff and his bunch got off easy in light of Frank Conners' pride. "I reckon that made Barney Graham a happy man."

"Not near as happy as it made John Trotter."

"Oh, yeah, why's that?"

"Well, John's one of the strongest union men around."

"So?"

"If you was engaged to marry a man's only daughter, you'd want him on your side, wouldn't you?"

"Lacey Conners is engaged to marry John Trotter?"

"It shouldn't surprise you none. They growed up together. Folks here been expecting it all along. I forgot you've been away."

"When?"

"Probably be a few months. They're putting it off 'til spring in hopes things will get better in the mines. Yeah, they are just the nicest young folks. That Lacey, she takes care of that family like a mamma hen."

"When did they get engaged?"

"Oh, I'm not rightly sure. Could have been sometime in August. I'm usually good with dates. That's something you train yourself to do when you work with the railroad."

Ezra talked on, but Coy didn't listen. He looked out the open door of the engine and watched the rails pass. They matched the pace of his mind as it raced to shut out the news. Lacey had promised to marry John as soon as she found out that he had left town.

He made his way to Seth's old cabin, where several gallons of prime moonshine had been buried under the house. Coy was relieved to find them still there, and it was enough to keep him passed out or half insane for over a week.

When Coy finally sobered up, he had dragged himself out onto the front porch and slid down by the window, catching a glimpse of himself in the glass. "Damn, if you don't look a sight," he groaned out loud. "But you know, I think I know you," he said with a flash of insight. "You are that Coy Lynn Wilson who don't have a damn thing to lose, 'cause you don't have a damn thing to begin with."

Somehow the thought had given him a lot of comfort. He was back on familiar ground. Nothing to lose gave a man a lot of freedom. He had been wrong to get mixed up in Lacey's life. He couldn't offer her nothing but a hard life. According to

Seth's count, he figured he was on up toward sixth generation worthless. Someday with John, if they made it through the strike, Lacey would have something.

When Coy reached the cabin, he lit a coal oil lamp, put it on the kitchen table and spread out the money from his winnings. He hated losing that last bit to Perry, but it had gotten him away from Sawyer. And anyway, thirty bucks wasn't bad for one night.

He had been about half drunk and crazy with his thoughts the night he had wandered down to the hotel and joined in a card game. He had won a lot of money that first night, and on impulse he had taken the money to John Trotter. It had taken some doing to go to John's house late that night without being seen. He had asked him to step outside so Cora couldn't hear, pulling him around back in the dark so they wouldn't be seen. Looking back, it had taken a damn sight of courage for John to step out into the dark with him like that, not knowing which side he was on.

His plan had been just to give the money to John to buy food for the strikers, knowing that Lacey would get some of whatever was bought. When Coy turned to go, John had grabbed his arm to stop him. He had been so damn grateful. And that was how he had ended up spying on the company.

'If they find out, they'll kill you," John had said simply.

Coy had shrugged. He could still remember the puzzled look in John's eyes when they shook hands. "You're a good man," John had said.

He thought back with frustration on what he had learned in the last week. Mostly it didn't amount to a hill of beans. He had come damn close to killing Sawyer, and he might have to do it yet. Roy was a lot of blow. If he had ever done anything, it had grown bigger with the telling. Perry was dangerous only because he was a fool and didn't know it. Both would most likely go along with whatever Sawyer said. Sawyer took his orders from a thug named Shorty Green, but Shorty hadn't been around much. When he was, the other men made way for him. When he wasn't, they talked a lot about starting trouble, but so far it had been mostly talk. Several times they had threatened to beat up a few of the miners or fire a few rounds into camp houses, but it was nothing that couldn't be passed off later as liquor talking. Besides, right now it wasn't that kind of talk that worried him. When Sawyer had brought up Lacey's name, his

first instinct had been to go for his throat and stuff his filthy
words back into his mouth until he choked on them. It had
taken everything he had to sit there smiling at the bastard.
That's one son of a bitch I intend to keep an eye on, he thought,
as he spread out his bedroll on the kitchen floor and lay down
for another sleepless night.

15

The taste of blood and dirt filled John's mouth. He tried to open his eyes, but the eyelids refused to move. They were swollen shut. John didn't know how long he had been face down in the road, but he sensed that it was dark. *Either that or they have beaten me until I am blind,* he thought without humor. Feeling around until he found the running board of the truck, he tried to pull himself up. Everything inside screamed with pain, and when he let go of the truck, he slid to the ground with a thud. He thought he was going to pass out, and then he remembered Frank Conners, who had been with him. They had been to pick up a load of food from Monterey and had been hurrying to get back before dark. John had had a bad feeling about the trip and had tried to get Frank to stay home.

The thugs had been on them before they knew what was happening. He remembered now seeing one of them hit Frank with the butt of his gun. After that, they had laid into John. At first, he had felt each blow, heard the crunch of breaking bone, and felt the blood pour out of his mouth and nose. Finally, he had felt only pain.

John tried to call out Frank's name, but only a whistling sound came out. He put his hand to his mouth, only to realize that his teeth had cut a large gash below his bottom lip and it was torn loose on one side. It flapped and air whistled in and out when he tried to talk. As he began to crawl on his hands and knees around the truck, his hand felt something smooth and cool. Suddenly he realized what it was. The bastards had cut open the flour sacks and dumped them all over the road. A murderous rage came over him. He had never wanted to kill anyone in his life, but now he yanked viciously on the tail-gate of the truck, trying to pull himself up. *I'll kill them. I'll kill every damn one of them*, he thought just before he passed out from the pain.

When he came to, the air had grown cooler and dew had fallen, and he could hear footsteps behind him. *If they're coming back to get me, it won't be much of a contest*, he thought. As he groped around for something to use as a weapon, his hand fell upon a stick, and he seized it like a drowning man.

"John, is that you?"

He tried to answer, but his lip flapped about uselessly.

"John, it's all right. It's me, Coy."

John could feel Coy standing over him. As Coy kneeled down, John could almost feel his warm breath on him. He was afraid he might cry.

"Dammit, John, they damn near killed you. I'm going to put you in the truck, and we are going to get you to the doctor. Stupid sons of bitches were bragging about it back at the cottage. Bragging about leaving you up on the road to die. I had to wait around an hour before I could get away."

As Coy reached to put his arms around him, John grabbed him by the sleeve to stop him. He put a hand on his lip to hold it in place as he spoke. "Ffannk."

"What is it? What are you saying?"

"Ffannnk."

"Frank. Was Frank Conners with you?"

John nodded, grateful not to have to say more.

"Hang on. Just rest here. I'll look for him."

John sank back against the truck and listened as Coy searched along the road for Frank. In a few minutes he could hear the sound of something being dragged toward him.

"It's all right. He's alive, but he's hurt bad. I'm going to put him in the back of the truck, and then I'll help you up, John. We will have you both to a doctor in no time."

John waited, almost giving in to the pain he had fought so long. There was something he had to tell Coy, if he could just remember what it was.

"I'm going to put your arm around my neck and lift you up now," Coy said. "It's going to hurt like hell. When you are ready, just nod your head."

He could remember giving Coy the go ahead, but he must have fainted. When he came to, he was sitting next to Coy on the passenger side of the truck, and he remembered what he had to tell him. "Noooo," he sputtered.

"Sorry, John. I'm going as slow as I can. I know the road's rough."

"No doccor," John said, shaking his head.

"What are you saying? We have to get you to a doctor."

"Nooo doccor," he said reaching out to grab Coy's arm.

"Did they threaten to hurt you again if you told anybody about this?"

John shook his head no.

"Did they threaten to hurt somebody else?"

John shook his head yes. "Viction."

"Eviction. Damn. They threated to evict miners if you tell who beat you up?"

"Promise. No, doccor."

"Hell, John. Don't you know they could do that anytime they took a notion?"

"Home," he whispered.

They drove on a few minutes before Coy answered. "All right, John. I'll take you home."

John slumped back in the seat, finally relieved to be alive. "Food?"

"All gone. Scattered all over the road."

They rode on in silence. They were almost to John's house before Coy spoke again. "I can't go in with you, John. I'm sorry. I got to leave you here. You understand. I'll leave the truck as close to the house as I can. They'll have men out looking for you, so it won't be long before they find the truck."

John nodded.

"I'm going to move you over to the driver's side, and then I'll slip out. You count to ten and then blow the horn for help. I hate to do it this way. You know I don't have no choice."

John wanted to say thanks, but he felt the darkness spinning around him, and he was trying to count. The last thing he remembered was the sound of the horn when he fell over on the steering wheel. He hoped he had made it to ten.

Something felt cool on his eyes, and he reached up to touch the soft rag spread across his face. Instead, he felt a small, soft hand. *Lacey*, he thought and was afraid to say her name. He thought about how ugly he must look to her.

"John, are you awake?"

Lacey took the cloth from his eyes, and he looked at her through milky slits. At least he was not blind. She looked more beautiful than he thought anybody could ever look. A frown of worry creased her forehead, and her lips were puckered with concern. He closed his eyes and fought the urge to cry.

"John," Lacey whispered, touching his cheek gently. "It's been three days. We was all getting worried sick. You wouldn't let us send for the doctor. You kept saying, 'No, Doctor.' I had to do the best I knowed how. Barney sent for the sheriff. He's been waiting for you to come to so you could tell who done this to you. He's ready to go after then hisself if the sheriff don't do nothing. They still can't figure out how you drove that truck in the shape you was in. Let me get your ma. She ain't slept since they carried you in."

John held up his hand to stop her from leaving. "Frank." He was surprised when it came out sounding like a word. He felt his lips. They were rough with stitches.

"I had to sew your lip a might. It'll leave a scar most likely. Don't you worry about Pa. He's going to be fine. We carried him home yesterday. It's just going to take a while. Now, please let me get your ma. She's been worried sick."

"No!" he shouted. "First I want to talk to Barney." He tried to grab her sleeve as she rose to leave. The pain shot through his ribs and made him cry out.

"John Trotter, I swear. You lay back down there, and don't you move." She gently helped him back down. "You got broken ribs," she said reproachfully. "You want to put one of them right through your lungs?"

She smoothed back the hair on his forehead as though he was a child with a fever, and he reached up and took her hand in his, holding on to it for just a moment. "Thank you, Lacey. It ain't that I don't appreciate you taking care of me. I'm real grateful to you." She pulled her hand slowly away, and he could see her blushing. He wanted to say more. He wanted to tell her how it was almost worth getting beat up to feel the touch of her hand on his face. He wanted to, but the words wouldn't come.

"I'll get Barney, if you will promise not to move. I can tell you, though; your ma ain't going to like it."

He tried to smile, but his face wouldn't cooperate. "You can handle her for me, Lacey." She put her hands on her hips and cocked her head, trying to appear angry, then broke into a smile that made him want to be through with all this strike business and get on with his life.

Closing his eyes, John rested his head on the pillow while he waited for Barney. It was too bad Barney had involved the sheriff. It might have already caused trouble for some of the other miners. Not that the sheriff was likely to do anything against the gun thugs, but it might set them off just knowing he told. A roof over their heads was about all most of these miners had, and he didn't want to be responsible for them losing that, too.

Suddenly, Barney burst into the room like a man possessed. "Dammit, boy! You are some kind of mess. Those varmints whupped you good, didn't they. Don't worry, though. We'll get 'em. I done told the sheriff it was that no good bunch of gun thugs that done it."

John groaned and shook his head.

"Well, hell. It was them that done it, weren't it? I didn't see no need to wait 'til you come to tell it."

"It don't matter who done it."

"What the hell you saying son?"

"I mean, I ain't saying who done it."

"You don't have to say. I done told everybody it was them gun thugs."

"You don't understand. They threatened to throw a bunch of miners out of their homes if I told anybody who done this to me."

"Is that the reason you wouldn't let us get a doctor for you?"

John closed his eyes and shook his head, sick at all he had suffered only to have it come to nothing.

"Son, you are a damn fool! Don't you know if they wanted to throw us out, they'd do it whether you told or not. They ain't afraid of no sheriff. We are not only going to tell what they done, we are going to tell what they threatened to do if you told. I've been talking to some of them newspaper reporters that's been coming in here. The company's been trying to stop me. They make everybody that comes through town report to the mine office. Talking may not stop them, but it might slow them down a might."

John felt like a fool. Of course the mine owners could kick them all out any time they took a notion, just like Coy had said. They owned the houses; they owned the whole damn town. For the first time he saw what they were really up against. He felt like he was standing in a deep hollow trying to hold off a rockslide with a pickaxe. Barney's excitement over talking to the newspaper men only made him feel the weight of their inevitable defeat even heavier.

"You're looking peaked, boy. I shouldn't have pestered you with this. Don't you worry about a thing. I'll take care of this. Now, you just rest up a few days, and you'll be good as new. I need you, boy."

John thought he heard the door close, but he couldn't be sure. The rocks were getting closer, and everything was getting darker and darker.

16

"**A**in't that the pitifulest thing you ever seen!"

"Hush, Ruby, he can hear you," Lacey whispered. Patiently she spooned the bean soup into her pa's slack, quivering mouth. He had not spoken much that could be made sense of since they brought him in that night and his eyes occasionally rolled about in his head as though they had forgotten how to work. He spent most of his time propped up in a chair at the kitchen table while the rest of the household moved about him unable to fathom that they might never see the old Frank again. "Pa, you need to eat to get your strength back." His tongue flicked about through the spaces where his teeth had once been.

"Ooooh, Lordy, Lordy," Ruby moaned to the dirty dishes as she poured hot water on them from the cookstove. "He don't have no more control over hisself than little Rachel had when she was born. What on earth is going to become of us? I tell you, I don't know what's to become of us. It's been two weeks, and Pa ain't showing no sign of getting better."

"Ruby," Lacey hissed. "Hush up."

Ruby turned around, her eyes wide in disbelief, her lip quivering. Suddenly she was upon Lacey, hugging her to her generous chest. Huge tears fell on Lacey's hair and face. "Lacey, honey. Ain't I just the worst friend? I don't know where my mind was saying such things. Look at you, just plumb wore out with taking care of us and me making it worse with my goings on."

Lacey thought she might lose her breath in the stranglehold of Ruby's fleshy arms, and she gently eased them from around her head. "Ruby, stop that crying! I shouldn't of yelled out like that."

"Yes, you should of. It was ugly of me to say them things. Just plain ugly. Say you'll forgive me, Lacey. I just can't bear it if you was mad at me."

"Ruby, I'm not mad at you. It's just that Pa don't need to hear such talk. He's got to know he's going to get better. The men that done this to him has got to see they can't lick us that easy. You hear me, Pa?"

"It's too bad Pa can't say who done this to him."

"He don't have to say. I know."

"Well, hit ain't much doubt it was them leather jacket gun thugs the mines done hired, but which ones?"

"I know which ones. I know the very one that set it up. I know the one that beat Pa nearly to death."

"How do you know such a thing, and how come you ain't told?"

"John told me."

"He told you when he wouldn't name nothing to the sheriff about it, nor Barney Graham neither?"

"He didn't know he was telling. He said it near a hundred times when he was out of his head."

"Then why haven't you told it?"

"'Cause it would just bring more grief on this family if we was to try to get back at them thugs. They just as well kill somebody this time."

"Who was it, Lacey? What name was it John kept saying?"

"Don't you repeat this to a living soul. Before he passed out, John must of heart one of 'em calling this un's name, cause he kept saying 'Call him off. Call him off. He's going to kill him.' He said it like there was one that was doing the most of the beating, and the others was watching or holding him."

"Well, which one was it?"

"You know the one that was spying on me down at the creek bed that day? Might near scared me to death, and me acting like I didn't know he was there."

"Sawyer," Will yelled from the doorway. "It was that son-of-a-bitch Sawyer, weren't it, Lacey!"

Lacey looked up horrified, just in time to see Will take the shotgun from the corner and turn on his heels.

"No, Will, don't do it!" she screamed. "Ruby, stay with pa. I'm going to get help."

"Lacey, they'll kill him. Oh, Lord. He's the same as dead. I know it. My sweet Will. What am I going to do?"

Just then Frank relieved himself on the kitchen floor.

Lacey took an old pistol from the bottom of the wooden box where her pa had hidden it a month back. The gun was from the Spanish-American War and had been given to her pa before she was born. She loaded it with the only three bullets she could find. Before she went out the back door, she remembered Ruby. "I reckon you better start by cleaning up the kitchen floor."

Lacey watched the hotel windows for signs of what might be going on inside. Her heart was beating so fast she had to lean against the wall of the post office to keep from being sick. She had told Ruby she was going for help, but the truth was, with Pa and John laid up, she wasn't sure where to turn. Besides, there had been no time to go for help. Will was such a hot-head, he had headed straight to the hotel in plain daylight. Now, he stood in the street calling Sawyer out like a gunfighter in a Tom Mix movie.

"Goddamn you, Sawyer. Get your sorry ass out here," Will growled. He had the shotgun cocked and pointed at the hotel door.

Sawyer came out laughing, his gun at his side. "Well, if it ain't one of them puny, shit-faced punkin rollers. What do you want, boy?"

"You beat my Pa up an' left him on the road to die. A man ought to have to pay for something like that."

"Now, I can't rightly say I know what you're talking about, boy. Who would this pa of yours be?"

"You know who I'm talking about. Frank Conners. Frank Conners!"

The gun jerked about wildly in Will's hands. Sawyer eased his gun up to his side and cocked it.

"Well, I reckon all you union men look alike," Sawyer sneered.

Lacey knew he was baiting Will to shoot first so he could kill him outright. Just then two men came out of the twilight shadows, and she called out a warning to Will. The sound was drowned out by the scuffling as the thugs grabbed Will from behind and forced him to the ground. They stood over him kicking him in the sides and back with the toes of their high leather boots. Instinctively, she raised the pistol and fired the three rounds toward the hotel. She heard a cry of pain, and the men looked up frozen by surprise. She could see Will scrambling to his feet. As she turned to run, she prayed he would get away. The last thing she heard was someone calling for a doctor above the howling cries of a man in pain.

"You can just stand there in the yard, Sheriff Watson. Ain't no need for you and them deputies to come no closer." Lacey had covered her pa with domestic and set a bowl of warm water in his lap. She turned her back to the sheriff and sharpened the old razor on a worn strap. She had been expecting them all night. She had prepared herself for it a hundred times during the night, but now that they were here she thought her knees might go out from under her. She steadied herself against the arm of the chair.

"Now, Lacey. You know why I'm here."

"You're out mighty early bringing misery to folks' lives."

"I'm sorry about the last time, but Will's done brung this on hisself. They's plenty of witnesses to say he threatened to shoot a mine guard."

"And did he?"

"Did he what?"

"Shoot a mine guard."

"Well, no. Not exactly."

"That don't hardly seem possible. Did Will shoot this mine guard or not?"

"It was Sawyer what was shot. Cut a chunk right outta the side of his face. And no, it weren't Will directly."

Lacey was pleased to know it had been Sawyer she had hit and shocked to realize she was sorry she hadn't killed him. She tried to steady her shaking hand as she gently scraped the lather from her pa's slack jaw. His eyes rolled up into his head, and his mouth dropped open. She could feel the sheriff watching. She turned quickly and gave him a look like Saint Peter judging a sinner. "It ain't a pretty sight, is it sheriff?"

The sheriff looked away quickly in embarrassment, shuffled his feet and readjusted his stance. When he spoke, he stared off into the distance. "You know my name, Lacey. I've knowed this family since before you was born."

"Then why are you here? Have you sunk so low you're planning on arresting Will for a cuss-fight? The mines must be paying you right smart for tough work like that."

"That's about enough out of you, young lady. It may not have been Will that shot Sawyer, but whoever done it used your pa's pistol. We found the bullet. It was a .0457. Ain't nobody in town got a gun like that but your pa. He showed it to me years ago."

"So now you're accusing Pa?"

"Hell, no Lacey. Anybody can see your pa … I mean …"

Lacey just stared at him, giving him no relief. Inside, her heart was beginning to pound. How stupid it had been of her to use her pa's old Spanish-American War pistol. She thought they might search the house for a pistol, but she hadn't known how easy this one would be to connect to the family.

"Does your pa still have that gun, Lacey?"

"I don't rightly know, sheriff. Why don't you ask him?"

Sheriff Watson's face grew red with anger, and his cheeks bulged.

"Where's Will? Get him out here, and I'll ask him."

"Oh, Will's not here. He took Ruby and Ma up to Monterey on the midnight shopper to visit some of Ma's people."

"Lacey, I don't have no other choice. I'm going to have to search this house."

"I can see you ain't got no other choice. If it weren't Will, then it must have been a skinny little girl or a feeble old man that done it."

"Get in there boys and check out ever nook and cranny," Watson shouted.

The deputies scrambled onto the porch, eager to have it done and be out of there. Lacey cringed at the sound of overturned chairs and drawers being dumped out. It seemed an eternity before they finally came out shrugging their shoulders and shaking their head.

Sheriff Watson looked at them and then at Lacey. She faced him without blinking until he turned on his heels without a word. Grabbing the two deputies by their shirts, he pushed on ahead. She waited until he was out of the yard and down the road before she finally sank down on the porch and rested her head on her pa's knee. Weakness overtook her and shook her insides like wind in a sapling. Just when she thought she might break down and cry, she heard a sound above her. It was a soft, rumbling sound. Her pa's knee moved beneath her head, and she looked up to see a crooked grin on his face. A deep chuckle rolled up from his insides and sent spasms through his body. Suddenly, he focused his eyes on Lacey. Grinning broadly, he reached under the domestic and pulled out the pistol.

"Oh, Pa! Oh, God, Pa!" Lacey cried, throwing her arms around him and laughing in helpless joy. They held each other for a long time. And then she went to bury the gun.

17

"**I** admit I ain't proud of it," John spoke. "Truth is, I done a lot of thinking laying there waiting to die, just listening for the sound of them coming back to finish the job. It all felt so hopeless to me. Plain damn hopeless."

Coy didn't answer but continued to roll his cigarette slowly. Propping his legs on the porch railing, he flicked a lighted match into the night sky. It flared like a falling star and fell to its death. He thought of all the nights that he and Seth had sat on that porch and talked until the first rays of sunlight made their way over the ridgeline. It had been a deceptive kind of peace that existed only within a few square feet of a ramshackle cabin and a hard-packed dirt yard.

"They's been a lot of fighting, a lot of killing and a lot of good men stealing to feed their younguns," John said wearily. "I used to think the company cared about us. I used to think being a miner was a good way to make a living. Now, don't nothing make sense."

"You let yourself get too beholden to the company, John. You can't never let yourself get under the heel of nobody's boot. Times get hard; they'll crush you just trying to save their own asses. Grind you into the dirt like a bug and never look back to see what it was they stepped on. Folks here got to thinking the company needed them as much as they needed the company. They got to thinking this town belonged to them just because they put hard work into it. Don't nothing here belong to nobody but the company, and no matter how hard you work, John, you can't change that. Hell you can't ever let 'em know you care."

"I do care, Coy. I can't live without I care about something."

"I reckon that's where we're different. The only way I can live is not to give a damn about nothing."

"I can't hardly believe that about you, Coy. You must believe in the union just a little, or you wouldn't risk your life the way you've done."

"Well, it's something to do, I reckon."

"You're a better man than you give yourself credit for."

Coy shrugged. "No I ain't," he stated flatly. The irony of him coming out a hero in John's eyes struck him as right humorous, and he chuckled to himself. "Don't seem like you give up, though," he said after a moment of silence.

"No," John said matter-of-factly. "I'll fight it out to the end. I don't know no other way."

"Even if you don't stand a chance of winning?"

"You may laugh at me over this, but I'll tell you something, Coy. I'd go right back in them mines tomorrow if I could. I know that sounds like I'm tetched. It's just mining is all I know. All I ever asked was a way to make a living. My life was set out for me that way."

Coy could feel John looking at him in the dark and shook his head at the wonder of it. He had never had his life laid out for him. Every now and then when it did appear to be forming a pattern, he'd break loose like a wild mustang busting free of everything that held him.

"Coy, I'm right ashamed of myself for going on like this. Right ashamed of complaining when there's good men going hungry down there fighting for what they think is right."

"Won't nooby never know it less there's a raccoon or a 'possum out there listening."

"You are a good man, Coy. That's really what I come up here to tell you. Won't never be a way I can thank you for what you done."

"Consider it an old debt I owed you."

"What do you mean?"

"Remember that day down by the river? The day of the big preaching. You was the only one that shook my hand and spoke to me like I was somebody." They sat with a thick silence between them, sheltered from their emotions by the darkness.

"Just the same," John stammered, "I thank you."

"How's them ribs of yourn?"

"Well, they was a hell of a lot better before I made this climb up here!"

Coy snorted a laugh. "It does keep the church ladies from making regular visits."

"That's a blessing in itself, I reckon."

Coy was surprised to find that John had a vein of humor buried deep in him. They sat for a long while listening to the night sounds. Coy's cigarette was a glowing ember of light in the night air, and each man seemed afraid to speak and break the moment's peace. Finally, Coy ventured a question. "What do you figure's next?"

"Davidson mines posted a notice. They'll be opening if they can get enough scabs. Wilder's already digging a little coal. I figure sometime soon one of 'em is going to try to haul a load out of this holler."

"Could be trouble then?"

"If we let it go out, they've beat us for sure. If we try to stop it, they'll use it as an excuse to call in more guns. They're circulating a petition now in the county to ask the governor to call in the National Guard. Folks is scared with all the shooting that's been going on."

"Wouldn't the National Guard protect the miners, too?"

"That's what the coal company is saying. Makes me suspicion it right off. 'Course I'd risk a lot to keep that coal from going out."

"If the miners don't make trouble, them gun thugs will. It works in their favor to keep things stirred up. The more trouble, the better."

"Yeah, I reckon Will didn't help none, threatening Sawyer in broad daylight. Can't say's I blame him, though, the way they worked over Frank Conners. You seen him since they beat him?"

"No. I don't see much of the mine families."

"Sorry, Coy. I forgot. I promise you when this is over; I intend to let folks know what you done. I'll make it right."

Coy shrugged his shoulders as though it didn't matter. Talk of the Conners family made him uncomfortable. He was afraid that any moment John would mention Lacey's name.

"Lacey don't hardly leave his side," John said, catching him off guard. "Won't hear a word about him not getting better."

Yes, he could imagine her there feeding him, dressing him, watching after him like a mountain lion with a newborn cub. "Any word on who shot Sawyer?"

"That's one reason I'm ashamed of myself. While I was laid up whining like a pup after a teat, Lacey done went out and shot the biggest gun thug in town."

Coy jumped from his seat and overturned the keg he had been sitting on. "What the hell — ."

"Yeah, that was my reaction. Went running after Will. Took that old pistol of her pa's. That gun was knowed all over town. So next morning they come looking for it. She played it cool as a cucumber from what I can tell. Ain't that something and her not bigger than a tree squirrel!"

Coy couldn't think for seeing Sawyer's face the way he had leered at him that night trying to include him in his filthy talk about Lacey. Sawyer would go after them. Nobody in the Conners family would be safe now. And he would start with Lacey first. It was just the excuse he needed.

"Don't worry. She buried the gun. I tell you that gal is something."

"Sure sounds like it. Weren't you afraid for her?'

"Hell, yes. Scared the living daylights out of me when I heard. I couldn't say much, though. She come out of her tangle with Sawyer better than I did."

Coy decided not to bring up Sawyer's conversation over cards or the idea that he might go after the family. John seemed to feel the miners had won some kind of victory, and he wouldn't take that away from him. It wouldn't stop Sawyer's revenge, and it made him sad to think how much John and the other miners underestimated the power of the company.

"You know we plan to marry in the spring."

"Yeah, seems like I recollect hearing that," Coy said casually. It was a thought always in the back of his mind, a constant reminder that no matter how things turned out, Lacey was never going to be his. He was just there to keep her safe until the strike was over. Hearing it spoken out loud made him realize how much he had allowed thoughts of Lacey to creep into his mind. Thoughts of her long, soft hair in his hands, smelling of sunshine and spring water, and his face buried in her neck were still vivid.

"'Course you'd know."

"What do you mean?" Coy asked, fearing he might have revealed something.

"Well, it's just . . . I bet I done told you myself a dozen times."

"No, I just heard about it when I come back to Wilder."

"You're probably just being polite. Anyhow, if I have said it before, it's just because I feel like a lucky man. Sometimes I just have to say it to myself to believe it."

"No, doubt about it, John. You are one lucky man," Coy said truthfully. John talked on, but Coy couldn't keep his mind off Sawyer. He had to get to him before he tried something. It would have been better if Lacey had been a better shot. Now he would have to finish the job she had started.

18

"I swear, John. I don't know where you got these pinto beans," Lacey said. She stared down into the blackened pot and stirred it like a witches' brew. "I done cooked these things four hours and they're still like rocks. Here taste this." She thrust the spoon at him and he dutifully swallowed the contents.

John sat around the kitchen table with Lacey's pa and Will. They grinned as John grimaced and swallowed the beans like a dose of medicine.

"Lacey, I wasn't going to tell you this, but I seen John down by the creekbed just the other day. Looked to all the world to me like he was picking up rocks," Will said seriously.

"Well, I wouldn't be surprised from the looks of this mess." Lacey held the kettle lid up and winked at Will from behind it before she replaced it on the pot.

"Ain't you two about the sorriest younguns," Pa spoke up. "John don't pay them no never mind."

"I don't never pay 'em no mind, Frank. This time I do have to admit. Nothing against your cooking, Lacey," John said apologetically. "I have et some fine meals at this table. Lord knows though, this ain't going to be one of 'em."

They all laughed. It seemed to Lacey as she looked around the kitchen at the pale, thin faces, that it had been a lifetime since they had laughed like this. She knew that later they would eat the tough, stony beans and be glad of them, but for now it felt good to laugh. Her pa sat grinning at them all from his usual place at the head of the table. With his missing front teeth and his face green with slowly fading bruises, he didn't look like the old Frank at all. One side of his face still quivered and drooped, and his mouth sometimes dropped open spilling his food when he was eating. Lacey had taken to feeding him alone in the kitchen before she set the table for the rest of the family. He spent his days holding his empty pipe in his hand, staring out the kitchen window.

Ruby came in carrying Rachel and put her down on the floor next to where Ben sat idly tying cats-in-a-cradle out of string. "Keep an eye on little Rachel, would you Ben? Don't let her touch that hot stove."

"It don't feel hot enough to burn nobody," Ben said matter-of-factly. Lacey looked at Ben. He was as pale and thin as birch bark. They had had no extra milk for a long time, and what little they could get hold of went to the baby.

"Don't make sense to be sitting here in a holler full of coal and us having to burn slate to keep warm," Will said, slamming his fist on the table.

When Rachel jerked her arms about at the noise and puckered her lips, Lacey watched as Ben picked her up and cuddled her awkwardly on his bony lap. Ruby chewed nervously on her fingernails watching Will from the corner of her eye.

"Where'd you get this coal, Will," Lacey asked.

"Me and John dug it out of No. 1. Toted it out in toe-sacks. It was rough going, too."

"Will that place ain't safe," Ruby pleaded. "I've heard Pa say they ought to blast it shut to keep folks out of there."

"I'll admit it was singing a song yesterday, weren't it John!"

John shot a look at Lacey, and shifted his shoulders uncomfortably. "We didn't go too far in. We didn't have enough carbide to last long, and them timbers is plumb rotten in places. We mostly dug around the mouth, and that's why the coal ain't much good."

"You don't have to excuse it, John," Frank said. "We're proud to have it. That mines' been shut down since before you was born. You know, I heard they took the doors off of some folk's houses. I don't reckon we can expect the company to deliver coal if we ain't working, but taking the front door off a man's house is about as low down as I hope to hear about."

"They took the 'lectric lights out of a bunch a houses too," John said.

Frank shook his head in disbelief. "I can recollect the time when we used have them big Christmas parties up at the school house. Mr. Boyer and his wife used to hand out candy to all the younguns. We always had a big spread the womenfolk had fixed to eat. Them was good times. I knowed they was the bosses and we was just common workers," he said, his voice trailing off with a deep sadness. "Still I thought they cared about the miners and our families."

"You know they probably did care, Frank," John spoke up. "Thing is they stand to lose everything they got same as us. It makes a man do some desperate things. That's why we need the union. It keeps the company from breaking a man when he's down."

"Ain't never no excuse for breaking a man. They's starving us down here like a bunch of caged up animals. Beating up on folks and firing guns into homes with younguns sleeping in 'em. And why? 'Cause we won't work like dogs for twenty cents a ton. Unions is fine and I ain't regretting joining, John. I'm just sorry I lived long enough to see the day when folks couldn't be decent to other folks 'cause it was the right thing to do."

"Frank, I. . .," John stammered.

Tears welled up in Lacey's eyes, and she turned her back to the table where her pa sat. He had been like that ever since the beating. It was more than just having the fight knocked out of him. He seemed so hurt and confused by a world that no longer acted the way he had come to expect. The silence was broken by Annie coming through the back door screeching like a bird. She had been at Maude Sutters' all morning.

"Frank! Frank! You won't believe what I got here. Looky here what I brung you Frank!"

"Annie did you get somebody to walk you home?"

"Yes, of course, Frank. Maude's husband walked me right to the door."

"Why didn't Buford come in and set a spell?"

"He said he had to get back. Maude wants him to start packing up their belongings."

"Packing up? Where they a-going?"

"To Indiana, a course."

"Indiana!" Will shouted.

Lacey watched as Will and Ruby exchanged a quick glance.

"Their son come in day before yesterday from Indiana. You know that's why I went over there to begin with, Frank," Annie said like he was simple-minded. "Anyway he said he wouldn't have his ma a-living like this. That they could do a whole lot better up north. And she just up and told Buford to pack up. They was moving tomorrow. But looky here what she give me!" Annie laid the tobacco out on the table like a sack of gold. "Willard, Maude's son, give it to me. Maude said I could have a sack of sugar or this here tobacco, and I thought how proud you'd be to have a smoke. So I told Maude I just had to have that sack of tobacco for my Frank."

Frank fingered the tobacco sack with his rough, veiny hand, turning it over in wonder like he was getting familiar with the look of it all over again. Annie's tiny hand rested on his shoulder, and he reached up and patted it gently, tears hugged the corners of his eyes. "I know how much you like your tea cakes, Annie. Well, I mean it was right nice of you."

Annie beamed.

"Well boys. Let's have us a smoke."

Everyone laughed like it was the best joke. They all watched as Frank carefully packed his pipe and took the first puff, then exhaled with genuine pleasure. "Now that's as fine a smoke as I've ever had."

"How they getting to Indiana, Ma?" Will asked impatiently, as though he had waited as long as he could.

"Who son?" Annie asked, still too full of herself to be interested in anything Will had to say.

"Buford and Maude Sutters."

"Well, the way Maude told it, Willard has a Model-T pick up truck, and they was just going to pile their stuff in the back and ride right to Indiana in the back of that truck. Maude was real excited about going. You know, she always did like new things."

"Pa, me and Ruby and little Rachel is going with 'em. If they'll have us," Will blurted out.

Ruby reached over and took Will's hand and squeezed it hard under the table.

"When did you decide this, son?" Frank asked.

"Ruby and me been talking about leaving ever since the mine closed," Will said sheepishly.

"I got no reason to believe things is any easier in Indiana. Works hard to come by anywhere nowadays," Frank reasoned, chewing the stem of his pipe in concentration.

John watched Lacey for her reaction, and Lacey watched her pa, ready to step in if he got too tough on Will. She was surprised that Will wanted to leave. It hurt her that Ruby had never said anything about it, but then she thought of all the things she had never told Ruby.

"It'd be real hard going where you don't hardly know a soul. You wouldn't have no family around if you got into trouble or if you was to fall sick."

"We've thought about all that, Pa. It just seems like we don't have nothing here. We don't mean to pull out and leave the family. It's just we're young, and we want to make some kinda life for ourselves and for Rachel."

"Then I can't fault you for trying. Go on and see if they'll take you."

"You mean it Pa? You ain't put out with us for leaving?"

"Might be I should of done it myself back in '24 when I was younger."

"Thank you, Pa," Will said, rising to shake his father's hand awkwardly. Then he grabbed Ruby by the hand, and they ran out the back door. "Ben, keep an eye on Rachel," he yelled from the back step.

The family sat in stunned silence, listening to the sounds of their excited voices grow faint. Finally John broke the silence. "Lacey, I better get you up to Ma's if you're going to get any quilting done this afternoon. Don't worry, Frank. I'll have her back before dark."

"John, don't pay Will no mind. He never was one to stick with something."

"I've said this before, the union business, and mining for that matter, ain't something you can force nobody to believe in. You either do or you don't."

"Well, anyways, I didn't want no hard feelings between the two of you over this."

"They ain't none. I hope they do real well for themselves in Indiana. Lacey, you better get your wrap. It'll be getting cool by the time we head back."

When they were outside, Lacey breathed in the fresh, cool air. It chilled her through her thin shawl, and she shivered.

"Here take my jacket. You're shaking like a leaf," John said.

"No, I'm fine. I'm just not used to the cold, yet. We'll walk fast and it'll keep us warm."

"You always have the answer to every problem."

"It don't hardly seem like it to me."

"Did you know that Will was thinking about leaving?"

She shook her head.

"I know you'll miss him. Especially, Ruby and the baby."

"Things are just changing real fast. Seems like things couldn't ever go back to being the way they were before all the trouble started in the mines. I think Pa's right about that."

"Maybe things will be better."

"John, I didn't know you could be such a dreamer."

John blushed and looked down at the ground. "Lacey, what's the first thing you'd do if the strike was over?"

She thought about how long they had been without enough to eat and how they were going into the winter months with nothing put by. "I'd fry up a whole side of pork meat, crisp and brown, bake a pan of biscuits with milk gravy, open a jar of blackberry preserves and sit down and eat 'til I was sick."

"That sure sounds good. I was kinda hoping for some of them little green apples you used to fry with butter and some of old man Sewart's honey fresh from the hive."

"Oh hush, hush. I can't take anymore talk of food," she said grabbing hold of his arms like she meant to shake him. She was surprised when he pulled her gently to him and kissed her on the lips. She eased away from him. It was so rare he showed his affections that she sometimes forgot that they were to be married in the spring. An anxious look crossed his brow and made him squint at her as though he was trying to see her better through the gloom of a bleak November day. She held on to his hand and thought to distract him. "What would you do, John? When the strike is over, what's the first thing you want to do?"

He looked at her solemnly. "The first thing I want is to get back to work."

She nodded. It was the answer she might have expected from John. Still it was as ordinary as her wish for enough to eat. It seemed such a small reward for all their suffering.

"You're thinking I'm a pretty dull sort just wanting to get back to work."

Lacey worried that so much showed on her face. Sometimes even when she was thinking something else, her true thoughts would show by her expression, surprising and embarrassing her when someone pointed it out. She lied. "No, John. There's plenty of men around here that would wish the same."

"It's just that when a man has work, he can start to make something of his life. Your pa thought I might be mad at Will for leaving. Truth is I was jealous. When he leaves here, this strike will all be behind him. If he gets work in Indiana, him and Ruby can get 'em a little place of their own and get on with living. That's what I want for us, is a chance to get on with living. That's why I want to get back to work."

"I know, John."

"None of this has been fair to you, Lacey. I know you had dreams of how you wanted things to be. Curtains on the windows, a sitting room with a sofa, and a garden plot the size of this holler."

She laughed out loud at the mention of her garden. "You know how I love my garden."

"I always had it in my mind to give you those dreams."

"John, you are the sweetest man I know," she said truthfully.

"I have to see this strike through. I've made a promise to myself about that. Barney Graham and a lot of good men are risking their lives to see it through. I can't pull out and leave them."

They had reached his house, and they stood on the porch looking out over the hollow. Smoke came from only a few of the chimneys. It meant that they were neither cooking nor keeping warm. Of course, some of the houses were deserted. A few of the families had moved off company property where it was safer and they could keep a cow or some pigs.

"Is that what you was thinking I wanted you to do?"

"No, you're not like that. It's just that I want you to know that when this is over, if I'm still alive, I'm going to spend the rest of my life seeing that you have everything you ever wanted."

She reached up and touched him gently on the cheek. He was so thin and pale in the afternoon light. She never imagined that it would hurt to have someone love her so much. Suddenly, when she looked into his eyes, she had a feeling he knew she did not love him. It gave her the sensation of falling backwards off a cliff. "John, I...."

"You younguns get in here before you freeze to death!" Cora yelled from the front door.

It was just as well Cora had interrupted her. She had no idea what she was about to say. Was she going to lie to him or try to explain to him what he already knew? Somehow she didn't think it would make any difference.

"Lacey you get up here by this fire and warm yourself," Cora directed.

Lacey worked her way around the quilting frame that took up nearly the entire front room. She stood warming her hands at the small fire in the coal grate. "This feels good Cora. It's pretty chilly out there for November."

"I've still got a little sassafras. I'll make us some tea. That will warm you right up."

"Don't go to no trouble."

"Lord, honey. It ain't no trouble to boil a little water. John get Lacey a chair up here by the fire."

John dutifully moved a chair close to the fire and motioned for Lacey to sit down.

"Thank you, John. I think I would just as soon stand."

"Maybe so, but before Ma gets back in here, I advise you to sit down."

Lacey giggled at John's reference to his mother's willfulness. John grinned back at her sheepishly. They both hid their faces when Cora walked in.

"What are you two snickering about? Here Lacey, drink this here tea while it's hot. Honey, sit down here now. Take those shoes off and stick you feet right up next to that fire. Come on now, do as I say. Believe me I know. If you don't warm your feet, that's a sure way to catch a cold."

Lacey took off her shoes. She couldn't look at John for fear of breaking into a fit of giggling. "Thank you, Cora. This feels real good."

"John," Cora said, turning her considerable energy on her son. "You just as well find something to do with yourself until it's time to walk Lacey home. We are going to be right busy here with this quilt."

John looked helplessly back over his shoulder at Lacey as Cora ushered him from the room.

"That's the trouble nowadays," Cora remarked to John's back. "There ain't enough to keep the menfolk busy, so they're always underfoot."

"Cora the quilt turned out pretty. Where did you get enough batting to quilt it?"

"It come from some of them church women out of Nashville. You know, after I talked about 'em like dogs. Ain't that just the way! Makes me plumb ashamed of myself."

Lacey couldn't detect any signs of remorse in her voice.

"It might of been mean of me to take it when there was other folks that needed it. Anyway, I mean to see this quilt finished for you and John. If you're finished with that tea, pull your chair up here, and we'll get to quilting."

They quilted to the rhythm of the mantel clock. Lacey was content to listen to Cora as she worked, whose conversation was as precise and industrious as her stitches. Lacey looked around the room, which would be her home if she married John. It was as neat and scrubbed as Cora's boundless energy could make it. The curtains on the windows were made of domestic boiled white and trimmed with tatting. The sofa, pushed back against the wall to accommodate the quilting frame, was covered by embroidered dollies. The room radiated the industrious nature that was Cora. And John, too, Lacey thought.

"I picked this double wedding ring pattern," Cora was saying. "Aunt Arie, tried to get me to do a Jacob's ladder. I said, 'Aunt Arie, young folks just getting married should start out with at least one quilt with a double wedding ring. That's what my mama made for me and that's what I'm making for John and Lacey.'"

"It's beautiful, Cora."

"I knowed you'd like it. You're that much like me."

"It's the very pattern I would have picked."

"You know I never had a daughter, but you are as much like one as I could ever hope to have. John's lucky to find such a good wife."

Cora patted Lacey on the hand. Lacey could feel herself blushing.

"John's a good catch, too, of course," Cora said laughing. "Ain't a mother of a son alive that don't think that, I reckon."

Cora didn't seem to need a reply. She never looked up or paused from her perfect stitches. "He don't talk much for sure.

His pa was the same way, only with us, it didn't matter so much 'cause I done enough talking for the both of us. I expect you'll learn to do the same."

Lacey wasn't so sure about that. She never had been good at filling in the silence with idle chatter. She had her pa's economy of words.

"Don't let John's quiet fool you. He's always got something working in his head. Usually he's figuring on how to build something or fix up something. If he has a problem, he'll turn it over and over in his mind until he's seen every side of it a dozen times. He sticks with something, that's for sure. Won't give it up until he's sure they ain't no way to win and then he'll stay a while longer. It's just his way."

Cora deftly cut her thread and knotted the needle with one hand. She ran it through the quilt once and left it while she stood and stretched her back. "Can't sit like I used to. Gets me too stiff in my back."

"You work so fast. I've hardly got started on this side."

"Been quilting since I was seven. I don't hardly remember a time I didn't have either a needle in my hand or a frying pan. 'Course, since Luther died, I can't hardly pin myself down to nothing like I used to. When John was a baby, Luther made plenty of money so I didn't have nothing to do but take care of them. I always wanted a passle of younguns but the Lord didn't see it my way. So I must of knitted John enough booties and sweaters for a dozen babies. Lord, them was happy times! If I just learned to bake a different kind of cake and it turned out well, I was proud. Luther was handy with tools, and he had made me a walnut eating table. Prettiest thing you ever seen. We had a little cookware and a water bucket, and I had four quilts and two sheets. I made them sheets myself. Put embroidery all around the edges. Now, I don't hardly have a mind for nothing. Can't even quilt like I used to 'cause I can't see well enough."

"I admire your fine stitches."

"Lacey."

Lacey looked up and waited for Cora to speak.

"All that talk about John. I just want you to understand his ways. He'd marry you today, if it weren't for this strike. Some girls wouldn't want to wait."

Lacey didn't know how to answer. Maybe John had told her it was his idea to wait until spring when maybe the strike would be over. Of course, she would expect any young girl to be impatient to marry the man she loved, just as she must have been impatient in those early days to marry Luther. Yes, John would always have a plan in his head for their lives. Her life with John would stretch out before her like the tracks of a train. When times were so hard it was a wonder where the next meal was coming from, how could she be frightened by the thought of marrying a man so honorable, so steady? "I wouldn't want John to break a promise to the men who are counting on him," Lacey said weakly, feeling like a hypocrite.

"Well, this could get a whole lot worse before it gets better. I reckon the company expected to break us by now."

"Are you worried about John getting hurt again?"

"Lord, yes. Every time I hear a gun shot or dynamite going off, it makes me might nigh sick. I expect to see them come carrying him in here again, only this time he'll be dead. I'm afraid they won't settle for just beating him up next time. It don't do me no good to worry, though. I worried about his pa every day for twenty-five years. Besides, I know better than to get between John and what he believes in. He's a standing up kind of man like his pa. Always was, even when he was a youngun."

"What do you thinks to come of all this, Cora?"

"Well, I don't see none of them mine guards a-growing pale and thin a wearing themselves out scrounging for something to feed their families. You know they's already plenty of sickness around and it ain't hardly winter. They say May Russet's got pellagra. That's what the Doc called it."

"What's pellagra?"

"Honey, it ain't nothing but not having enough to eat."

It shocked Lacey that folks she had known all of her life could be starving. It was true. She had seen her own family wither under the strain of meager rations. Pride had kept them from letting others know just how bad it was, but it seemed there were others worse off than them. She felt anger well up in her for all the suffering the company had brought on them.

"Lacey?" John poked his head into the room tentatively.

"Come on in John," Cora called. "I reckon I've put Lacey through enough for one day."

"I enjoyed it, Cora."

"Law me. I don't know what got into me. If I wasn't rambling on about the old days, I was complaining about today. Ain't nothing a young person hates more than that. I ought to know better. You should of told me to hush up with my whining." Cora took Lacey's hands in hers and patted them affectionately.

"Now, you know Lacey ain't going to tell you to hush, Ma," John said.

"I know that John. Why do you think I like to talk to her so much?"

Lacey laughed and gave Cora a big hug.

"You two better head on. I didn't realize it was getting on toward dark already."

A knock on the door brought them all to attention. John walked to the door and stood a moment. He eased the door open. Joe Morgan spilled through the opening like water from an overturned bucket. "Joe, what on earth is the matter?" John asked.

"I come as fast as I could. Had to work my way around through the woods. It weren't safe to take the roads."

"What's happened, Joe?" John asked with more patience than Lacey thought possible.

"They've set fire to the Davidson tipple. It's a-burning like the fires of hell right now."

"Who done it, Joe?"

"Ain't nobody a-saying, but the company's got every guard and deputy they can get hold of up there trying to put it out. The company's real mad about this one. They was scheduled to open tomorrow."

"Could it of caught off that old slag heap?"

"John, that slag heap's been burning for years. It'd be mighty unlikely."

"So they're blaming the union."

"That's a $20,000 tipple, John. You think the company would burn their own tipple?"

"Don't hardly stand to reason."

"Yeah, well, I'm afraid this is just what they've been looking for to bring in the militia on us."

Just then gunfire rang out. John was on the porch before anyone saw him go out. "John, get back in here," Lacey called, running after him. They stood in stunned silence as a truckload of gun thugs sped past them on their way to Davidson shouting and firing their guns into the air. In the distance they could see the black smoke of the tipple.

19

"We been gone a long time, Lacey," Ben said. He tossed another rock into the creekbed. It hit a boulder with a cracking sound and bounced into the water.

"I know," Lacey said without looking at Ben. They had been away for two hours looking for hickory nuts. It was the first time she had left the house since they had brought Pa home and since she had shot Sawyer. Lacey knew it was foolish for them to be so far from home, but she was sick of being careful. As she looked down at her thin arms, she was amazed that they could feel so heavy. Her whole body felt weighted to the ground where she sat. The weeks of caring for Pa, of scrounging for food, and worrying about Will had left her numb, with not enough energy left to grieve for all that she had lost.

It wasn't right that she should still care about Coy. It wasn't right that she should listen for his name to be spoken or to catch sight of him on the street. He was no better than any of those other gun thugs. He played cards with them; he drank their whiskey and had taken the side of the company over her own people. The worst part was knowing he didn't really care about the company. He was just trying to get back at her pa and at her too, she guessed. She could understand him leaving, running off like that when her pa had called him a thief. What she couldn't understand was him coming back just to get even. It was contrariness in his nature that always set him on the wrong path. And yet there was something that would not allow her to hate him.

"You know what, Lacey?"

Lacey was startled from her thoughts by Ben's words. She felt that she had been away for days, and it seemed strange to realize they were still sitting by the creekbed. Ben had built a small bridge of rocks and sticks spanning a trickle of water between two boulders. His back was to her, and his thin shoulder blades were sharp beneath his shirt. His color had faded from the summer sun and when he turned to look at her he was as frail as a baby bird that had fallen from the nest.

"Lacey, you know what?"

"What, Ben?"

"I think when I grow up, I'm goin' to build me a bridge just like this; only a real one. That's what I'm going to be. A bridge builder."

He looked at Lacey with the same look he had had the day he showed her a bluebird's nest full of sky blue eggs. It was a look that said some things are too wonderful to be believed. It stunned her that he could be thinking of the future when she was struggling so hard to survive each day. Then she felt ashamed of herself. Six months ago, life for her had been filled with hope, and now she forgotten what it was like to be a child.

"You don't want to be a miner?"

He looked at her shamefaced and shook his head. "Reckon Pa would understand?"

He was as serious as though he planned to start that day. "A man's got to do what a man's got to do," Lacey said with equal seriousness.

"That's what Coy always said."

It had just slipped out Lacey knew, but they both stared at each other for a while in silence, sharing the longing for the magic that was Coy. "Did you ever tell Coy about wanting to build bridges?"

"Sorta. When we was working on Seth's place. He told me I sure was a good carpenter. That maybe I ought to build things for a living when I growed up. I just kinda decided today that bridges was the thing I'd like building the most."

Lacey could tell that Ben's words contained a mixture of love and hurt. He had trusted Coy and wanted his praise to still mean something. "Coy was right. You are a good hand at building things, and someday you'll build a bridge that people will paint pictures of it will be so pretty."

"Do you think so, Lacey? Do you really think so?"

"You know I wouldn't say so if I didn't believe it." She had half expected him to be embarrassed by her praise, but instead he stared off dreamy-eyed. She wanted to draw a circle around him and pray God to protect him always from the hurt of a dream that might not come true.

"Do you think Coy was lying when he said I was a good builder?" Ben asked.

"No, I don't think he was lying about that, Ben."

"He lied about being my friend."

"What makes you think he lied about that?"

"Well, cause now he hangs around with all them guards that work for the company and he don't never come around or ask about us or nothing. If he really was a friend, he wouldn't act like that would he, Lacey?"

"I don't know, Ben. You know how Pa treated him. He wouldn't exactly be welcome at the house."

"I know. Still it ain't right to act like you like somebody if you don't. You oughn't to tell folks stuff if you don't mean it. It ain't honest."

Ben was hurt, Lacey realized. As hurt as he had ever been by anyone in his ten short years. He had worshiped Coy, and Coy had let him down. He had heard the talk around town about Coy and Lacey didn't know what to tell him. She was too hurt and confused herself to defend Coy, even for Ben's sake. Maybe Ben had been his best friend. Maybe Coy had loved her. She could see why in the eyes of a child it all seemed a lie. It seemed like a lie to her, too.

"It's getting late, Ben. Why don't you run on back to the house and tell 'em I'll be there directly to fix supper."

"Ain't you coming?"

"In a minute. Here, take this poke of hickory nuts with you."

His eyes looked at her pleadingly.

"Don't worry. I won't be long. I'm just going to sit here a while longer."

Ben dug his toes into the dirt and made fretful expressions over his shoulder as he turned to go.

"I swear you'd think I was little Rachel or something the way you're looking at me," Lacey laughed. "Now, go. I need you to tell the folks I won't be long or they'll be fussing for sure by the time I get there. I'll be all right. I'm not ready to head back just yet."

As soon as Ben was out of sight, Lacey couldn't imagine why she had had her mind so set on staying by the creek a while longer. It really wasn't safe to be out by herself, but as she wrapped her skirt around her knees and rested her chin against her arms, it felt wonderful to be alone. With a houseful of people needing something from her all the time, it felt good to soak in the quiet of a fall day. The afternoon sun on the leaves made them smell like warm biscuits from the stove, and the thought made her hungry. She searched around, crawling on all fours, for a rock to crack the few hickory nuts she had saved. She cracked a handful and leaned back against a large rock to savor the tiny morsels. The sun teased her with its warm rays through the last remaining leaves of fall. Closing her eyes, she savored the good feelings as she felt herself slipping away, lost in the simple quiet and warmth.

When she awoke with a start she had only the sense that time had passed and that some noise had awakened her. As she strained her ears to recapture whatever sound had brought her back, the crack of a stick behind her made her turn. Sawyer stood over her; his eyes were red-rimmed from corn whiskey. One side of his face was covered with a filthy bandage and the other side with several days' growth of beard. He worked his clenched teeth until his jaws shook with the fury that was in him.

Terror kept Lacey frozen to the spot where she had been sitting. Her legs refused to push her body up into a running position, and no scream would come. Sawyer watched, waiting for the first move. As she slowly moved her hand over the ground behind her in search of the rock she had used to crack the hickory nuts, Sawyer's face split into a vile grin, and his tongue flicked across his lips like a living thing. Suddenly, Lacey was scrambling on all fours, clawing at the rocks and dirt beneath her. She felt his full weight land on her, knocking the air from her lungs and forcing her face and body into the bruising rocks. His foul, hot breath made the bile rise to her throat, and saliva ran from the corner of her mouth and mixed with the earth beneath her.

"You ain't so smart now, are you, gal, being off down here all by yourself. Where's the rest of that puny-assed family of yourn? Word is the whole bunch of yourns sure does stick together. You see I got me this hole in the side of my face, and I sure have been mighty curious as to who put it there."

Sawyer suddenly raised his weight off of her, straddling her on his knees. Instinctively, she started to crawl away, but he put one large fist in her backside. With one hand he flipped her over, then put both hands on her shoulders, pinning her arms to her with his knees. He put his mouth close to her face. "Now, I'm just afraid the young ladies won't find me as handsome as they did once. What do you think, Lacey? Do you think I'm as handsome as ever? You always did favor me, I know." His breath was as hot and foul.

She tried to pull far away from his breath. Screams churned up from her insides, but caught in her throat, gagging her with their force.

"I seen you down here before, showing yourself off, wanting somebody to see you with that dress hiked up around your legs. You want to show me them legs again, Lacey?"

She could feel him reach back and run his hand along her leg, fumbling with the material of her dress to get his hand underneath. She kicked at him with all the strength left in her, flailing her legs about under his weight. Suddenly, he rose up over her and leered down at her. With one vicious yank, he jerked her dress up around her waist, and tears of rage and helplessness sprang into her eyes and streamed down her face into her hair. Sawyer threw back his head and laughed, and Lacey closed her eyes in horror and humiliation. She tried to shut out the sickening sound.

Without warning, Sawyer fell full weight upon her, knocking the breath from her, and she gasped for air as his dead weight pressed her into the ground below. The stubble from his unshaven face cut into her cheek, and just when she thought she might pass out, Sawyer's body was wrenched violently from her. Her body slowly responded to her commands to flee, and she was able to pull herself up to a sitting position, pushing her dress back down around her knees. When she looked around her, she saw Coy dragging Sawyer's body away, and realized he must have come up behind Sawyer and struck him on the back of the head. Now, she watched stunned as Coy bludgeoned Sawyer's face into a shapeless, bloody mass with the butt of his rifle. She could hear the bones cracking and see the blood and flesh shoot into the air, but all she could feel was relief. Finally, Coy stopped, and then turned to her, his jaws tight with hate and his breath ragged. "Are you all right?" he asked, trying to catch his breath.

She didn't know how to answer. He had saved her life, but she was frightened by what she had seen in his eyes. As he started toward her, the gun still in his hand, she tried to scream, but it came out a whimper. Scrambling backwards on her hands and pushing herself with her feet, she fought to escape him. He stopped. Suddenly, he looked down at his hands as though just realizing that he still held the bloody gun, and then he dropped it into the weeds and wiped his hands on the ground.

Lacey stopped crawling and sat watching him. She didn't know what to make of him being there, beating Sawyer, and saving her life. It was impossible to know what he meant to do next. Exhaustion had crept into every limb and she couldn't think clearly. "Is he dead?" she whispered hoarsely as though it might have been a trick.

"If he ain't, when he comes to he is going to wish he was. Are you all right?"

She nodded, but she wasn't really sure.

"We better get out of here then."

"Out of here?"

"Yeah. Outta here. His kind runs in packs."

"Are we just going to leave him?"

"He'd do the same for me," Coy said, grinning warily.

"Like he left Pa and John?"

Coy nodded. Then he rolled Sawyer's body over the bank and into a laurel thicket and tossed the rifle into creek.

Suddenly, she collapsed into helpless tears as her fear caused her to shake uncontrollably. Reaching down, he pulled her up to him, and then held her, cradling her like a baby.

"It'll be all right. You're safe now. Just hold tight. I'm going to take you up to Seth's place to rest."

"What about the rifle? I mean shouldn't we carry it off somewhere?"

"The way I hear it you're pretty experienced handling that little detail."

She looked at him puzzled. "How did you know about the gun?"

"Don't worry. Your secret is safe. The gun's his. We'll leave it. Maybe they'll think he beat himself up with his own gun."

Coy grinned down at her the way he had so many times, and she gave him a weak smile and buried her face in his shoulder. She couldn't fight him. It was all too confusing, and her mind reeled as they headed through the woods up the ridgeline.

As they started up the steep incline to the cabin, Lacey could feel Coy's heart beating under the soft flannel of his shirt. She thought of the last time she had struggled through the storm in the dark to make it up the winding path to Seth Ramsey's place. They had not spoken again since they had started their trek, although Coy had stopped at times to rest and would look at her face as though to ask how she was doing.

"I can walk now, Coy. Really, I'm all right," Lacey protested.

"I got you. Don't worry. I've toted sacks of sugar that weigh more than you up this hillside."

"Please, Coy. I want to walk. I should be getting on home. Folks will be out looking for me if I'm not back soon." She had to get away from the nearness of him. There were too many questions to be answered and she needed to think. Her head reeled with the mixture of emotions that swirled around her in the presence of Coy. She felt gratitude for his having saved her life, but she was angry with him for leaving her without a word and then coming back only to spend his hours with gun thugs and scabs.

Coy's brow puckered into a frown, and he gave her a puzzled look, and then sat her down gently. She held on to him, testing her legs, and was surprised to find that they could hardly hold her weight and wobbled beneath her like a newborn colt.

"Here sit down under this tree a while and rest. You've been through a lot today. Is that what you want? To go back now?"

They sat down under the tree where she had fallen the night of the storm. "Yes, but. . ." She could wait no longer, and the words spilled out. "Why, Coy? First, you up and run off, and then when you do show back up here, you side with them company men. That night I seen you on the hotel porch I prayed to die. I prayed that if it truly was you standing there that God would let me die. I couldn't help what Pa done to you but you should of knowed it wasn't my feelings. I was so proud of you that day. You know I come to you that night," she found herself saying, surprised at her own anger. "I made it to this tree. It was storming, and I turned my ankle on a root."

He knelt before her and hung his head into his hands. She could hear a low moan escape his throat, and then he looked up, his face was twisted with pain.

"The next day I heard you was gone."

"Oh, God, Lacey. I didn't know."

"Maybe I should've tried harder to get to you," she whispered, softened by his anguish. "Ben come after me and helped me back home."

"No, I should've come after you."

She reached out and touched his face, something deep within responding to him. He rubbed his cheek against her palm and gently kissed the inside of her hand. For a brief moment they were lost in what might have been.

"When I come back" he said his voice hoarse with emotion, "I'd made up my mind to do whatever it took to have you." He paused for a long time, staring off over her shoulder. "I found out on the train coming in that you planned to marry John in the spring."

"I was hurt," she answered weakly, stunned by the foolishness of it.

Coy nodded.

"It still don't explain why you took to hanging out with them gun thugs."

"I wanted to do something to make it up to you. To make things easier for you and look after you while all this was going on. I figured I had done lost any chance of us being together. None of the miners would have accepted my help outright. Least of all your Pa. They never would have trusted me. So one night I'd won a lot at poker, and I just up and took my winnings to John. Offered the money to him to buy food for the miners. He asked me if I heard anything interesting from them thugs, would I tell it."

"John. You made a deal with John to spy on the company?" Her mind could not take in what he was saying. "You knowed I was going to marry John, and you offered to help him anyway."

"He was so damn grateful," Coy said as though that was reason enough for what he had done.

Coy's simple words went through her like the blade of a knife, and she sat stunned by the foolish, reckless, desperation of his actions. He seemed always driven to do the very thing that would bring him to the cliff-edge of destruction even when it was for all the right reasons.

"You could of been killed."

"He took me at my word when I said I wanted to help. He never asked me why."

"That's John's way." *Just as it was Coy's way to ride the reins of his own fury*, she thought.

"I gave him what money I could scrape together. Mostly from gambling. He seen to it that the miners got it. I knowed he'd take care of you."

"He makes sure we get food when he can. I always worried that he favored us." She thought back to when John had first brought food to the house. He was always greeted heartily and often stayed to share supper with them. Then she thought of the day Coy had ridden up with a wagon load of supplies and her pa had lashed out at him, calling him a thief. Her heart ached for him as it had at that moment.

"He's an honest man but he ain't a saint." Coy laughed out deep and laugh. "I sorta counted on him favoring you."

The sound of his laughter vibrated through her. "Oh, God," she cried throwing herself into his arms. "Coy, you are such a crazy fool!"

"A man's got to be good at something."

She smiled up at him, helplessly caught in the web of his charm. She wrapped her arms around his waist and they walked the rest of the way up the hill to Seth's cabin.

Coy spread the bedroll by the fireplace and gave her a look of apology. "I've just been batchin' it since I got back." He eased her down onto the bedroll and then went about making a fire in the grate. Then he left the room, and she could hear him putting wood into the cookstove and breaking kindling for a fire. It felt strange not to be doing it herself, not to offer to help, but she felt powerless to move. She looked around the almost empty room. An old trunk sat in the corner piled high with yellowed newspapers, and two chairs stood before the fireplace like gateposts.

Coy came back into the room and stood over her. "We don't have much time. They'll be looking for you."

It was true they had probably found the body by now, or at least they had begun to miss her at home and would go looking. She shouldn't have come at all. She should have headed straight home. It had been so reckless of Coy to bring her here, but she had not resisted. Then she realized that he was asking her if she wanted to stay. He knelt before her and looked deep into her eyes waiting for some sign. Her breath caught in her throat as he reached out and removed the combs that held her hair in place. It tumbled about her face and he caught it in his hands. When he lowered her to the rough fabric of the bedroll, she tried to think of all the reasons she shouldn't be doing what she was doing. The blood roared in her ears and the room spun around her.

Coy unbuttoned her dress slowly and slipped it over her head. When he sat up to take off his shirt, his skin was dark and smooth in the firelight. She reached up for him, and he came to her, his breath ragged in his throat. Gently, slowly, desperately he kissed her and for the first time in her life, Lacey thought only of the moment. She took in the feel of him like breathing in air, and she memorized the muscles in his arms as he held himself above her. The curve of his back was like carved wood beneath her fingers.

They lay clinging to each other for a long time, as the room grew dark with the fading sun and the dying fire. She ran her hands one last time through his coarse black hair, down the sharp edge of his cheekbones and into the well of his neck.

"I'll always love you," he whispered, rubbing his chin against her hand.

"And I will always love you," was all she could say.

Then he dressed quickly and went into the kitchen. She could hear him rattling about. She slipped her dress over her head and ran her fingers through her hair and tried to subdue it with her combs. Her cheek felt hot and flushed from their lovemaking. By the time she joined Coy in the kitchen, he was pouring strong, black coffee into two cups. She couldn't remember when anyone had done such a simple thing as pour a cup of coffee for her. It was such a sweet thing to watch, an action she thought she would love to see again and again for the rest of her life.

"Sit down. I hope you can drink it black."

"Thank you, that's the way I like it." She sat down; somehow nervous in a way she had not been when they had been naked together. She sipped the scalding liquid, and it was wonderful. "Oh Lordy, this is good. I didn't think anything could be this good."

"Well, there is something about nearly getting killed to make simple things seem better."

"Oh, God, Coy! Ain't I the worst person in the world? I hadn't even thought about Sawyer since we got here."

"I'll take that as a compliment." He leaned over and kissed her, his lips warm from the coffee.

His kiss stirred feelings deep within her, and she could not look at him. She kept her eyes on her coffee, drinking great gulps until she could control herself. When she looked at Coy, he was staring at her with a worried frown.

"What are we going to do, Coy?"

He smiled and sweetly touched her hand, drawing circles in her palm with his finger. "First, I reckon I better get you back home."

"I'll go down by myself. I don't want them tying you into this thing. If I hadn't been so foolhardy as to send Ben on none of this would ever of happened."

"It would have happened sooner of later. Sawyer wouldn't have given up that easy. I'm just glad I was there. Does it bother you, what I done to him?"

"Yes," she said truthfully. "I just don't want nobody suffering for it. Them thugs is not likely to take well to have one of their own beat senseless. They might make trouble for all of us just to get even. I couldn't bear it if my foolishness brought more trouble to folks."

"I'll walk you down and then I'll go check on what's left of Sawyer."

"Good."

They sat in silence for some time. Finally, Lacey got up to clear the table. "What about John?" Coy asked when her back was turned.

She could not face him. "I don't want to hurt him."

"What about what happened in there?"

"We have to find a way to tell him without hurting him."

"You can't always make life work out perfect for everybody. You got to think of yourself. You got to think of us."

Suddenly, a knock on the back door brought Coy to his feet. He pulled her up close behind him just as the door opened and someone yelled, "Coy."

"John," Coy answered. "You scared the life out of me."

"Sorry, Coy. It's Lacey. She's gone and can't nobody find her. Ben left her down by the creekbed hours ago. We done searched high and low. Turned over ever rock." John was ashen faced in the lamplight. "That ain't all. I found Sawyer's body under a bush not ten feet from where Ben left Lacey. He was beat bad. You got to help me, Coy." John threw himself into a chair and covered his face with his hands. "I didn't know where else to go. I thought you might of heard something from some of the men. If something has happened to Lacey, I don't think I can live. I should of killed that son-of-a-bitch myself before this."

"John, Lacey's all right. She's here with me."

Lacey stepped out into the light. John looked up at her, incredulously. Then he looked at Coy. Lacey walked over to him and still he did not speak. Then she looked around at Coy uncertainly, and John threw his arms around her waist and cried like a baby. "Oh, my God, Lacey. I thought you was dead. You know I couldn't go on if anything ever happened to you. Oh, Lord, help me. I thought you was dead."

Lacey stroked the top of his head and put her arm around his shoulders. Her heart broke at the sound of his forlorn cries, and it shamed her that she had never imagined him capable of such feelings. "I'm fine, John. He didn't hurt me. Coy come along just in time."

"Coy, you're the one that beat Sawyer up!" He jumped up to shake Coy's hand. "You saved my Lacey! I don't know how to thank you." He pumped Coy's hand and then impulsively he threw his arms around him.

Coy looked over at Lacey uncomfortably. They had both caught the "my Lacey." Coy started to speak. Lacey looked at him pleadingly.

"Just glad I was there, John."

"And this is not the first time you were there."

Coy's eyes widened in surprise.

"Have you forgotten already? It ain't been that long since you saved my hide."

Lacey could see Coy's body relax. He, too, had been thinking that John had somehow guessed that their being together was no accident.

"Sit down and tell me what happened," John said. They sat down and Lacey poured them coffee.

"Not much to tell. I just come upon Sawyer. He, uh. . .well, he had Lacey pinned to the ground."

"That no good son-of-a-bitch."

"I hit him with the butt of his gun. He must of put it down when he jumped Lacey."

"He looked like you might of hit him more than once."

"I wanted to make sure I had his full attention. Is he dead?"

John looked at Coy with such gratitude and admiration that Lacey had to turn away. She got the coffee pot from the cookstove and refilled their cups. "He moaned when I poked him, so I let him be."

"I brought Lacey here 'cause she was real shook up and I didn't think I could go carrying her in to her pa."

"Of course, you done the right thing. I reckon I had better get her back though. Her folk's is fit to be tied. You up to it, Lacey?"

"I'm fine, really. I just feel sick over the trouble I've caused. Who else knows about Sawyer, John?"

"Well, nobody. I kept it to myself. I figured it couldn't do no good to panic folks, but they won't wait much longer before they go for help. We best be getting back."

"We can't just leave Sawyer there, John," Lacey pleaded. "Can't you get rid of him somehow?"

They both looked at her like she was crazy. "I'll do it Lacey," Coy broke in. "You go on now. I'll take care of things."

"Let me do it," John protested. "I'm the one that should have been watching out for Lacey."

"You take Lacey home. Tell her folks she was hiding out in the woods. I'll go by the hotel and sneak Sawyer's stuff out before anybody finds out. We'll load him in the wagon and haul him outta town. They'll just think he drifted out of town like he drifted in. I'm sure he don't have no kin to speak of."

"You don't think he'll come back just to get even?"

"Maybe, if he makes it. I have a feeling he wouldn't want to face his buddies after the licking he took and after what he tried to do to Lacey."

"You're probably right. I'll meet you at the creek in an hour. And thanks again for what you done."

John shook hands with Coy and took Lacey by the elbow to lead her out.

She smiled weakly at Coy. "Yes, thank you, Coy for everything," she said as John guided her into the night.

20

"**N**ow, that damn tipple fire didn't start from no slag heap, Myles. I will admit to that much. That slag heap's been burning for years, and it ain't never done nothing but stink up the place. Besides, it's too far away to catch the tipple."

"I know that Barney. I just had to find out from you. You think some of your men did it?" Myles Horton asked calmly, nodding his head.

John was amazed that Myles could remain so unruffled in the storm of Barney's anger. John had been through it already with Barney when they had first heard that union men were being blamed for the fire. Myles Horton had driven in from Monteagle at Barney's request. Horton was from a place called the Highlander Folk School. Myles said they taught ordinary people how to handle labor strikes. A lot of folks around there thought they were a bunch of Communists and didn't want anything to do with them. Barney had told John it didn't matter as long as it helped the union.

"Well, hell. What if it was Myles? We have tried and tried to arbitrate this strike, and the company won't even talk to the union. You know Doctor Homer Watkins? He's a fine man out of Nashville. He's done a lot to help feed folks, and get the word out about what things is like here. He offered to arbitrate the strike and the company wouldn't even let him in to talk. Men get desperate when they see their kids a-starving."

"I'm on your side Barney, but you know the sheriff's got a petition in to the governor to bring in the National Guard."

"Myles, some folks think that might make things better for the union," John spoke up. "They're supposed to protect everybody. Be neutral."

"I wish it worked that way, John. You see the government usually sees the union as the troublemakers. Whatever the company does is just to protect itself against the union. All the shooting that's been going on here, the fans that were blown up inside the mines and now this tipple burning have all been blamed on the strikers. They company is just trying to protect its property."

"You know that no striker could have blown up those fans. They would have had to crawl fifty yards inside the mine to the fans after they got past the mine guards outside. Them guards is so testy, they would of shot a rat trying to get into that mine shaft."

"I know that, John. You have to understand how it looks to the outside. They only have the company's word on what happened."

John slumped against the straight-backed chair in Barney's kitchen, feeling once again overwhelmed by the forces that seemed to be crushing them from all sides. Barney moved about the room hitting one fist against his other palm.

"Barney!" Myles almost shouted. "It is important you tell me everything you know about the illegal practices of the company."

Barney looked up as though he wasn't sure whether he was prepared to share what he had discovered. "You'll make sure this gets in the paper?"

"I'll do everything I can. You can count on that." Myles took out a pad of paper and a pen and laid them on the table.

Reaching into his denim jacket pocket, Barney pulled out a bundle of crumpled papers and spread them on the table before Myles. He had obviously decided to trust Myles. "Here's the workslips for twelve different miners. Some of them are for the year before we went on strike when the men didn't hardly make enough to buy powder so they could work. You can see it shows the items that the company deducted from the miner's pay, rent, lights, powder, and funeral fund. That's standard stuff. A miner always has to pay for his own powder, carbide, and tools. Whatever supplies it takes to get the job done.

Nothing unusual about that. Now, look right here. They've scratched through whatever the slip had printed on it and wrote in *Banner*. That's the *Nashville Banner*. They were charging us eighty cents for a damn newspaper when we had men going hungry."

"Did these men ask to have a newspaper?"

"Hell, no! They didn't ask. The point is they never got it. Not a one of these men ever laid eyes on a *Nashville Banner* the whole time the company was deducting it from their pay."

"That's real interesting, Barney. I think we might have us a court case here. You put those workslips in a safe place. Don't be carrying them around. They could jump you any time, and we wouldn't have a shred of evidence left. Yeah, we might have us something here. I'll check the records at the Banner to see if they ever had orders for that many papers for the Fentress Coal and Coke Company. What else have you got? You said something earlier about the Red Cross."

Barney sat down in the kitchen chair and pulled it up close to Myles. He was obviously excited to have someone who would listen to his side. John envied his doggedness. To Barney the strike was not something to be endured until it was won or lost. It was his reason for living.

John felt guilty because he was tired. He hated the hunger, the violence and the constant fear. He just wanted a chance to work and to build some kind of life. Of course, that was what Barney wanted for all of them. He had been thinking, though, that might not be possible in Wilder no matter how much he, or Barney or anyone else wanted it. Of course, it was just this thing with Lacey. It had shaken him real bad.

She had nearly been killed, and he hadn't even been there. If Coy hadn't known about Sawyer, she probably would be dead now. He hated to admit it, but it bothered him more than a little that it had been Coy who had saved Lacey's life. Lacey might see him differently if it had been him. Coy didn't even have anything at stake in this strike, and he had risked his life twice. He owed Coy a lot; there was no doubt about that. It was right small of him to be jealous. Maybe, it was just that things seemed to be getting out of hand, racing out of control with no way to know how bad it was going to get before it stopped, or if it was ever going to stop. He wanted to be strong enough to hold out. He supposed there was no way of knowing till it happened.

"We ain't getting no relief!" Barney shouted angrily. He jumped up from his seat, knocking over his chair, but he didn't even stoop to pick it up. He paced the room nervously. Myles waited patiently. Barney looked at John.

"The thing is Myles," John said, watching Barney out of the corner of his eye. "They been giving the stuff to the scabs. They sent stuff in to give to the strikers, but the people that run the Red Cross here is all company people. They're mostly the wives of company men."

"That shouldn't be too hard to correct. The Red Cross won't like hearing about such as that going on."

"If that bothers 'em, then see how they like this," Barney interjected. "Some of the womenfolk couldn't go up to the aid station to get clothes for their babies 'cause they didn't have no shoes to wear. They had to wait till a neighbor got back to borrow a pair of shoes. I wonder if they noticed that every woman that showed up there had on the same pair of shoes."

"Is any relief getting out to the union men?"

"Some, but it's not near enough to keep folks fed. They's pellagra all over camp. It's getting colder and pretty soon the snows will set in. You can't hardly get nothing over this mountain in the wintertime, and there won't be no way of getting things in or out. There ain't been no newspapers in the holler since the strike. Ain't no way to get the word out about how bad it is here except by word of mouth. That's why we're counting on you Myles."

"They can't stop me from talking to the newspaper. I know the law, Barney. That's one thing they don't have a right to do."

"They don't pay no attention to the law. If they want to stop you, they'll find a way. They can at least make you wish you'd never heard of Wilder."

"I appreciate the concern, Barney, but I'm not worried about me. It's you that needs to be careful. You could be in real danger."

"You men want something to eat?" Barney asked changing the subject. "I think we got some cornbread and molasses here."

Barney searched around the warming oven and found a few scraps of day old cornbread. John knew it was probably the only food left in the house, but he couldn't stop Barney from giving away every bite of food he came across, even when his own family was hungry. Barney always figured the other guy needed it more. The Potter children had long since joined their mother up north, but Barney had children of his own to feed.

"My wife ain't here Myles, or I'd have her fix you something decent."

"I appreciate that, Barney. The truth is I ate already on the ride over here. I'm not a bit hungry."

"Are you sure? John?"

Both men shook their heads.

"Myles, what did you mean Barney could be in real danger?" John asked. Barney shot him a look of disgust, but John ignored him.

"You have to know, John, that what Barney is doing doesn't exactly make him popular with the company."

"John knows that Myles," Barney said. "They damn near beat him to death last month."

"It's more than that, ain't it, Myles?" John asked.

"There are rumors. Several people have heard a bunch of those hired thugs the company has working for them bragging."

"Bragging about what, Myles?"

"That they're going to get Barney."

"Oh, hell! Myles, what did you think they would say? That they wanted to make me president of the company? They're just trying to scare me off."

"I checked into the background of some of these men, Barney, and they're nothing but criminals and hired guns. Some of these men brag about having killed men. You're finding out too much about the company. They are bound to try to shut you up somehow. Besides they know you are the backbone of this union."

"I won't give up, Myles. I can't let them know they've got me worried. These men count on me. If I was to tuck tail and run, what do you think would happen to this union? Too many good men have suffered too much for me to worry about my own hide at this point. I knew going into this that it was dangerous."

"I'm not asking you to give up. I respect what you are trying to do here, or I wouldn't be here. I'm asking you to be careful. Watch your back."

"What exactly did you hear, Myles?" John asked.

Myles looked at John for a long moment. A frown sliced his forehead, and a sigh eased out of him like a whisper. "They're going to try to kill him, John. They never expected the union to hold out this long. I think they know the men are holding on because of Barney's leadership. I'm pretty sure they think the only way to stop the strike is to kill Barney."

John looked at Barney. The look on his face said that he already knew, and it didn't make any difference.

"John, I hate you have to walk me all the way over to Aunt Aubrey's," Lacey said.

"I'm glad to do it, Lacey."

"Well, you know how Ma is when she takes a notion for something. With Will leaving tomorrow, Ma decides to take to her bed. Says she knows she won't never live to see baby Rachel again. She remembered how Aunt Aubrey used to keep some ginseng root all the time. Nothing would do, but I run up there and get some," Lacey said apologetically.

"Really, it's good to get outside. I get the fidgets with no work to keep me busy and in the house all the time."

"I'm glad then."

They walked on, veering off the main road to Davidson and up a footpath that led through a stand of pines. Aunt Aubrey lived up a holler on the edge of a hillside on just enough flat land to hold her tiny house. She was as old as the holler, and everyone called her Aunt Aubrey. It was a dreary, overcast day without a hint of sun trying to peek through. John thought it fit his mood after the morning meeting with Myles Horton.

Lacey walked ahead of him on the path. The color was rising in Lacey's cheeks, and the mist was curling the loose hairs around her forehead. She was so beautiful as she turned around to speak that he could only stare at her. "Are you all right, John?" she asked.

"I'm fine. I just hope you don't catch you're death out here."

"John, you sounded just like your mother."

John could feel himself grow warm all over. He hated himself for sounding so stupid.

"I didn't mean it that way, John. Your mother fusses over me like I was one of her own."

"Yeah, well. . . I just worry more now about well. . . anything happening to you since the thing with Sawyer."

Lacey looked like he had struck her in the face, recoiling at the mention of Sawyer's name. He didn't know why he had said it. Of course, she was trying to put it out of her mind and he wasn't helping things. He couldn't put it out of his mind, he knew that much.

They had gone back after dark, just him and Coy and found Sawyer. He had moaned and cried out for help when they had picked him up and tossed him into the back of the wagon. They had carried him a good ten miles from Wilder before they left him by the side of the road, tossing his stuff out after him. John thought maybe he should have felt some regret about leaving him there, but it was exactly what Sawyer had done to him. An eye for an eye? It had to be done. He never wanted to think about it again, but he knew that he always would. He would never bring up Sawyer's name again. They walked on in silence, not sure which way to take the conversation.

"You know Ben begged to come along," Lacey said tentatively.

"Why didn't you tell him to come on? You know he's always welcome."

"He's just so pale and thin, now. He freezes all the time, even in the house. I worry about him. A lot of folks are getting pneumonia. He chafes at me keeping him in so much, though."

"It's hard on a boy his age to stay put. He don't understand what's going on. This strike is hard enough on grown ups who are fighting for something they believe in. Younguns don't have no say. They just have to go along."

"He's really not one to complain. I reckon that hurts me even more."

"I'm thinking this strike can't go on much longer."

"What makes you say that?"

John didn't want to tell her about the death threats on Barney Graham or about the petition in to the governor to call in the National Guard. "Oh, I just feel like something will bring it to a head soon."

"What do you thinks going to happen, John?"

Just then a noise from behind made them both turn with a start. Coy stepped out of the trees onto the path. John had the gun drawn before he had time to think. Coy put his hands up palms out.

"Hold on there, John. It's just me."

Lacey came around him on the path. She rushed toward Coy and stopped herself in mid-stride. "John," she stammered. "I was afraid you would shoot him."

"It's ok, Lacey," Coy laughed. "I should of made myself known."

John stared at them. "Sorry, Coy," he apologized, but he was still trying to make sense of Lacey running toward Coy that way.

"It's all right," Coy said, turning to Lacey. "It's the smart thing to do nowadays. If it hadn't of been me you woulda been glad he had a gun."

"He could have shot you," Lacey answered.

John noticed that there was real fear in her voice. Coy and Lacey exchanged a look that made his heart stop.

"John," Coy said, breaking his attention away from Lacey. "I tried to catch you before you left your house. They're getting ready to haul out the first load of coal from the Wilder mines."

"I knew it would be any day now. They've had the cars loaded, just waiting."

"We got to hurry. They could be pulling out right now."

"Coy, if they're loaded and rolling, there ain't nothing we can do to stop them."

"It's what they're planning to do that we have to stop."

"What are you talking about?"

"The guards are going to let the train go on through, and then they are planning on blowing the trestle and make it look like the strikers did it."

"That sounds right stupid. Why would the strikers want to blow the trestle after the coal goes out?"

"They wouldn't, but the guards figure won't nobody outside Wilder know the difference."

"Where's it going to be?"

"They're setting the charges about two miles up from here."

"Let me round up some men and we will head up that way."

"There ain't time."

"Well, at least let me get Lacey back home. I can't leave her here."

"I'm telling you it could go any minute."

"I'll go with you," Lacey spoke up

"You can't do that. It's too dangerous," John said.

"I want to go with you. I promise I won't be no trouble. I'll stay back out of the way."

John looked at Coy, who was fidgeting nervously with the urgency of his mission. He reluctantly gave in. "We'll find a safe place to leave you and if anything goes wrong," he said taking Lacey by the shoulders and looking her in the eye, "run and don't stop until you get home. Understand?"

Lacey nodded.

They headed out at a fast pace straight through the woods and over a small ridge to the tracks. "We'll stay in the woods and follow the tracks till we see something," John said. "It's a mile and a half to the first trestle but keep an eye out for guards."

"You take the lead. You know this place better than me," Coy said.

"Do you have a gun?"

Coy patted his jacket in answer.

They walked in silence. John glanced back occasionally to make sure Lacey was keeping up. He hated the idea of bringing her along. There was no telling what might happen if they ran into armed thugs, but he couldn't just leave her there on the trail to walk home alone, not after what had happened to her already. Maybe she was safer with him.

They crested a low ridgeline and were standing looking at the trestle before they realized it. Suddenly, they heard voices from under the trestle. Coy grabbed Lacey's hand and pulled her back behind the shelter of a thicket of trees. They lay on their bellies peering over the ridge. John strained to hear what the men were saying, but it was impossible. "I'm going to go scout around. See if I can't find out how many of them there are."

"John, if they see you they won't hesitate to shoot you," Coy said

"I know."

"And they'll say they caught you setting charges under the trestle."

"Well, you can't go for sure and let them find out who's been spying on the company."

"Listen," Lacey whispered.

Coy looked at John. "A train."

They waited helplessly as the train drew nearer. Finally, it was upon them whooshing and clanging, overpowering them with its noise. And then it was gone, taking its sound with it. They stood in the echoing silence and watched as two men climbed the ridge on the other side and disappeared

"They've lit the fuses," John said. The horror of the realization propelled him over the ridgeline and toward the trestle in a desperate effort to stop the charges from going off, his heart pumping fiercely from the effort and the fear. The blood roared in his ears like the sound of the train that had just passed as he willed his legs to push him faster. He heard someone coming up behind him and could only hope that it was Coy.

The first shock wave hit him just as he heard someone scream, "Coy! No don't go." The second wave sent him hurling backwards, head over heals and smashed his face into the rocks and dirt. He thought he could feel blood running from his nose and soaking the ground beneath him, but when he tried to move his hand up to feel his face the earth swallowed him up.

"John. John," someone called from faraway. The voice sounded familiar

"John, can you hear me?" Coy asked.

"John, it's me Lacey."

He was coming back to them. He could feel himself headed toward the sounds of their voices, and he remembered now heading down the hill toward the trestle when the dynamite had exploded. His body had been hurled through the air, spinning over and over until it hit the ground. He felt strange, but he wasn't sure what was wrong. He didn't think that anything was broken.

Then he opened his eyes, and Coy and Lacey were kneeling over him. Suddenly, it hit him like the blast of the second charge. As he had been running toward the trestle, he had heard Lacey calling after Coy. She had tried to stop Coy from being hurt. She hadn't called his name. She had called Coy's. What a fool he had been to think that Coy had done all of this for nothing. He had wondered why a man like Coy would risk his life to spy on a company when he hated mining, and hated Wilder. He was in love with Lacey. And she was in love with him.

For how long? he wondered. He tried to think back to all the signs he must have missed. That day at the revival when they had encountered Coy by the river, she had been like a frightened deer when he spoke to her. And that night at the movies when she had searched the crowd looking for someone, she had been looking for Coy. That night he had found her at Seth's cabin, he hadn't thought about how strange it was that he should take her there. He had been too glad to find her safe.

And today when Coy had appeared on the trail, Lacey had almost thrown herself into his arms.

"John, we got to get out of here," Coy urged. "They'll have every guard in town up here soon."

"I'm all right," John said pulling himself to his feet. His knees buckled under him.

"Here, put one arm around me," Lacey said. "And one around Coy."

John started to draw back but found he was too weak to stand. Finally, he gave in helplessly and allowed them to carry him down the hill.

21

The tiny flame from the coal embers added only a little light to the gloom of a cold February day. Coy and Lacey lay on a quilt in front of the fireplace, the quilt wrapped around them. Lacey rested her head on his arm while her thoughts drifted, lost in the moment. They had been meeting like this for months every time she could get away. She had risked everything to be with him, and for the time they were together, it was worth it. She knew the torment would come later, but she brushed aside the thought as Coy kissed the back of her neck.

"Did you have any trouble getting here?"

He always asked the question and she always lied. "Not much. There's a National Guardsmen on every foot of railroad track, so I took to the woods."

"Ah, they're not so bad. Some of those guys are younger'n I am. I seen some of them giving candy to some of the striker's younguns. I don't think they'd harm a woman."

She didn't tell him about the things they yelled at her if they saw her walking along. The names they called her and the whistling. Once a bunch of them had ridden over the ridge on their horses, surprising her. She had huddled in a clump of bushes breathing like a frightened rabbit. The memory made her shiver.

"Are you cold? I can put more coal on the grate."

She shook her head but pressed her body closer to his. It made her feel guilty that they lay warm by the fire. Coy had all the coal he wanted. He got it from the company. At home, they had burned the wood from their shed to keep warm, and now that that was gone, they had been ripping boards from the back porch. Some days when it was bitter cold and ice formed on the insides of all the windows, they stayed huddled in bed all day. Ben had developed a cough that had hung on for months, and he had stopped asking to go with her when she went out. As his eyes followed her around the room before she left, she found herself making up excuses for her leaving.

She had not told him about meeting Coy nor tried to explain to him what Coy was doing. In the first place, she felt it was too dangerous for anyone else to know. And then, she wasn't sure Ben would believe it. His trust in Coy had been too shattered. No matter what Coy thought, the National Guard hadn't made things easier as some folks had hoped. They just represented another power over the strikers and were there to protect company property, not striking miners. They had been called in the day after the trestle had blown back in November.

The strikers had been blamed, just as John knew they would be. Barney Graham had told some people from the *Knoxville News Sentinel* that it didn't make sense for the union to blow up that trestle after the coal had gone out, but it hadn't made any difference. The militia had set up headquarters in a company house, and all their men were being quartered in company houses. There seemed to be more guards in town now than there were people to guard, and trestles were still being blown up, although they had not yet arrested one person for it.

"Wait right here. I got something for you," Coy said.

He jumped up and padded naked into the kitchen, yelping each time his feet touched the cold floor. His skin was still dark even in the winter, and muscles rippled in his thighs as he walked. Lacey looked down at her own pale flesh. The bones jutted from her hips and her ribs were covered by the thinnest of membranes. She wondered how he could bear to touch her, and yet, he seemed to never tire of her. Each time they met, he held her like she was a tiny flame he was protecting from the wind.

He had become for her everything that she had prayed for that day on Buck Rock. He lifted her up away from all those things that had always been her life, and he gave her relief from the never-ending need to care for the lives of her family. For the time they were together there was only Coy. He would not allow her to talk about Wilder or the strike but kept her entertained with stories of far off places like California. She could only imagine if they were true or things he made up for her amusement. She knew that Coy was not without flaws, and sometimes she thought he enjoyed the strike too much and played it like a game. She couldn't help but wish that he would talk about the future so she could be sure that she was part of his plans, for she had broken every rule and betrayed every value to be with him. She didn't like herself for it, and she felt overwhelmed by the thought of hurting so many people, of losing them. It was only when they were together that she felt she could endure any punishment God saw fit to send her, if they could just stop time and be together.

She could hear Coy rattling around in the kitchen, poking wood into the cookstove and banging the pots around. When he came back into the room, he was carrying something wrapped in a kitchen towel, and laid it before her like a treasure. She knew he loved doing this. Each time they met, he brought her something, presenting it to her like she was a queen. It never failed to leave her breathless, even from the first day when he had given her the hawk he had been carving by the creekbed. Slowly he unfolded the corners of the towel, revealing six perfect tea cakes sprinkled on top with sugar. Lacey drew in her breath with surprise. "Where did you get these?"

"You'd be amazed what some of them womenfolk will do when there's fresh meat in town. You should see some of them young girls making eyes at them National Guardsmen, bringing 'em cookies and hanging around."

"Scabs and company women," Lacey said, balking at his gift.

"So we'll have the last laugh! They ended up in the belly of a union woman."

That struck Lacey as really funny, and she grabbed a tea cake with both hands and took a huge bite. Coy mimicked her, stuffing nearly a whole cake in his mouth at once. "Wait! Hold on a minute," Coy said his mouth full.

He jumped up and went into the kitchen, coming back with a steaming cup of black coffee. Gently he pressed it to Lacey's lips, and she sipped the hot, potent liquid. It ran warm and delicious through what seemed like the whole length of her body. The combination of coffee and sugar made her lightheaded and giddy. "Coy this is too wicked," she said, but found herself giggling out of control as she said it.

"Yeah, I think that's what I like most about it. Sitting up here eating their tea cakes and drinking their coffee. You and me Lacey. We'll fool them all. They think they know us so well, but we're neither one what we seem. And they will never ever know that will they?"

Coy seemed lost in a dream world, a place where he had defied the odds and won. She wondered if that was what he loved about her. Their falling in love and being together had been against all odds. She was the daughter of a respected man in Wilder. She was engaged to another miner, a union man, an engagement Coy had never asked her to break. He spied on the company, living off money he won from gambling with gun thugs and guardsmen, and even their meetings were a dangerous gamble. She was something he was not supposed to have but did. If her family found out about them, she'd be kicked out of the house, and if the company found out about Coy working with the union, he'd most likely be killed. When he looked at her again, it was with eyes so hungry she felt swallowed up, lost in his voracious need. Then he was Coy again, licking crumbs from the corner of her mouth and pressing his perfect lips to hers.

It was late afternoon before they finally got dressed. Lacey slipped her dress over her head, and Coy buttoned it for her like a child being dressed for school. This was the time she hated most. It would be a week at least before she would be able to find an excuse to see him again. Sometimes, she and John would come up, when John needed to see Coy about some union business and didn't want anyone to suspect anything. She was uncomfortable coming with John and always swore she would never do it again. She didn't like using him that way, and sometimes she even felt that he had to know about them. But maybe what she thought she saw reflected in his eyes was just her own guilt.

Coy walked Lacey to the back door. "I can walk down with you as far as the oak tree."

"No. There's no point taking the chance."

"Lacey, before you go. I have to tell you something."

"What is it Coy?"

"I have to go away for a while."

The blood rushed from Lacey's head, and she thought she might faint.

"I don't want to go, but Ellen wrote last week to say that Seth was real bad sick. She wants me to come up there for a visit. Says he talks about me all the time."

"Oh," Lacey said. "I hate to hear Seth's sick." Actually, she felt relief that Coy's reason for leaving was so believable. "I know you think a lot of him."

"That's just it. I wouldn't go for nothing less, but Ellen feels like he might not make it through."

"How long do you think you may be gone?" She could feel Coy hesitate.

"Maybe a month."

She pressed her head to his chest. He had said a month. Just a month. Why did she feel like that was an eternity? A lifetime. She looked up at his face so handsome in the afternoon light and knew the answer. When he was not with her, she could never believe that he really existed and that she would ever see him again. It was only when they were together that she could really be sure. Tears forced themselves out the corners of her eyes.

"Hey, let's not have that!" Coy said, holding her chin in his hand and grinning down at her. "I'll be back before the redbuds bloom. I promise you that. We'll head up to Buck Rock first thing."

The thought brought a smile to her lips. She would hope for an early spring. Coy kissed her gently and then more fiercely as they held on to each other as though their lives depended on it.

Suddenly, a noise at the back door brought them back to earth. They pulled away from each other and turned to look. Lacey's eyes met Ben's as he stared at her in disbelief. She started to call out to him, but she could only watch as he turned and ran back down the hollow.

_____ *22* _____

"Teacher Tells Church of Arrest At Wilder," Barney read out loud. "Ain't that Myles a case! He's not about to let this thing rest. This is from a piece they wrote in the *Knoxville News Sentinel*."

"What all does he say about the arrest?" John asked. He pressed his hands closer to the small stove that warmed the general store where the aid station had been set up. He felt chilled to the bone from being out all day on the aid truck. They had received a truckload of clothes collected by Vanderbilt University in Nashville, and some of the students had even come over to help give out the clothes. It was amazing to him that so many people he had never met could care what happened in a little mining camp like Wilder. Barney was the one that had always believed that people would care if they could just get the word out.

"Well, first he says that the press has been unfair to the miners by just giving the operators' side and that the strikebreakers was the ones that stood to benefit. And let's see . . . that the evidence pointed to the fact that men in the employment of the companies had blown up the bridges. Horton says the charge on which he was arrested was 'obtaining evidence of this kind to teach in his school.'" Barney chuckled as he read the charges.

"I heard they tucked tail and ran when Colonel Boyd come in and found out what they'd done," John said laughing.

Barney and he could laugh at the arrest now, but John was sure had Barney known about it at the time he would have charged in to try to save Myles. There was no telling what would have happened, for most of the National Guard troops stationed there were just boys with high-powered rifles looking for something to happen. For many of them, it was their first taste of power, freedom and alcohol. They weren't even sure who Myles Horton was, but he had been seen in the company of union officials. He had been held all night at the hotel and released unharmed the next morning when Colonel Boyd had returned to find out what had happened in his absence.

"They didn't have a reason in the world to hold him, but Boyd was the only one had enough sense to know that. They just knew that he had been coming in and out of here bringing food and clothes and talking to the strikers."

"You think they knew he was responsible for stopping the company from evicting eighteen striking miners?"

"I don't know. Boyd probably did, but he also knew that Myles did it strictly legal. By the book."

"What about the two cases we got in court right now?"

"There's a right smart on that in this newspaper piece from the *News-Sentinel*. One of the cases has to do with the bath house. Seems there was a law passed back in 1921 that says the company is supposed to furnish a bath house for every fifty miners at no charge."

"Along the last, they was charging us $1.25 a month."

"Well, it used to be more than that. I remember when they was taking out a $1.75. I reckon they just got plumb ashamed of themselves," Barney said, looking over the top of the paper he held with a grin. "The other case is about them making miners buy the *Nashville Banner*."

"I bet they never thought when they was handing out them work slips like it was the law that they would someday be used against them."

"These cases ain't hardly more than a match between a giant's toes, I reckon, but with enough of them we can have the old guy kicking and screaming, can't we John?"

John smiled and nodded his agreement. He wished he cared how it came out. The truth was nowadays, he was just going through the motions of being interested. To Barney he was the same hard working, union man, but inside the fire was gone. He looked out at the two Guardsmen standing on the porch. As they passed a pint of whiskey between them, he thought about asking them for a swig. He looked over in the corner where his mother stood going through the last of the boxes of clothes that had not been given out that day. She was separating them by size and folding them neatly in stacks. Looking up, she stopped to stretch, her hands planted firmly on her hips, her eyes inspecting him closely. He had caught her doing that a lot lately. He squirmed under the scrutiny, and his chair almost tipped over when he stood up suddenly. Barney looked up from his paper surprised. "I think I'll get out for a while. Walk over to Lacey's."

"I would have thought you had had enough of being out after standing in the back of that truck all day and it colder than Jack Frost," his mother declared.

"I reckon it ain't never too cold for courting, Cora. Ain't that right, John?" Barney asked.

John just wanted to escape without any more questioning, but he thought he ought to answer Barney. "It'd have to get a right smart colder than it did today."

Barney laughed and slapped his knee with the paper in his hand. John turned to go without looking at his mother.

"You be careful, John," Cora called to his backside as he closed the door.

John walked between the Guardsmen and down the steps. They had parted making room for him to get by without comment, and he was relieved to be on his way. There was still plenty of daylight left, but the cold wind cut through him in seconds, and his right knee ached with the freezing temperatures. It had hurt since the day the trestle had blown up and he had been thrown to the ground on a pile of rocks. *Guess I've probably chipped a bone,* he thought. When the pain was at its worst, he walked with a slight limp.

The pain had become a constant reminder of that day. Not that he needed one. The memory of it never left him. He hadn't been hurt that badly. The wind had been knocked out of him, and he had a few scratches and bruises, but when he came to himself his whole world had crumbled.

He could still hear Lacey's voice calling "Coy, Coy." He wasn't sure why that alone had told the tale, but it had. Since then he had pieced a lot of things together. It was clear to him now why Lacey had agreed to marry him: Coy had left town. Maybe they had had a fight, and she probably thought he wasn't coming back and had done it out of spite. It had been terrible knowing that she didn't love him, but he had had hope. Knowing that she loved someone else was a torment he could hardly bear. And yet, he was afraid to confront her with the truth. Instead, he resorted to behavior that disgusted him. He often took her with him when he met Coy. Sometimes they went to Coy's place to talk, and he would watch them for any sign that would prove his suspicions. Did they look too long at each other? Did they steal glances at each other or brush too close when they passed? He hated himself for it, but still he did it.

He had been so lost in thought that he was standing on the Conners' front porch when he came to himself. It was so quiet and dark inside he wasn't sure anyone was at home, but he knocked softly and waited. What was he doing there anyway? Lacey must be laughing at him for being such a pathetic fool, and that was what he was for sure. He just couldn't give her up, not until she told him to straight to his face. He couldn't tell Barney, but he was looking into a program for miners and sawmill workers that were out of work. President Roosevelt was starting a program in Cumberland County to give land to people just like him that were out of work. It was a chance to build your own house and then farm the land. He didn't know much about farming, but a piece of land would be a prize he could offer Lacey. Hadn't he promised her the biggest garden spot he could find?

The door opened a fraction, and Frank peered through the crack until he could decide who was there. "John, boy. Good to see you. Come in."

John noticed that he was whispering and wondered if Annie was having another one of her attacks. "I hope it's no bother. I just come by to see Lacey."

"Well, John. I don't know if I can get her out here. She won't leave Ben's side."

"What's the matter, Frank? Is Ben sick?"

Frank nodded.

"What is it?"

"Pneumonia fever."

"Is it bad?"

"You can't tell with these things. Last time he pulled out of it fine. This time he's a lot weaker. Lacey ain't left his side day and night. I ain't never seen her like this. Them two's always been close."

"Reckon she'd let me in to see him?"

Frank shrugged his shoulders and pointed to the room. John stopped at the door and listened, but he could hear nothing. He knocked softly, and when no answer came, he gently opened the door.

Ben lay so lifeless on the bed that John could not be sure he wasn't already dead. Lacey knelt by the bed, her face pressed to Ben's hand. She seemed to be whispering something over and over but John could not make it out. "Lacey, it's me John."

He didn't think she had heard him until slowly she raised her head and looked at him. His breath caught in his throat when he saw her pale skin and the deep circles under her eyes, which were shining wildly like an animal caught in a snare. He had seen a fox like that once. It was caught in a barbed wire fence, fur and flesh all matted together, and it had been driven mad by pain and fear. Even after he had unmatted the hair and flesh and set it free, the animal had just lain there paralyzed by its own fear, as though it had already accepted death and didn't know how to handle having its life handed back to it. Finally, it had hobbled off with the look of terror still in its eyes. It chilled him for Lacey to look at him the same way the fox had looked at him, but he wanted to go to her. When he took a step, she pulled back in fear. "Lacey it's me. Are you all right? Let me help you."

Just then he saw Ben stir, and Lacey held tighter to his hand as if to hold his back from death. "Lacey, let me help you. You need to get some rest, or you'll be sick, too. I'll look after him while you sleep."

She didn't speak, but her eyes followed him as he moved closer to the bed. They widened as he reached out and touched Ben on the forehead. He didn't have a high fever but his breathing was troubled.

"How long has he been like this, Lacey?"

She looked at him with a puzzled expression, and he realized she didn't know how much time had passed.

Finally she spoke. "It's come again, John. His lungs never were strong after that last time."

"He's stronger than you think, Lacey."

"No, this is all my fault. I'm the cause of this. I should of took better care of him. You know I always looked after him."

She shook her head in despair and tears poured from her eyes. "I did this to him," she whispered.

"Has he eaten anything?" John asked to distract her.

The look on her face told him that there was nothing in the house to eat. "Why don't you come out for a while, Lacey? You need to keep up your own strength if you're going to look after Ben." She looked stricken by the thought of leaving. "All right Lacey. I'm leaving for a little while. I'll be back soon, and I'll stay with you until he's better. If you don't want me to help that's all right, but I'm going to be right out here if you need me."

She didn't look at him as he left. He backed out of the room and closed the door. Frank met him outside.

"She wouldn't come out, would she, son? I told you she wouldn't budge."

John didn't ask if the doctor had been there. He knew there wasn't money. "I'm worried about her. She's blaming herself for this."

"Well, Lacey was keeping Ben in the house, not letting him go out 'cause he had a cough and he don't have no coat. One day when she wasn't here, he took off and stayed gone two or three hours. The next day he took sick. I reckon she figures if she had been here, he wouldn't have gone out."

John didn't ask why one of them hadn't kept a closer eye on him. It probably hadn't occurred to them. Lacey was right. She had always watched out for Ben. Annie sat in a rocker by the coal grate, a quilt wrapped around her shoulders. There was no fire in the grate, but she had pulled her chair close as though it was still possible to get some heat from it. The room was silent except for the ticking of the clock on the mantel.

"John," Annie called.

"Yes, ma'am."

"I wish you could get Lacey out here. I need her to fix me some of my heart tonic. My heart is a bothering me something awful. It's just a-fluttering like a hummingbird. You can might near see it beating through my clothes. Frank can tell you. He felt it. I said, 'Frank put your hand right here on my chest.' Tell him, Frank."

"Yes, Annie," Frank answered patiently.

"Frank, I have to go take care of some things, and then I'll be back to see about Lacey."

Frank nodded helplessly. John didn't have time to explain why he was leaving. He didn't look back as Frank closed the door behind him.

John waited in total darkness. The frozen ground beneath him made his bones ache, and he wasn't sure how much time had passed. Every sound from the streets had died away, and he was sure that even the guards had gone in on a night like this. Taking the crowbar from his jacket, he wedged between the floor joist and the board that formed part of the commissary floor. He hoped that he had guessed correctly and he was underneath the storeroom.

As soon as he left Lacey's, he had known what he intended to do. He had never stolen anything in his life, but Ben needed to eat. There was nothing wrong with that boy that starvation hadn't brought to half the younguns in Wilder. What he really needed was meat. The only place within twenty-five miles that John could get meat was the commissary. It wasn't like he could go out and kill a rabbit or a squirrel. They had all been hunted out. Any local livestock had been borrowed by the meat committee months ago. What he was really hoping for was a side of bacon or some canned meats.

The wood groaned and creaked under the pressure from the crowbar, and he cringed as the wood splintered. At the very worst, someone would be inside guarding the commissary, and he would be shot dead on the spot. Then again, one of the guards he had seen so often leaning against the porch railing could shoot him in the back as he was trying to get away. He tried to shake off the picture of his body thrown into the air by the impact of the bullets. He didn't want to risk trying to widen the opening by removing another floor board, so he forced his body through the narrow space, straining to pull himself up. The effort and the fear left him breathless.

Pulling his gun from his pocket and holding it cocked and ready, he rested, listening for sounds outside the storeroom door. It was quiet outside, but inside the storeroom he could hear a rustling noise. Laying his gun by his side, he reached into his jacket for a candle. He hoped the noise was mice. It was dangerous to have a light but he had no choice. He couldn't risk fumbling around in the dark knocking things over to find what he wanted. The sudden burst of flame from the match seemed to fill the whole room with a blazing light. A strange noise came from the far corner of the room. His eyes were still blinded by the light, and his instinct was to put out the match and run. Instead, he shielded it with his hand to light the candle. He held his gun in one hand and a candle in the other as he approached the corner. John's approach set off a terrible squawking and flapping of wings that stopped him immediately. Ten feet in front of him sat a crate with two fat, terrified hens. *My God, I'm the fox in the henhouse,* he thought as he dowsed the light and backed off. He waited for the hens to settle back down. They probably had been brought in on the train and somebody would be expecting them for Sunday dinner. He hated to disappoint whoever it was, but he needed them more and, besides, he couldn't have them alerting the whole camp.

As John crawled on his belly toward the crate, he thought about why he was doing this. If he was doing it to impress Lacey, he was glad she couldn't see him now. He slipped his hands into the crate and gently stroked the protesting hens. The thought crossed his mind that if Coy was there, he would probably just walk through the front door, throw the crate on his shoulder, and walk out in front of half the camp. With that thought, John slipped his hands around the hens' throats and quickly squeezed the life out of them, and then stuffed them into a toe sack he had brought with him. Without relighting the candle, he worked from memory to fill the sack with a side of bacon, canned meats, and tins of milk. He had a hard time stuffing the sack through the opening in the floor, and it was a relief to finally drop to the ground alongside his bounty. Despite the cold, he was sweating in the frigid February air. When he peered out into the moonless night, it had just started to snow, and he hurried on before the snow got deep enough to leave tracks.

As he watched Lacey spoon the chicken broth into Ben, John felt proud of himself. His plan had been foolish but he had been so full of himself he had even stopped in his escape long enough to pick up a few chunks of coal for the fire. After all, it was hard to cook a chicken without a fire. He had cut through the woods and headed straight to Lacey's from the commissary. It was dangerous to go straight there, but it was more so to be caught out in the middle of the night with a load of easy-to-identify commissary goods. Frank had let him in without a question, and Lacey had been coaxed away from Ben's side to prepare the food that John assured her was just what he needed to get better.

Finally, Ben swallowed the last of the bowl of broth, and Lacey eased his head back on to the pillow. Turning to John, she gave him such a smile of gratitude, it made his heart turnover in his chest. "Now, you get some rest," he managed to say, and she stood up and let him lead her into Will and Ruby's old room. Lifting her into his arms where he wanted to hold her forever, he laid her gently on the bed. "He's going to be all right, Lacey. I promise you that."

Tears ran from the corners of Lacey eyes, and she seemed to want to speak. However, only a moan escaped her lips. He brushed back her hair with his hand, suddenly aware of how rough they must be, and she took his hand in hers. He sat holding her tiny hand through the dawn, watching her face long after she had fallen asleep. There was sadness in her features even as she rested. It was as though the life had drained out of her as Ben grew stronger. He would stay until she woke up. No, he would stay for as long as Lacey wanted.

23

Lacey sat on the front porch, her knees hugged tight to her chest and her face turned up to the late April sun. She felt lightheaded from the delight of the moment. Ben played on the porch nearby where he had sat for hours constructing a swinging bridge from string and sticks. He tied it between the rungs of the porch and walked it over and over again with his fingers, testing its strength and construction. Never quite satisfied, he constantly adjusted it, retying a string here or replacing a slat there. He was still as "poor as Job's turkey," Lacey thought, but he had made it through the winter. They had all made it through the winter. Things had been quiet in the hollow since February. Folks were getting by somehow, day by day.

Will had written to say he'd finally found work in an auction house loading and unloading trucks. Sometimes he got to hold up the stuff as the auctioneer sold it. It sounded like the very thing for Will. Lacey could picture him swaggering and strutting in front of the folks. Ruby was cleaning house for some rich folks that let her bring Rachel along and they gave her stuff sometimes. Will and Ruby were fixing up their place real nice. Lacey missed them so much; it made her wince at the memory of Will's letter. She missed so many things these days. There had been a time at sixteen when she hadn't realized she had so much to lose.

Ben looked up and grinned a lopsided grin. At least, he had been given back to her. He didn't talk much, lately, to her or to any one. Maybe he wasn't ready to trust her again. Maybe he never would again. She tried to explain to him about Coy, and she had tried to explain why she had lied and deceived him, but it had sounded pretty shallow in the telling. She wanted him to know that Coy had really been spying on the company because he loved them and wanted to help somehow, but as she told him, it hit her what a crazy and dangerous thing Coy had done. *So much like him,* she thought. Word had come by one of the train engineers that Coy would be home in two weeks. She was to meet him on Buck Rock to catch the first redbuds in bloom. He had good news for her.

Frank carried a straight-back chair from the kitchen through the open door and placed it in the spot where his old rocker had been. They had burned the rocker during the winter to heat the house. "It's a fine day, ain't it gal?"

"I was just thinking that Pa," Lacey answered

"Yeah, winter sure is hard on folks."

"Winter is just part of nature, Pa. I wouldn't call what we've been through this winter a natural happening."

"I reckon you are right about that. Nature's got a cruel side, but she can't hold a candle to what folks can do to each other. You are awful young to have to see such ugliness in folks. When you think about it, though, it's just as well to be tempered young. Won't nothing seem as hard in life after this."

Somehow Lacey felt sure that what he was saying was true, but he couldn't know the changes that had taken place inside of her that year. Outside, it had been a year of suffering and starvation and violence. She had lost much of the world she had known since birth. Inside, she had known both deep sorrow and great love, at times sacrificing her values and betraying her loved ones to have it. And she had discovered a part of herself that she both cherished and despised.

She looked up to see John coming up the road. Spring had been good for him, too, for his limp was not as pronounced as it had been. She waved to him, and he acknowledged her with a nod. He came almost every day to check on them and to ask after Ben. She had wanted to tell him it wasn't necessary to come everyday, but she hadn't the heart after all he had done for them and especially for Ben.

"How you doing Frank?" John called as he walked into the yard.

Frank nodded.

"That's a good-looking swinging bridge you got there, Ben. I used to walk one like that when I was a boy and we'd visit my Granny Tate. I believe though, now that I look closer, yours is a whole lot finer bridge."

Ben grinned and went on working. Lacey motioned for John to sit down next to her on the step.

"How's Ben been a-feeling, Lacey?"

"Better every day, John," Lacey answered. "Thanks for asking." It was the same thing she said every day when John asked the same question. It always seemed to satisfy him.

"And how's your ma?"

"About the same."

"Still spending most of her time in bed?"

Lacey nodded. "I try to get her to sit out in the sunshine, but she says she feels too weak to sit up."

"Probably do her good to get outside. Looks like it agrees with you. Your cheeks have a blush on them already."

Lacey put the back of her hand to her cheek and felt the heat. She smiled. "I always forget that it don't take much sun to burn a person after a long winter. I just can't make myself go inside."

"It looks good on you."

John looked at her longingly, like she was the one who had almost died with pneumonia. He seemed to know that she was somehow tied to Ben in ways that he couldn't understand. He knew instinctively that if Ben had died, her life would have somehow gone away with his. Maybe that was why he had struggled so to save Ben. Night after night he had sat up with her, holding Ben as he coughed until he was too weak to cough anymore. Once he even reached down Ben's throat and pulled out the phlegm that threatened to choke him.

"John, what do you hear from Myles Horton?" Frank asked.

They so rarely brought up the strike these days that Lacey looked at her pa. It was as though their resistance was so fragile they dared not talk about it. Many of the miners had gone back to work. She didn't hold it against them, but some folks did, though, and it was turning families against families, even brothers against brothers. Lacey strained to think what John had said about Myles Horton. She had never met the man but

John spoke highly of him as someone who was trying to help the miners.

"He's gone to Nashville to try to convince the governor that they intend to kill Barney Graham."

"Lord, son, if the governor was here he wouldn't have to be convinced. Shorty Green has done bragged about it to everybody in Wilder that would listen."

"Myles took pictures with him of Green holding two guns. Says he has proof that he ain't nothing but a criminal and a murderer."

"You think the governor will listen?"

"Well, Governor McAlister is a new governor. He might be more reasonable than Governor Horton. Still, he's more likely to listen to the company whining 'cause this strike has cost them $75,000 dollars. They claim the strike has driven them into bankruptcy."

"They could have settled this strike for a lot less than $75,000."

"They never expected us to hold out this long. They thought they could break us inside of a month."

"You going to talk Barney into leaving town until this is over?"

"I've tried. He's known for a long time that they intended to kill him, and the men have been trying to get him to move over to Twinton. He walks by them guards every day on his way home from a union meeting just to show 'em."

"He's knows that's what he has to do, son. He knows he's the only thing holding this union together."

"The company knows that too, Frank. That's why they're out to get him."

"So he's going to see it through to the end."

"It appears that way," John said sadly. "And you know the sad part. If we won the strike today, there wouldn't be enough work for all of us. Coal has just bottomed out."

"It'll pick back up, son. Things always do."

"It will be too late for Wilder, Frank. Too many little mines like this opened up when coal was big. Wilder is a dying place."

They sat in silence, stunned by the forces working against them and one man's courage in the face of death.

"It makes a man half ashamed of himself," John spoke softly.

He seemed almost to be speaking to himself. Lacey had never heard such despair in John's voice. "Why John, what are you talking about?"

"I feel like I'm letting Barney down talking like that."

"You don't have nothing to be ashamed of John. You know what you know. Sometimes facing up to it is as brave as a man can get."

"But Barney is willing to die for what he believes in."

"You have risked your life more than once for the union. Are you forgetting the night they almost killed you and Pa? And the time you tried to stop them from blowing up the trestle."

John hung his head between his legs, his hands covered his face.

"I know how much you care for Barney," Lacey said. She put her arms around his hunched shoulders.

"I was afraid. All those times, I was afraid of dying," he whispered.

Lacey heart ached for the pain she knew John was feeling. "You think you should be willing to die for the union?"

John nodded.

"I think Barney is afraid to die, but he's made his mind up to it. I think he decided that a long time ago. Maybe before all of this even started."

"You know, I think you are right," John said. He raised his head to look at Lacey. "He told me early on that he intended to win this one or die trying."

"For some folks there are things tougher than facing death. Sometimes just picking up and carrying on takes a whole lot of courage."

John looked at her as though he wasn't quite convinced. For Lacey, there could be no doubt. Life was the harder choice.

"I want to thank you for the seed 'taters, John."

"Lacey don't thank me. Them come from the Wilder Emergency Relief folks. And them seeds too," John said modestly. The truth was, he had never been as proud of anything. He had carried the small bag of potatoes in and unwrapped them on Lacey's kitchen table like he was delivering gold. Lacey had been so happy, she had laughed with delight and hugged him with pure pleasure. She had thanked him over and over again

"Well, they were a wonder to get," she said.

In her excitement, she took him by the hand as they walked along, glancing at Ben to make sure he was still with them. He tagged along never too far from Lacey, silent and self-absorbed. John watched Lacey smile to herself and breathe in the warm April night air. They were on their way to church, and it was a perfect clear night. John should have been a happy man to have Lacey there by his side doing what they had done so many times before, but he knew something she didn't. Coy was back. He had seen him getting off the train yesterday.

Coy had been unmistakable, tall and lean in his double-breasted serge suit and wide brimmed, felt hat. His time away had served him well. As John stood out of sight watching Coy, he wondered what damage Coy had inflicted on the lives of the folks on the other end of his visit. Wherever he had been, wherever he had dropped in for his latest stay, surely, he had left them wounded, too. Or did he save it all for him? He hated such self-pity, but the sight of Coy so handsome and so self-assured took away any hope he had built up over the last few months. He had meant to confront Coy and have it done but he had ended up by ducking out of sight and keeping Coy's arrival a secret. He had long ago sacrificed his pride for one more day with Lacey.

"Folks are here early tonight," Lacey remarked

"It's the weather. They're tired of being in all winter."

"It's almost like it used to be, John."

He smiled wishing it could be true. John shook hands with the men gathered on the porch. "Howdy, Joe. Good to see ya."

"Yeah, I reckon I should be home watching the house."

"You had trouble?"

"Fired into my place the other night," Harvey Long spoke up.

"We've been expecting them to ride through, again," Joe said.

"Things have been quiet too long, I guess," John speculated.

"We think they're building up to something, if you know what I mean," Harvey said.

John nodded. He knew what Harvey meant. He just didn't know what to do about it. He could hear hymns from inside the church. "We better get in here, men. We'll miss the singing." Taking Lacey by the arm, he guided her into the church. The room was full, and people moved down to make room on the pew for the three of them. They sang "Amazing Grace." John was shy about singing in church but tonight he joined in the familiar words, which gave him solace from the nagging worries.

Something was in the air. John looked at Lacey who sang softly without looking at her hymn book and he watched his ma three rows up singing with relish, putting her heart into every word. Even Frank and Annie were there tonight. John felt a sense of pride standing with all the people who had fought so hard to hold their lives together. They all seemed to know that their being there on this night was somehow a triumph. They has struggled and suffered and they had endured. Now they were going to have their moment there tonight in that song. John sang the words loud and strong: "Amazing grace! How sweet the sound, That saved a wretch like me! I once was lost, but now am found, Was blind, but now I see. 'Twas grace that taught my heart to fear, And Grace my fears relieved; How precious did that grace appear The hour I first believed!"

John looked around the little chapel. They had all believed. They had believed that somehow justice would come from their struggle that their simple wants of work and enough to feed their families could be had if they all stood together. Despite their sacrifices, it had not been enough. They were just a few families standing against a giant company. He supposed they had never really had a chance all along, but somehow, he didn't feel like they had failed, for they had stood together. It had brought out some bad in the best of them and a lot of good in most, and they had helped each other out even in the worst of times. They had shared food, and clothes, and coal, when there had not been enough for their own families, and they had been helped out by folks they had never met who lived hundreds of miles away. Such memories gave the words of the hymn special meaning and he could hear the voices around him join in acknowledging their bond. "Thru' many dangers, toils and snares, I have already come; 'Tis grace hath bro't me safe thus far, And grace will lead me home."

John recognized the sound of gunfire above the singing voices around him. "Nooo!" he screamed. The crowd became silent around him, and then they all turned to look at him. The sound of gunfire seemed to go on forever. "It's Barney," John said at last. "They've killed him." No one questioned how he knew, but he was as certain of it as anything he had ever known in his life.

Lacey put her hand on his shoulder. "Be careful, John. If they're bold enough to shoot Barney Graham in daylight, there's nothing they won't do."

He patted her hand as he brushed it off his shoulder. Men were already rushing out the door and down the hillside toward the center of town. John was met by Joe Morgan and Harvey Long.

"Damn, John," Joe said. "Sounded like a machine gun going off."

"Except, I could hear the sound of a half-dozen different guns," Harvey said breathless from running.

John didn't speak. As they topped the rise, they could see a crowd of people already gathered and several guards had them held off with guns. John didn't see Shorty Green, but the lights of the commissary were ablaze. Although they had shot Barney Graham in the middle of town, with it barely dusk, they had used the lights of the commissary to give them a better chance. Not that they needed it from the sound of all the gunfire.

Anger made John push his way to the front of the crowd. When he reached the guards, they tried to push him back from Barney's body. One of them, Doc Thompson, was a good friend of Shorty Green. He had a machine gun and waved it at John.

"There ain't no use in starting anything, John."

"Let me through, Doc," John asked through gritted teeth. They looked at each other for a full minute, then John pushed by him. He stopped at the sight of Barney's bullet-riddled body sprawled on the ground in front of him. His clothes were torn and soaked in blood. As John knelt over the body, he could see that Barney's head was a mass of gashes, some of them two inches long. On the ground next to him lay the broken pieces from the butt of the gun they had used to beat him with after they had shot him. Running his hand gently down the body as though he could somehow still cause the man pain, he found a gun under Barney's hand. John picked it up. The safety was still on and it was not Barney's gun. They had obviously planted it on him.

He looked up at Doc Thompson with the purest hate he had ever felt toward anyone. "How many of you did it take to bring him down, Doc? Who fired the first shot, Shorty Green? Where is the son-of-a-bitch? Hid out like the low-life skunk he is?"

"I'm warning you, John. Don't cause no trouble. It was self-defense, pure and simple. He had a gun."

"The safety's still on. Besides, it ain't even his gun."

The guard just sneered, unconcerned by such evidence. "Just back away from there now, John. We'll take care of things."

"You already took care of it. How many rounds did you get off from that machine gun while he was coming at you?"

"I didn't have this gun 'til after he was shot. I went into the commissary and got it just before you got here."

"He's a-lying," someone yelled from the crowd.

John started to pick up the body.

Doc brandished the gun at him. "Leave him be."

John thought about picking up the gun next to Barney's body and putting a hole through Thompson. He pictured himself grabbing the machine gun from Thompson's arms and blasting away at the guards, bursting through the commissary door and splattering Shorty Green's brains all over the sacks of flour and meal and bolts of new spring dress prints. The thought gave him great pleasure, but he knew he would be dead before the first round left the chamber. "I'm taking him to Doctor Collins to examine."

"You can take him when I say so. Now, get out of here."

John eased the body to the ground but refused to move. He kept his eyes on the guards, who pranced around but made no move to haul him away. Then he sat down next to the body and waited as the crowd milled about, restless and angry. He could hear occasional mumbled threats of revenge, but no one made a move. As he sat there, John thought about Barney's wife and children and wondered if someone had gone to tell them. He doubted if Barney's wife could even get out of bed to see what they had done to her husband. She had been ill for months with pellagra. John thought, Barney had given away too much food his own family needed. Barney had given his life for the union, and John wondered if the union would be there to take care of his family now.

John looked up to see Doctor Collins standing over him. "Son, lets get this man over to my office where I can examine him."

John nodded numbly, realizing that his legs ached from sitting on the cold ground. He looked at his pocket watch. It was nine o'clock, an hour and a half since Barney had been shot dead in the streets. The guards were finally letting them take the body. Several men filed in past the guards, scooped up Barney's body, and carried it across the street to the doctor's office. John followed silently behind.

"All of you wait out here while I look this man over," Doctor Collins announced to the men gathering outside the office. "I can't think with a roomful of people standing over me."

The men that Barney had led huddled in whispered silence near the office door. *There was nothing the doctor could tell them that they did not already know*, John thought. Barney had held the men together with the shear will of his determination and the company hadn't known how to fight a man who was willing to face anything they handed out to keep alive the simple belief in a fair chance to work and live and raise a family. In the end, the only thing they knew to do was to kill him, and kill him they had. When one bullet would have killed him, they had riddled his body, when one blow to the head would have done the job, they had broken their pistol handles over his head. It was almost like they were afraid that he was more than just a man.

Suddenly, John felt more alone than he had ever been in his life and he turned and walked off into the dark toward home. He didn't need to wait for the doctor's report to know that he had lost the best friend he would ever have.

A thousand people filled the cemetery and spilled out onto the road and hillsides around Highland. John stood alone on a knoll a hundred yards from the mourners. He had come alone to say his piece to Barney away from the crowds and the dignitaries. He squinted into the bright May sunshine to look over the crowd at all the people whom Barney had touched. A thousand people had not been able to stop the death of one man, and now they were here to mourn his loss. The doctor's report said there were ten bullet holes found in the body and four cuts on the head. Several witnesses had seen shots fired from atop the commissary and from a nearby house. There was no doubt in John's mind that Barney had been set up for an ambush. The grand jury was questioning Jack Green, the man they called Shorty, in Jamestown at that very moment. His bond had been set at two thousand dollars.

Some of the men had come to him the previous night to ask him to take over leadership of the union. There were still those who thought the union had a chance to win, but John didn't believe it. Some of them thought that too many people had fought and suffered for the sake of the union to give it all up now, and Barney would want him to carry it through to the end.

"Forgive me, Barney," John whispered. "I know you thought that if a man wasn't willing to die for what he believed in, he didn't really believe it. I believed in the union, Barney. I really did, but we have come to the end. Twenty-six union men have been shot. Men have died on both sides. Families have been torn apart. While folks were blowing up bridges and trestles, destroying property and shooting at one another, we somehow managed to destroy a way of life. I don't think we can bring that back no matter how long we hold out. I thought I would live out my life in Wilder. I never pictured living anyplace else. Now, I know that's not the way it's to be. Barney, I got to move on. Been wrestling with my conscience for some weeks now. Truth is, I know I'm not the man you was, but I hope you won't think less of me for it."

"They's a lot of important folks here to speak at your funeral, Barney. William Turnblazer, President of the UMW District 19 come down. Howard Kester, head of the Wilder Emergency Relief is here. You know they say he run for state senator last year. And there must be a thousand people standing around everywhere they can find a place. They loved you Barney. They all loved you. Won't nobody here ever forget what you done."

John shifted on his feet and twisted his crumpled cap in his hands, wiping the tears from the corners of his eyes with the back of his hand. He stood in silence, not knowing what else to say. He thought that after four days the anger over Barney's killing would have worked itself out, but suddenly he felt it well up again. This time he was surprised to feel it directed at Barney.

"Why didn't you listen Barney? Why couldn't you have been more careful?" John stamped his foot on the ground and threw down his cap in frustration. He dropped to his knees and beat the ground with his fist in silent rage, and then it all passed over him and was gone, leaving nothing but emptiness. Picking up his cap, he put it on, nodding respectfully in salute to the man he had admired so much. "Well, I've said what I come to say. I reckon there's nothing left to say but good-bye, Barney. You always was a standing-up kinda man." Slowly he walked down to join the other mourners.

Joe Morgan, Harvey Long and the others were waiting for him. They were waiting with the coffin for John to come. Silently he picked up one end, and they hoisted it onto their shoulders. Then they carried it from the cemetery in Highland to the place where Barney had been killed and back again. Six hundred people marched two by two in a line that stretched for miles. When a man grew tired of carrying the coffin, another man stepped in to spell him. The parade of mourners lasted well into the afternoon. In the end, after the parade and after the speeches, after the hymns and the tears, there had been nothing left that anyone could do but lower Barney's body into the ground. John stayed until dark to shovel the dirt over Barney's coffin. He stayed long after the last mourner left. It was the least he could do. It was all he had left to give.

24

It was a beautiful spring day. The sun sparkled off the tree tops and reflected the brilliant green of new leaves, and the air carried the fresh, crisp smell of new growth. Lacey breathed it in like a promise. She could almost imagine that it was spring like any other spring. It had the same smell and feel and warmth, but she knew it couldn't be.

The strike had been broken with the death of Barney Graham. Shorty Green, the man accused of the shooting, had gotten off with self-defense. The trial had been a sham. A lot of ugly things had been said about Barney being drunk and starting the fight.

She knew that John had been deeply hurt by the murder and by the way the trial had been handled, and he hadn't come around for days after the funeral. He had refused to talk about it then, and they sat on the porch in silence and let the time tick away. The union men were black-balled from the mines so John wouldn't be going back to work for the Fentress Coal and Coke Company. He would have to leave Wilder. Somewhere inside all of his silence, she knew he was making plans.

Lacey could see Coy coming through the trees a hundred yards before he reached Buck Rock. The white of his shirt flashed in the sunlight, and at one point he stopped and searched the rock for her. When he spotted her, he waved excitedly. Holding her hand up as though testing the wind currents, she waved back shyly, hesitantly. She held her breath knowing that he was running the last twenty yards and that at any second he would be coming up behind her. She turned before she heard a noise, but he was already there, breathless from the climb. The sight of him almost made her knees fold under her. Somehow, she had thought it would be different. She imagined that he wouldn't have the same affect on her after two months.

Coy wore a white dress shirt open at the collar. The sleeves were rolled back to show the dark skin of his arms. His pants and shoes looked fashionable and new, and he had put on a little weight. His time away had served him well. He smiled at her, his hands on his hips trying to catch his breath. He held out a hand to her as though he needed her help. Her thought was that she would not go to him, that she would first off tell him what she had come to say.

Always when they were together, he would not let her speak of the future. He would not allow her to plan or imagine or worry about what the next minute would be like. It was his way to live for the moment and she had accepted it so she could be with him. But she could not accept it any longer. She had made a promise to herself during the long winter as she watched Ben struggling to get well despite the hunger and the cold. The promise grew stronger in her as she watched her pa struggle to hold on to his pride in a world he could no longer control, and as she watched John and the other good people of Wilder grieve for the way of life they had lost. Her promise had been like a thread tying her to all that she had known and had shared. Each person and each event made up another stitch in the fabric until it began to form a pattern. She would not leave until she had said what she had come to say.

Suddenly, he was coming to her smiling his self-assured smile, and she found herself meeting him halfway, stopping so near to him, she could see his heart beating under his shirt. She felt, suddenly shy and awkward in the bright sunlight as he cupped her chin in his hand and raised her head until she was looking into his eyes. He was so handsome, dark and flashing like a storm on a hot August day. She had that old feeling that she had dreamed him up out of her imagination. After all, he had come to her after that day a year ago when she had stood out on Buck Rock and wished for someone to love, someone who would free her from the life that had been set out for her. She had been tired of taking care of so many people, of being responsible for their happiness. She wanted to know what it was like to be carefree and joyful and even wicked.

Lacey wrapped her arms around Coy's neck and he scooped her up off the ground, kissing her face and neck. Her hair was tied back with a ribbon and he untied it with one hand, taking great handfuls of her hair and touching it to his face.

"God, you are so beautiful," he whispered.

She couldn't answer. The warmth and smell and feel of him was such unbearable pleasure it closed off her throat. He carried her to the pine thicket where she and Ben had sat many times and laid her on a bed of pine needles and tenderly undressed her. When he lay beside her naked, she felt like she was in a dream. She knew that nothing she would ever know in life could be as wonderful as the dream of the two of them together in that moment, making love with the fresh smell of pine needles, the sunlight on their bare skin and the shrill cry of the red-tailed hawks circling overhead.

Coy brushed a strand of hair from her face. "I have missed you so much. You are so beautiful. Did I tell you that?"

"You always say that," she said.

"And you never believe me."

Lacey shrugged.

"You can't stop me from saying it."

"I'm so thin and pale," she said, her nakedness making her feel shy and vulnerable in the bright sunshine.

"You have perfect skin," Coy said, sitting up excitedly.

Lacey watched as Coy searched the pockets of his pants. She blushed as the sight of their clothes so carelessly discarded earlier.

"I have the perfect thing for your perfect ivory skin," Coy said smiling triumphantly. Dangling from his fingers was a gold locket.

Lacey drew in her breath in surprise. "Do you like it?" he asked as expectant as a child.

"Oh, Coy. It really is the most beautiful thing I have ever seen."

"Here, let me put it on you."

"No, I couldn't take it. It must have cost a fortune." She blushed, embarrassed by what she had said. It was a sign of all she had been through that her first thought had been how much food the money for the locket would have bought. It struck her that Coy had not asked how they had made it through the winter.

"Only the best for one so beautiful."

She lowered her eyes from his gaze unable to resist his charm. "I don't have anything to put in it."

"Wait, I can take care of that."

She watched as he took out his pocket knife and opened the blade. Gently, he cut a strand of her hair. Then reaching up, he clumsily cut a strand of his own hair. He laid them side beside on his leg. Her hair curled like a garden snake while his lay stiff and coarse like rails of track. She looked on in amazement as he wove the two strands together and coiled them inside the locket. "This way even if we can't be together all the time, a part of us will be together always." He fastened the locket around her neck and smiled his approval.

Her hand went up automatically to feel the locket. She wished she had a mirror so she could see it on.

"Don't worry, it looks wonderful."

"I've never had anything so pretty." Tears welled up and overflowed her eyes.

"If I have anything to say about it, you'll have nothing but pretty things for the rest of your life. I guess you can tell, I done all right for myself in Kentucky."

"You never said how Seth was doing."

"Oh, he's fine as frog's hair. That was mostly an excuse to get me up there. Seth's got himself a business."

"What kind of business?"

"It's a little dry goods place."

"Where did he get the money to open a store?"

"It seems his first wife's father left it to him years ago. Seth never knew anything about it 'til he went back up there."

"A general store don't sound much like Seth, does it."

"You ought to see him. Damn! He's gotten so respectable he dresses like a preacher on Sunday."

"What about Ellen?"

"She helps out at the store. Acts so refined you would think she'd been a school teacher all her life."

Lacey laughed at the thought of Seth and Ellen putting on airs. "I'm happy for them."

"You should be happy for us. Seth wants to take me on as a partner."

Lacey heart jumped in throat. She reached for her clothes, turning away from Coy as she slipped into her underclothes and pulled her dress over her head. Walking to the edge of the rock, she looked out over the hollow. She could hear Coy getting dressed. He walked up and slipped his arms around her waist. "What's wrong, Lacey?"

"Do you think you would be happy running a store?"

"It doesn't have to be forever. It's a good start for us. We could save up a little money and then do whatever we take a notion to do."

She smiled at the thought of Coy behind the counter selling flour and meal to little old ladies. It wouldn't be long before he "took a notion" to do something else she was sure. He would soon grow tired of being confined to a store. Nothing could hold Coy's interest for long. Even the excitement of the strike and risking his life had bored him soon enough. "You know Barney Graham was killed a few weeks ago," she said testing him.

"Yeah, I heard about that."

"The union is pretty well beat."

"That's why this store couldn't have come along at a better time. You can leave Wilder now. We can get out of this town or what's left of it."

"You know Ben was sick all winter. He nearly died of pneumonia." She didn't tell him how he had caught the pneumonia that had nearly taken his life. She didn't tell him that Ben had come after her, barefoot and without a coat to see where she going all those times she had lied to him.

"I hate to hear that, Lacey. I always liked the little guy."

"He's doing a lot better, now. You know John still has a little bit of a limp from that day he tried to stop the trestle from blowing up."

"Wasn't that the damnedest thing?" They stood there silent for a moment, and then Coy took her by the shoulders and turned her around. He looked at her for a long time. "What's bothering you, Lacey?"

She looked at him and there was not a single part of her that did not ache with the pain of what she was about to say. "It was a long winter, Coy. Those long hours I sat by Ben's bed watching to see that he was still breathing, I had time to think things out." He looked at her puzzled.

She walked to another spot on the rock to be away from the nearness of him. "A lot of good people fought with everything they had to stand up for what they believed in. They stood together even if it meant dying."

"They couldn't win, Lacey. There was too much against them from the beginning."

"It don't change nothing. Don't you see that these people only know one way and that's to live by the values they were brought up with? They're good people, Coy. They supported each other and took care of each other through hard times."

"You worked just as hard as any of them, Lacey."

"Coy, if you could have seen the look on Pa's face when he come home day after day of looking for work. What it done to him not to be able to feed his family. Did you know that John drove the aid truck for three days straight once without sleep? Stopping at every house begging for food."

"Lacey, I've seen you dig in the ground for hours to find enough roots to make a meal. I've seen you take a squirrel as bony as a twig and make a stew out of it. You've got nothing to be ashamed of. Now, what's this really all about?"

"All those times we were together, Coy. You know I lied about where I was. I lied to my folks, to Ben. I made up dozens of stories so we could be together."

"What real harm did that do, Lacey? There was no other way."

"They trusted me, Coy. Don't you see? I did things I never thought I would do to be with you. I hurt and deceived people who counted on me."

"John?"

"Yes, John. He's never done a harm thing to me, and I have wronged him in every way I know how. I was never with him that I wasn't figuring how I could get away to be with you. There can't be a lower way to treat a person. I thought I could do whatever it took to have you even if it meant betraying everything I ever believed in."

"Lacey you haven't done anything wrong. Life wasn't meant to be taken so seriously."

"That's just the difference in us Coy. I think it *was* meant to be taken seriously. I think when we don't take it seriously, there's a price to be paid. My mistake was in thinking I could pay it."

"Lacey, what are you going to do?"

"I'm going to marry John like I promised."

Coy bounded toward her and grabbed her by the shoulder shaking her furiously. "Lacey, you damn fool. You know you don't love John. You never will."

"I know," she said. She closed her eyes and dropped her head. "That night in Ben's room when he was so near death, I made a promise. If God would save him, I'd give you up."

"You thought Ben was the price for having me?"

She nodded.

He let go of her and turned away, his fist clenched. "Why did you meet me today? It wasn't just to tell me this."

"I thought it was."

"Why did you let me make love to you?"

"There will be a price to pay for that too. If not today, then someday."

"Dammit, Lacey!" he exploded, turning on her angrily. "You are such a little fool! How do these people have such a hold on you that you think you owe them your life? That pa of yours just uses you to run that house because his wife can't. And she uses her illness to get out of facing up to things. I know you feel responsible for Ben, but he has to grow up sometime."

"They're not asking anything of me that I shouldn't be willing to give."

"What about John? Have you thought about what its going to be like married to him for the rest of your life? It sure as hell won't be like it was for us a few minutes ago."

Lacey blushed, knowing it was true. "I made a promise, Coy."

"You want me, Lacey. Admit it. You'll never love anyone but me. Say it Lacey. Say it!"

Tears stung her eyes. "I love you Coy," she said unable to look at him. "I'll always love you."

He surprised her by taking her in his arms and kissing her on the lips, and then he looked down into her eyes. She wanted to say, *I'm sorry Coy. I didn't mean it.* She wanted to plead with him to take her with him. But she had made the promise and she would keep it.

"Then come with me now."

"I can't Coy. Wanting something don't make it right. Sometimes the price is too high."

"You are wrong Lacey. You'll realize it one day. It will come to you in the middle of the night when you wake up next to John but you were dreaming of me. You'll know what a fool you've been. You'll ache for me so bad you're going to think you're losing your mind. Every time you look over your shoulder you'll hope it's me. Every time you hear a train you'll wonder if I'm on it. Every time you feel that locket against your skin, you'll wish it was me. And one day, Lacey, I'll be back." He let go of her and headed off toward the trail. "I'll be back, Lacey. You be looking for me," he said giving her that lopsided grin. And then he was gone.

For a long time she looked at the place where he had been. Then, she walked to the edge of the cliff and reached under a tree root to something she had hidden earlier. Standing as close to the edge as she could, she could feel the wind pick up around her.

Slowly she looked at the carving of the red-tailed hawk in her hand. Its wings were still trapped in wood. It would never be completely free. Then she raised her thin arms to the sky and hurled the hawk into the sky. It tumbled over and over again in its fall. Finally, it crashed into the treetops, unable to fly.

Postscript

"Won't nothing seem as hard in life after this," Lacey's Pa told her, and he was probably right. Wilder left a permanent mark on the lives of the people who survived those difficult and dangerous times. The story of these people is one of hope, courage, and determination in the face of insurmountable odds and utter destitution.

What the people of Wilder could not have known was that their struggle was doomed by enormous forces sweeping the nation and the coal industry during the Great Depression. The coal industry had enjoyed an almost uninterrupted boom since the First World War. The demand for coal had been so great that wherever a railroad track ran, a coal mine flourished. Several generations had grown up knowing only life in the coal camps, dependent on the coal companies. Many enjoyed a better life than they had known as hard scrabble farmers.

When the coal industry began to decline, the companies waged a desperate war for a piece of the shrinking market. The war meant lower wages, increased danger, poor safety standards and more time underground for the miners. More often than not, it meant bankruptcy for the smaller companies as more of the business went to larger companies that were closer to market.

Although the union in Wilder struggled to survive after the death of its leader, by fall many of the union, government and civic leaders were looking for ways to help the people get on with their lives. Some of the people went to work building the Norris Dam, the first dam in the Tennessee Valley Authority system. Many of the young men went to work for the Civilian Conservation Corp. Some people went to the Cumberland Homesteads where they built a whole new community. A Federal Resettlement Project started by President Franklin D. Roosevelt, the Cumberland Homesteads not only provided work for the unemployed, it allowed even the poorest families to own their own farm.

As for Wilder, some deep mining continued through the 1950's but eventually the camp disappeared. Only a few stone foundations and rotting crossties give mute testimony to what once was. Of the town, nothing remains — nothing at all. The memories of what happened there, however, live on in those who endured. Sometimes these memories are passed on to sons and daughters who can only hope to keep them alive through stories like this one.